Sky's The Limit
In Mexico

Jacey K Dew

Chapter 1

"Fuck him." I side eye Bree, gaging her erratic moods. Is this one of the steps to acceptance? Has she reached anger? Or, is this the alcohol speaking? Maybe sleep deprivation, and exhaustion? Early onset jetlag? "Fuck her."

"I think they did enough fucking; that's the problem." My attempt at a joke falls flat. Delirium had me thinking that was a good idea, at least, before I opened my mouth, and said it. "They're problem; not ours." There is no saving us from my bad joke attempt.

I watch her nervously as she sighs, and sinks deeper into her seat.

"This was supposed to be our honeymoon." She reminds me solemnly; I know.

"Which he paid for, and lost out on, so the man whore could be with his whore." I recap unnecessarily to the brunette next to me. "His problem. Our benefit." I attempt to swing it into a positive, but I can't help but feel like I keep swallowing my foot.

A deep pit settles in my chest. I ache for the ability to know the right things to say to her to make her feel better. But, I really don't think anything will really make her feel better.

Finding out, just hours after your wedding, that your husband has been cheating on you, and wishes for divorce so he can be with the mistress, isn't something that you just get over.

Deep green eyes take a moment to stare into my soul. Fear creeps in as I start to think I've gone too far. "As much as I love hearing you swear. You're starting to weird me out." My smile creeps up wildly. I basically never swear. I think she appreciates it a small bit; might make her smile or get her out of her mood for a minute. If it helps, I don't mind swearing. "Remember, calm collected Skylar. I'm the messy, swearing, spontaneous one."

"It's a spite vacation. Anything could happen." I shrug. Sinking back into my seat, I get comfortable again.

"Ooo," a spark of her excitement returns. "Are you going to be spontaneous now?" I can practically feel the jabbing joke elbow hitting my ribs.

"Only for the next week." I point my finger at her, and shake my head. "Don't get used to it."

The entire situation is the only reason I am here; not including the messy wedding night break up, and cheating scandal. Though, that certainly helped convince my parents this was a good idea.

This vacation, my first one ever out of province, and country, promises more adventure than I've had in forever. More adventure than I'll have until I retire; until after my parents are both dead or in an old folk's home. I'll franchise the café, and travel the world until I die; or something like that.

Bree had a prepaid, and nonrefundable vacation spot open for the taking. Not even my parents could see reason to dispute a practically free vacation, while I support, and help Bree recover.

Bree sighs deeply in an exaggerated boredom; drama queen. "Are we there yet?"

"Don't start." I warn with a hint of humor.

Her phone screen lights up; the brightest thing here with the dim green spotlight lighting the bus provides above each seat. "We've been on the bus for like two, and a half hours now."

"Dropping everyone else off, getting us to our hotel safely. A little longer, and we'll be there. You just need a little more patience, and maybe a nap." I have to admit that I'm getting impatient as well. My butt has started tingling, and aching. I've taken to shifting positions every couple minutes in a bit to help keep my butt or legs from fully falling asleep.

"Yes, mom." She groans.

"You're the one who picked a hotel so far away from the resort." I point out.

They could have had a little more forethought to where the hotel was, and how far away from the airport it is. Tulum and Cancun aren't exactly that close. They should have known travel would take a while, even if they hadn't known about the extra stops along the way.

"HE picked it." Bree blames Christian. "He wanted something away from Cancun, and the partying, and in the Mayan Riviera. The hotel had amazing reviews; apparently. Smaller than a lot of the gigantic resorts, but still has all-the-things." Bree mocks the reasoning she must've heard Christian repeat numerous times in the planning, and thereafter.

"What are all-the-things?" I detour.

She shrugs. "I don't know. I just made sure it had a beach, and free booze."

My eyes roll almost involuntary. Of course, Bree goes to another country with the main priorities of drinking, and getting a tan.

Then again, that's why most people go somewhere tropical; to get a tan. Why people go to Mexico for the totted all-inclusive packages; for the non-stop drinks. I can't really blame her for being a typical tourist.

We travel in comfortable silence.

I watch the outside for as much as I can see; the whole foot, and a half visible in the darkness. The night is so dark here. Likely because there aren't as many street lamps out of town as there are back home.

That changes as we turn down a road between lit columns holding up an arch.

I get fidgety in my excitement. This should be it; a better lit road down leading to a hotel. We'll be there in a minute or two.

I elbow Bree softly. "I think this is it." We're the last people on the bus, so this has to be us logically.

I start gathering our scattered belongings, and garbage. Bree isn't as concerned, so I do hers as well. I don't want to have to stay on the bus any longer than I have to. Especially not to wait on her getting her things together, which she should be doing now.

It would be rude to leave an unnecessary mess.

As I finish tucking garbage into a compartment in Bree's carryon backpack, the bus comes to a stop. I brace myself on the seat in front of me, so I don't fall from my semi standing position.

"Ladies, last stop. Thank you for riding with us today. We sincerely hope you enjoy your visit. And, remember those all important Spanish words we learned earlier." The bus guide puts all his enthusiasm into our send off, just like he has done with each group, but he forgoes the bus speakers to speak to us directly.

"Cervezas!" Bree shouts.

Of course, that's the only word she remembers. He plays along, and shouts the word back excitedly.

I bet he's mostly excited to be finished for the night; if he's actually done, and not just going back for another load of customers. If it's the latter, then he at least gets a bit of downtime between here, and the airport.

The man helps us grab our bags from under the bus, I make sure we have everything, and then tip his open hand.

Everyone we've come across wants their tip after helping us. It came as a surprise the first time with the runner who helped us find our bus after shouting the name of our flight company, I had thought he was with the company, and was supposed to do that as a job. He gave me the nastiest look when I didn't understand why his hand was out, and why he was continuing to stand there after helping us. I felt hustled when he explained he wanted his tip. Had I known he'd require a tip, I would have never agreed to let him show us to our bus.

I'll have to adjust my budget to allow for tipping. I hadn't thought to budget for it since everything was all-inclusive; I thought it would be included. I had also heard that tipping was mostly a Canadian, and U.S. thing, so again, it wasn't a thought.

We walk down a pathway beside a gigantic fountain. The hotel lights are our beacon, and we may as well be the moths.

We get inside the hotel, and interrupt the workers from their personal conversations; if their postures have anything to do with the conversation. They stand at our attention as soon as they notice us. Back lit by a golden wall.

I gawk around while Bree checks us in; everything is under her, and Christian's names here. We didn't think it would be necessary to change it here, which I hope isn't an assumption that will come back to bite us.

The walls are crème coloured, maybe white in the daylight, with large brown tiled floorings. A metal chandelier hangs over a round wooden table with an elaborate flower bouquet. While the chandelier provides some light, the pot lights lining the ceiling light things up the most.

Loud music plays in the room beside us. They are playing Feliz Navidad. Slightly confusing this early, Halloween isn't even here yet, but maybe they're just playing music people might know or have requested.

Distracted by mariachi music, it takes a moment for me to realize Bree is calling my name. "They need to give you a wrist band."

"Sorry." I apologize for my delay, and hold out my wrist. They place an orange plastic wrist band around me; loose enough that it won't be a bother, but tight enough I won't be able to slip it off without a discomforting effort.

"Show your wrist bands to the staff when asked, or when you're getting a drink, or going into a restaurant. That's how we know that you're supposed to be here. Here are your key cards." She hands the both of them to Bree, who then transfers one to me.

"And remember to book any excursions with the representative for your booking company at those desks there." She points behind us. At the opposite side of the room, there are a couple desks with computers, and chairs on each side. "Your rep arrives at eight am, and leaves at six pm. You'll need to book at least one day in advance, and it's first come first served. Some excursions book up faster than others.

Payment will be added automatically to the credit card you purchased your vacation with, if you wish to pay otherwise, you'll need to bring that payment with you when you purchase the excursion. Same goes for the à la carte restaurant. You'll need to book the day in advance with your rep; no extra charges apply." She takes a slight pause after her scripted ramble. "Michael will show you to your room. If you have any questions, please don't hesitate to ask. Enjoy your stay."

A tall lanky man, presumed to be Michael, comes out from around the desk, and leads us out of the lobby, and down a long stretch. There are no doors or window coverings, just large open rooms, and columns, and holes in the walls. The open concept allows for a cooling breeze to filter through.

An open corridor leads to the guests rooms. Lights provide enough light to see to the pool, but no one is in there.

It's then that I notice no one else is around. No other guests to mention.

My gut sinks with dread. Please tell me Christian didn't cheap out on the honeymoon hotel, and grabbed whatever was cheapest; somewhere that no one goes to because of kidnappings or food poisonings.

Michael leads us up to a door on the third floor in a building. A location I wouldn't be able to locate if someone asked. He slips a card into the slot, and opens the door.

Once we are into the little entry, we quickly notice something awry. The shower is running, a suitcase is opened, clothes are everywhere, and the bed is messed up.

"We need to leave." Michael whispers. But, he doesn't have to finish telling us the words before we are already out the door. Michael closes the door behind us wide eyed. "There's been some mix up. We'll need to go back to the lobby."

Bree looks about ready to blow, so I step in. "No problem."

Colossal confusion crosses the woman's face when we all return. "Someone was already in that room." Michael informs her.

"What do you mean?" She asks.

"A guest is already staying in that room." Michael lays out plainly.

"No." She denies, still dazed from our return.

"Yes." Michael confirms.

"The computer said it was empty. That was supposed to be their room." I feel like the situation has broken her mind for a moment; I don't blame her. When you follow procedures, and the computer says no one else is supposed to be in the room already, then you expect the room to be empty for the arriving guests allocated for that room.

"We'll get them another room." Michael turns to us. "Leave your bags with us. We'll put them in your new room for you. There's a band playing, and some other guests just in there. Some snacks, if you're hungry." He directs us to a relatively closed in room with the mariachi music. "We'll come, and get you once everything is sorted."

"Thank you." I grab Bree's arm, and pull, then push her towards the music before she can have any sort of meltdown.

Columns open into an orange room with wooden tables, and chairs. A buffet table divides the middle of the room with space on either side to get around. A stage with a three man band, dressed in mariachi gear, is in the far corner straight ahead.

We sit in an exhausted huff away from the band, and away from the other guests; all two of them.

After spending an entire day traveling, the last thing I expected was not being able to flop straight into bed, and crash. It's past my bed time; I'm not eighteen anymore.

I scoff at myself. It's not like I'm fifty, I'm not even thirty, though some days I certainly feel like I am. Oh, the changes that just a few years can bring.

A lovely warm breeze brushes us from the openings in the walls.

Bree leaves me to help herself to the buffet snacks. One heaping small plate of guacamole, and salsa fresca, and one heaping pile of house made taco chips. She places the two plates right in front of her. But, after one longing gaze from me, she pushes both more towards the middle of the table.

"Thanks friend." I say appreciatively. I hadn't been hungry until she sat down, and started eating. A confounding thing after gorging on all the snack foods, airplane, and airport food all day.

I dip a chip in the green pile, and dive it to my mouth. Fresh avocado like I've never had before. Better tasting guacamole unlike what I can get back home. Something about having to ship it half way across the world tarnishes the taste. Fresh is always best, straight from the source, or close to it.

The salsa fresca tries to fall off my next chip. I catch some tomato chunks and onion pieces before they can hit the table. I toss the salsa into my mouth, and follow it with the chip.

The taste is addictingly fresh. We demolish the two plates quickly.

Too exhausted to talk, we sit with the silence between us, until Michael grabs us to take us to our room.

The door opens, and I'm relieved to find the lights are off. Nothing looks disturbed. Our bags are just inside the doorway.

"We're very sorry for the mix up." Michael explains, "we switched our systems last week, and we're thinking something got mixed up along the way."

"That's alright. No problem at all. It happens." I tell him.

"There's maps next to the phone. Feel free to call to the desk should you need anything." He leaves us to it with a bid to have a good night.

Bree rushes into the bathroom first, and closes the door.

Of course she has to pee.

I walk further into the room, finding the light switch for the main portion of the room.

Two separate beds are pushed together in the middle of the room; each has their own dull coloured patterned bedding. A large metal head board covers both beds. Twisted metal appears like branches.

The room is small. Just enough to hold the makeshift giant bed, and a side table on each side. There is a white, low but long, dresser across from the bed on the other side. A small TV stand directly beside it, with a TV on top. I don't assume that will get used at all while we're here; I don't plan on spending my vacation watching movies.

As I close the curtains to the pitch black outside, I see what appears to be a patio. I'll explore it further tomorrow, but with Bree in the bathroom, and the late hour, I just want to go to bed.

I strip, and quickly redress in a tank top, underwear, and sleeping shorts. Placing my phone on the right side table, and inserting the charging cord from my bag.

Bree flushes, and exits shortly after, and I take her place.

She is in bed by the time I leave the bathroom. Bree's taken the left bed, which leaves me with the one closest to the patio. I assume she may have made the choice based off my phone, but I wouldn't have cared with either bed. I turn off the light before blindly finding the bed.

I pull back the covers. The top layer feels a bit scratchy, but the sheets underneath are soft. I lie down, and get comfortable.

A thought comes to me. "Oh, I should set an alarm." I roll over to grab my phone.

"You want to set an alarm on vacation?" Bree sounds incredulous.

"Yes. Nothing ridiculous, but I want to make sure we can get to the booking agent before there's a crowd." I reason.

"There's not going to be a crowd." She denies with a groan twisted into her words.

"I don't want to take the chance that we'll have to wait an hour to get the excursions we want. And, what if they only have a certain amount of tickets for what we want." We had agreed to try to do a couple of excursions while we are here.

I don't want to only see the airport and the hotel while we're here. It seems like it would be a waste to go a quarter of the way around the world, and not go out, and experience anything else. You could literally go anywhere in the world at that point, and get the same type of experience.

"You can get up, and pick thing whatever you want, but I'm sleeping until noon." Part of me hopes she's joking, but my experience knows she's perfectly capable of sleeping for so long. "Night."

"Night."

The first snore from the other bed sounds off as I put my phone down. Even after such a long day, I don't know how she could possibly fall asleep so fast. It's quite the talent.

"Sweet dreams." I say to the sleeping body.

It feels amazing sinking into the soft pillows at least.

It's exhausting doing nothing on a plane all day. Then again, being up for longer spurts than normal will also have the same effect.

A horrid though enters my mind as I haze away, could the mystery guy in our room have been Christian?

God, I hope not.

Chapter 2

I shut the alarm off as soon as it sounds. Excitement has me wide awake immediately.

A soft day light fills the entire room from behind the curtains.

I look over to Bree's side of the bed. There is a long mirror, and a white doored closet I had missed last night.

Bree is still a lump in the bed; undisturbed from my screeching siren.

Throwing back the covers, I hop out of bed; eager to take a peek of the outside we were blind to last night.

I draw the curtains enough to get me access to the sliding door. Opening the door just enough to take a step out.

There are two plastic forest green chairs on the tiny white plastered patio. A railing made of wood, and rope keeps us from walking off the edge.

Our view of the center of the hotel area isn't much. A thatch covered walkway roof blocks much of the view to the right, and in front of me, the tops of the trees block the rest. If I stare hard enough, I can catch glimpses of the pool.

Directly down are a couple of umbrellas made out of thatch. They seem to belong to the private patios of the rooms on the first floor.

I can't help but wonder what the view in the other room would have looked like, if it would have had more to see.

My quiet peaceful moment comes to an end when my bladder

protests. I walk back inside, grab up my toiletries, and start getting ready for the day.

Without Bree's consciousness, I have no idea what the day will bring. The varying choices have varying clothing requirements.

If she does wake, and decides to go to the beach, I can always get dressed in my bathing suit then, but right now I feel like I need real clothing.

I dress into jean shorts, a tank top, and a light long sleeved flannel button down shirt; part of my attempt to avoid a sunburn. Briefly debating putting on sunscreen, I decide not to, and will see how well my skin handles the Mexican morning sun.

I drop my sandals at the door as I come across them in the bag.

Walking over to Bree's bed, I call her name, but she doesn't respond; three times. Shaking her a bit gains me a groan.

"I'm going down to book the excursion, then I'm going for breakfast. If you're mobile by then, come join me."

"Sleep." She mutters.

I roll my eyes. Maybe she'll remember this when she wakes up, maybe she won't, but at least I can tell her that I tried to tell her.

Before I leave the room, I make sure I have the key card. Nothing would be worse than getting locked out of my room without the key card, especially if Bree decides to leave the room.

I take note to the 344 written on our door. I hadn't even thought to get the room number last night. I doubt I'll be able to find my way here without getting lost.

I pick the direction we came from last night, and backtrack my way to the stairs. They lead to the interior of the building alcove.

It's like a picture, walking out to an empty resort. Not one person is sitting at any of the tables or in a blue cushioned lounge chairs. Not one person is in the pool. No bartenders are in the wet bars. It just looks like a slightly moving picture of the perfect resort.

I walk the path back to the entrance. There's two desks, but only one rep; the one for our booking company. While the other desk is empty, ours is already busy with a couple.

"Good morning. Grab a brochure, and take a look, while I finish helping these people." She tells me.

I do as she says, and grab a brochure. The pamphlet is filled with a variety of activities to do. Everything I could imagine, and more is in here; from swimming with the dolphins to dinner on a pirate ship. With our limited time here I know we will only be able to do, maybe, two or three of these things.

Something itches right above my eyebrow. I wipe my forehead with my forearm. Liquid glistens, and drips from my arm. God, I'm sweaty. Why, am I so sweaty?

The heat assaulting my body could definitely be an answer. It's a humid heat, unlike the dry heat of our summers. Maybe it's not fully my contribution; I can hope to avoid that embarrassment if others are having the same issue.

The list is over whelming. I want to make the most of our trip. I wanted to see ruins, and go swimming, and whatever else. I know Bree isn't into the ruins, so I know she won't pick them. Which means I should start there if I hope to see some this trip.

The section with the ruins lists a few, most I've never heard of before. One option catches my eye at the bottom of the list; a half day journey to the Tulum ruins, and half day at the Xel-Há for snorkeling. Something for me and something for her, and it maximizes what we can get done in our short time here.

"Hey," a voice calls beside me. I turn instinctively to find out who's talking, and who he nondescriptively said hi to. A chest greets me, positioned to face me. "Hi, I'm Will." I hadn't realized he was there.

"Skylar." I answer as I look up at him. He's tall. My eyes are at his chest height. His bright blue eyes catch me next; framed by wild surfer hair.

"Any ideas for a bachelor party; that won't get a groom in trouble?" He tags on the last part for clarification's sake, I'm sure.

"Umm," I huff, and look at the list. With his notation, I decide to nix anything that would be considered wild party central. "I'm not sure. I mean, you could turn any of these into a bachelor party; if you wanted to. There was a water park on here. You can repel into a cenote after touring a ruin. Or, a dinner, and pirate show on a pirate ship."

Will stops me there. "A pirate ship would be awesome, but Silvia would kill me for not taking her with us." He sounds a bit disappointed.

"Could you do a joint bachelor/bachelorette party?" I wonder.

Bree did hers partially together. A barbeque at their house after the girls went to play pool, and the guys went to a casino. It worked well for them.

"Hmn…" Will's thoughtful expression reveals the thought never crossed his mind.

"How the hell did Will Bogtrotter beat me here?" A femininely deep voice booms behind us.

"Silvia scares me. She threatened to feed me my balls if I screw up." The tall woman laughs at this, and nods her understanding.

Silvia, who I assume is the bride, sounds like she's got a temper; or maybe Will brings out her worst.

"Well, at least we now know a threat that works to keep you in line." I'm scrutinized as she looks me up, and down suspiciously. "Pick out something yet?"

"Yes, dinner, and a show on a pirate ship." He announces. I'm a bit surprised he picked that option, unless he's considered a joint party.

Her eyes go wide, and she slowly shakes her head. "No way, no, you can't do that. Sil will-"

Will cuts her off. "Do nothing. Skylar, here, suggested we do a together party. You know that would work best for everyone."

I wonder at the undertones. Does Silvia not trust her groom? Perhaps there's been cheating in the past, and she doesn't feel like she can trust him. That's a great way to start a marriage; zero trust. Though all the trust in the world has also proven it can be a bad thing.

"That's not a horrible idea. No wonder it wasn't yours." She sticks her hand out. "I'm Mel."

"Skylar." I shake her offering.

"Are you going to be there?" She asks with, what sounds like, more suspicion, and a pointed look at Will.

"Oh, no. I'm just suggestion girl." I flash both hands up in a sign of peace. "I wouldn't want to intrude."

"What's one more?" She eases off, and I think she more means to be polite with her insistence, than to truly invite me along.

"Two more." I say.

"Two more, your husband can talk guy stuff with the guys, and you can join us girls." Mel smiles, and I feel like she's being genuine now. Perhaps she's not viewing me as a threat anymore. No one would be that insistent for just being polite. But, I'm still hesitant to join in someone else's party. It feels intrusive, and weird.

"Oh, no husband." I wave off. "I'm with a friend; a girl. This was supposed to be her honeymoon, but her husband confessed to cheating on her, and wanted a divorce to be with the mistress. A bachelorette party might not be the best idea."

"Ouch. Nope, I suppose not. That really sucks." Mel commiserates. The other couple gets up to leave. I reflexively turn at the shriek of their chairs.

"Looks like it's your turn." Will says.

"Great." I smile at the both of them before taking my turn.

The lady at the desk helps me book up the dual excursion. She tells me that we'll need to be ready for a six am departure. And suggests we pick up biodegradable sunscreen at the shop; apparently a bid to help preserve the environment. Once done paying with my credit card, I get up, and thank her.

As I leave, I tell Will and Mel politely, "hope to see you around."

"It's a small resort. We'll run into each other again; probably later on today, at the least. Have fun tomorrow." Mel's initial suspicious frostiness has lifted into friendliness.

"You too." I say back.

It occurs in my exiting reflection that Will might be the cheating groom. Mel would have reason to be suspicious with his friendliness to a solo female. He never did say whether he was planning it for himself or for another. Might explain the dynamic between him, and Silvia.

I decide to walk back to the room. It would be more comfortable to go to the dining room with Bree. I don't mind solo breakfast but I would prefer to have some company for the first time. Then I can share the awkwardness of having no idea what to do.

But, with Bree passed out deeply that option looks less likely.

I remember the maps that Michael mentioned last night. I find a whole stack of them on the table, and grab up one. The map serves as an informational guide as well.

The buildings have names, and the names have hours listed beside them. Gawking at the time constraints, I realize that we have less than an hour and a half before they close up the breakfast buffet. Then they won't open for lunch until an hour after that.

The dotted snack locations seem to be open for most of the day after eleven, the same time lunch opens up, but I don't want to trust snack foods to fill me up. Although, they do seem to be the only option for food for a three hour period in the afternoon.

Looking at the list, it appears nothing is open for the hour in-between breakfast, and lunch.

There's only one thing to do, and I know Bree will forgive me; eventually. I pounce on the bed beside right beside her, and jolt her awake. "Get up. Get up. The buffet closes soon, and won't open back up until lunch."

"What the hell, Sky!?!" She yells. Angry with me for her sudden wake up call. Quickly, her head perks up, and her body relaxes as my words sink in. "Did you say they are closing the food down?"

"Yeah, they've got hours listed on the buffet, and all the food places. And if you don't get up, and down there now, there will be nothing to eat until lunch. And if you miss the two hour lunch window, then you're relying on a small list of snack foods until supper."

"Well that's dumb." She grumbles with a sigh of resignation. "Fine."

Chapter 3

The barest scraps of food residue on my plate gives evidence of the fruit, scrambled eggs, and pancakes I pulled from the buffet table. My plate was filled before I could even get to the second section. I'll have to try to get further down the line next time; remember to pace myself, and portion out my servings to the smallest tasting sizes.

Bree went further, and managed to find a custom omelette section, and some cookies.

I down the last gulp from my mango mimosa as Bree chomps on her last cookie. The waiters clear away the dishes as soon as we look like we're getting up.

We thank them, before Bree leads us out. As soon as we leave the doors we are on a raised platform type deck a few feet up from the beach.

Thatch umbrellas are pegged into the ground as permanent structures. People are already claiming the lounge chairs underneath.

All the people that were missing earlier had suddenly appeared for breakfast. I guess everyone sleeps in on vacation, unless they have an excursion.

I'm glad to see a bunch of other people here. It provides some comfort.

There's a little set of stairs leading down to the beach, with a shower at the entrance. I assume it's to wash your feet off once you're done on the beach so you aren't tracking sand everywhere.

I pull off my flip-flops as soon as the sand starts digging into them. They are of no use to me when they are weighed down by the sand.

It seems beyond surreal that I'm here right now. Everything is so different from what I know, and what I've seen in my life. I've never be even been to a beach before. The closest I've ever gotten to something like this has been pictures, and magazines.

Bree runs straight for the water with sandals in hand. The ocean is super calm and there are no crashing waves. No one is in there swimming around.

As I approach I look for some sort of a sign that says we shouldn't be swimming in the water, but there are none. I assume that means we should be safe from sharks.

I stop feet from the edge of the water to gaze at an alligator in the sand. Someone was up early carving a life-size alligator. I almost wonder if it's the gentleman in the boat advertising fishing trips, and snorkel tours just metres away. It doesn't seem to me like any of these tourists would be that ambitious this early in the morning, despite it being probably close to ten o'clock.

The resort seems to run on a different time schedule than the rest of the world. A steady stream of relaxing means life doesn't start until nine o'clock.

I stroll out to meet Bree in the water. I have no plans on going too deep without a bathing suit. Although Bree is quite the distance out, the water only slowly raises; reaching her thighs right above her knees.

Fish swim all around me without a care; a sure sign they must be used to people. It would be wonderful to have some goggles with so many fish around. They look grey, and brown from above the water, but I wonder if looking at them from the sides would reveal more colours. It might be cool to have them swirl around my head.

I stop and seethe when my toe stubs on to something hard and sharp. Looking down, there appears to be a large dead coral reef just in front of me.

Just as I start wondering how I'm going to get to Bree, and how she managed to get over on the other side of this reef, the men in the fishing boat start screaming, and yelling. Their attention is on me.

I have no idea what they're saying, or whether they are speaking English or Spanish. But, I figure yelling is not ever a good thing when you are in the ocean. I imagine whatever it is it means trouble. My mind goes straight to a shark. That could be why there's no one out here. Maybe all the fish attracted a shark.

"Bree? Bree!" I call to her. "I think we need to get out of the water right now." When she looks back to me, I point to the boat, and the men shouting.

She walks hurriedly back to me. I cringe as it looks like she steps on the reef in order to get over it.

We get out of the water as fast as we can. I look back over to the men in the boat, and they seem to be going back to their own business.

A man shouts to us from one of the lounge chairs. Bree shouts back, "what?" She didn't catch what he said either.

The man beckons us over with his hand so we listen, and go to him. Maybe he knows what's going on.

"There's sea urchins in there." He explains. "You're lucky you didn't step on them. They're having some sort of an infestation. They don't have any signs up because they don't want to scare anyone, but a man stepped on one yesterday, first day of his vacation, now he's going to be laid up for the rest of it. Not the way you want to spend your vacation."

"That's awful." I exclaim. And, in some places, would be a potential lawsuit.

"Ouch, so I guess beach swimming is out." Bree sounds so

disappointed. It was one of her key points of going on this vacation.

"If you really want to get in the water, try to avoid the rocks, and reef, wear your sandals, and watch where you step." The man advises. But, I get the idea that he still wouldn't recommend it. I know I wouldn't.

I look between Bree, and the man. "I think I'll just take my chances with the pool instead." I joke; half serious. "Thanks for letting us know. I had no idea what they were shouting at us about."

"No problem. Enjoy your vacation." He moves himself to get comfortable again.

"Thanks, you too." I tell him. Bree and I walk back towards the resort. "That was close. We were lucky we didn't step on anything. Could you imagine? If that happened, if either of us got hurt, I don't think my parents would ever let me have vacation time ever again."

"Pfft, you'll just have to threaten to quit." Bree makes it sound so easy.

"I'd be disowned if I tried that stunt." I wash my feet off in the little shower before stepping onto the stairs. Bree does the same.

I figure out quickly that it may have been better to deal with the sand. My sandals squish from the added water. But, I suppose they don't want the sand tracked all over the resort either.

"Well, then I guess I'll just have to get divorced again, and get them to send you on vacation with me out of pity." She jokes.

"Awe, you'd do that just for me?"

"Only you."

"Thanks bud."

"Hey look, it's the gift shop." Bree declares. I almost missed the small glassed in room. It looks almost completely empty.

We go inside, and are greeted by a worker. There isn't too much to the gift shop, a couple shelves, and a bench with things on them, so we find what we need immediately. The worker explains without our own vocalised question, that they are renovating so they don't have much right now.

I don't mind, as long as they have what we need. Bree finds the toothbrush she needs, and I find the biodegradable sunscreen we need for tomorrow.

"What's that for?" Bree asks as she pays for everything.

"Our excursion tomorrow needs it; we're not supposed to use our regular stuff because it isn't biodegradable. It's to help preserve the environment." The worker looks happy with my explanation. I keep my tone pleasant to hide my slight annoyance at the unexpected expense. If Mexico prefers people to have biodegradable sunscreen, then that should be something they tell you before you get here. It should be akin to common knowledge. I didn't even know such a thing existed nor that our regular sunscreen wasn't biodegradable.

Not that it's a bad idea, because it's probably a wonderful idea, it's just inconvenient learning about it at the stage of the trip; especially after having bought new sunscreen back home specifically for this trip.

"Where are we going?" Bree asks as we leave the shop.

"Tulum ruins." She makes a disgusted sound. "You said I got to pick, because you didn't want to get up with me. Besides, I was nice. It's a two part excursion; ruins in the morning, and snorkeling in the afternoon."

"Okay, fine. That sounds like half fun." We're silent for a minute as we head back toward the room. "Pool now?" Bree asks.

"Of course." I reply.

After the failed beach attempt, I figured the pool would be next. There's not much else going on right now to fill the time void.

We venture back to our hotel room to get changed. I leave everything unnecessary in the room.

Instead of going to the right, outside of our room, we go left. We figure we have to try and figure out some better ways to get in, and out of our hotel room. And as it turns out, just one room over is an exit out towards the pool area, and a much shorter escape route.

There are two wet bars in the pool, but only one of them seems to be open. The only guests in the pool look closer to the open bar than to the other side of the split pool.

I stake out a table, and set of chairs. Claiming it by setting my sandals on the chair. I don't let myself feel guilty about it since it's not busy.

Bree does the same with her own before she jumps right into the pool. My mouth opens, and shuts as my mind clicks in that she may have just made a mistake, then realize in quick succession to warn her, but the warning would be too late at this point.

"Cold!" She shrieks when she surfaces. Bree grasps onto herself in a hug.

I laugh at her expense. "What? Did you think it would be warm?"

"Yes!" She grumbles her way over to the wet bar.

A drink sounds great, but after seeing Bree's reaction, I ease myself in. It is colder than I expected, but I could also just be warmed from the sun. Giving it a moment, will surely acclimate me.

The water's resistance makes me go in slow motion. The water slowly lowers as I approach the bar area.

Seeing a ladder closer to the wet bar, has me regretting getting in so soon. I could have walked around a little, and dropped in right at the bar. Part of me didn't have to get wet and cold.

Bree has a margarita in hand as she talks to a freshly familiar sun bleached blond. As I come up to sit beside Bree, I put a hand on her shoulder, for just a moment, to let her know I'm there.

Will's eyes light with recognizance. "Hi again. So this is your friend? Sorry about your dick of a husband."

A long arm reaches out from behind Will to snack him upside the head. The hit is hard enough to knock his head to the side.

"Tactless idiot. Sorry, Will talks first, thinks later." A brown haired, green eyed man explains. A friend of Will's, I assume.

Will shrugs. "At least I'm honest."

"Too honest." His friend complains.

"Sounds like a certain blabbing friend of mine." Bree jabs back at me with a glare. She's ticked off. I guess, rightfully so. I have no business telling her business to anyone I see, no matter the circumstance.

"Sorry," I apologize bashfully.

"Let us buy you a drink." Will's friend suggests.

"It's all you can drink." I point out. Will smirks. A peak of his teeth show as his amusement does.

"Uh, let us order you a drink. What do you girls like?" Green eyes insist.

"Margarita." Bree says as she points to the one in her hand.

They all look at me expectantly, but I tell them, "I have no idea what they have yet. We just got in late last night." I haven't been around a resort before, and it's been years since I've been to a bar; restaurants tend to have their own versions, and names for things. Embarrassment heats my cheeks.

Bree passes me a laminated menu from the bar top. "Skylar's a girly drink drinker." She offers with a touch of derision. I lost my eagerness to drink the nasty alcohol drinks around the same time I quit going to bars.

"Do you like piña coladas?" Will asks.

"Yes." Sometimes, depending on how it's made. I've had both good and bad ones.

"Daiquiris?"

"Yes." Mostly in theory. I've never had it from a restaurant, only from the premade mix Bree's bought before, and who knows if she makes it how it's supposed to be made.

Will looks over to the waiter. "Two Miami Vices." The waiter gets right to work pouring his mixtures into two blenders, and setting the blenders on.

"What's a Miami Vice?" I ask. It's not something I've ever heard of before. Might be a specialty of the resort.

"The only thing I'm ever drinking again." Will announces. "It's half strawberry daiquiri, and half piña colada."

I contemplate the flavours in each, and then together. "Sounds delicious."

"It is." He gushes.

"So you know why we're here." Bree flashes a momentary glare my way. I look up, and away in faux distraction with the blenders to avoid the gaze. "What brings you here; vacation with the guys?"

"I'm getting married." Green eyes states.

So, he's the cheater.

I have to stop myself, to remind me that it's only my assumption that he's cheated. There's never been any actual mention of it.

Maybe Silvia is controlling, and he's the poor nice guy who lets her walk all over him.

Maybe she's suspicious of him in the way that cheaters always accuse their significant other of cheating since they figure out how easy it can be to get away with it, and she can't trust him out of her own behaviour. Maybe that's where Will fits in.

Maybe she's been cheated on before, and so she's always going to be suspicious of any significant other cheating.

The bartender shuts off the blenders, and pours a half cup of each of the slushes into each cup. Order doesn't seem to matter, as he two hands each pour. One drink ends up with daiquiri on the bottom, and piña colada on top, while the other is the opposite. He hands both cups to Will.

Will leans in as he hands me my drink, and hushes his voice a little. "I was forced against my will. Kidnapped. Help me."

The groom to be elbows Will in his ribs. He pulls back as he sputters a little cough, and his hand goes to the sore spot.

"We've been best friends since we were in diapers, so he had to be my best man. But, I'm marrying his sister, so that also makes me the hated boyfriend of his baby sister." The groom explains the complicated dynamic. At least a few pieces of the puzzle are explained. Silvia may not be so bad, if the animosity between her, and Will is because of sibling rivalry. All that speculation could be for absolutely nothing. "Whether he likes it or not, he has to be here."

"Worst nightmare ever." Will scoffs.

"Best marriage ever." Green eyes smiles as he mocks Will.

Will mock gags.

I attempt to defend the groom against Will's antics. "Isn't that the best case scenario though? Your best friend marries your sister. So now your best friend is your brother.

You're not losing him to some girl that you don't know or like.

You can obviously then trust the guy your sister is marrying." I take a pause for effect, then smirk wickedly at the notion. "I know guys tend to complain about it, but I would think you'd want it to happen more. Unless, you think your best friend isn't good enough to be marrying your sister."

"Oooohhh." A deep groan comes from the remaining men behind them; who apparently started listening at some point. They are all around the same age, so I wonder if they may be here for the wedding as well.

The groom looks at Will with some pointed accusation. "Will, you got something to say?"

"Yeah, I'm afraid my bratty sister's going to scare off the best friend I've ever had." He smiles charmingly at the end, trying to sell the statement.

"Nice save." Green eyes points into Will's chest. "You've had eight years to complain about it, don't be an asshole, and wait for the *does anyone have any reason why these two should not wed* part." His voice deepens with his exaggeration of the most famous drama filled part of the wedding vows.

"Oh come on, now you've gone a spoiled it, it was going to be the perfect revenge for breaking my arm." Will switches his direction from me to his friend half way through the sentence.

Green eyes frowns, and furrows his brows in confusion, but his expression quickly turns into a sneer. "Dude let it go. You didn't have to try jumping through those bushes to get away from her. That was your fault." Their inside joke brings up more questions than answers. Bree and I watch the exchange, hoping they continue to explain.

"It wouldn't have happened if she hadn't been chasing me in the first place." Will insists.

"With a frog, don't forget that important detail." The groom side bars with us to explain. "Will's afraid of frogs. Silvia was chasing him with a frog."

"Dude!" Will shouts.

The exclamation doesn't deter the groom from spilling more. "So he ran from her. He tried to jump through a hedge but there was a cement block at the base he knocked into. Broke his arm. He refuses to let go of it. And, swears it's all her fault."

"Your fault." Bree decides to pass the guilty judgement to Will.

"You didn't have to jump into the bush. That was your decision." His friend adds to the reasoning. I can't help but agree with them, nodding to it, it certainly sounds like it would have been Will's fault he broke his arm.

"You weren't there." Will narrows his eyes at Bree.

"No, but I was, and she's right." Green eyes says.

"I regret sharing my Miami Vice secret with you." Somehow, in my silence, this got turned around on me.

"It's on the menu; that's not exactly a secret." I shrug nonchalantly. I hope it really is on the menu, and not some secret menu item.

We're interrupted from one of the guys behind the two in our focus. "Silvia's going red calling for you."

"What?" The groom asks, but he turns around to a woman shouting from the other side of the pool.

"Volleyball!" We all hear; a bit faint from the distance.

"Looks like were being beckoned." The groom announces to the guys.

"We'll see you ladies later." Will smiles our way before he takes off.

"Nice meeting you." The groom says.

"You as well. Nice meeting you." I return politely.

"Bye." Bree says. She turns around to face the bar, and her

second drink.

The whole lot of men at the wet bar rush towards the other portion of the pool, leaving Bree and I alone with the bartender.

"He's cute." Bree nudges.

"They both were." I say. I know it's not what she meant. She means to get more information on Will, and I's meeting earlier, but there really is nothing to tell.

Her body tenses, and voice hardens. "I meant Will. He looked like he was interested in you. Other is getting married, so he's off limits. Not allowed to be hot." Bree declares.

I realize that I touched a nerve so I agree into my delicious drink mixture.

I'm not going to argue with her. He can be hot, just untouchable. But, she won't see that right now. The resulting insinuation would hit a little close to her heart.

Chapter 4

Pushing a zombie-like Bree through her morning routine bright, and early has me feeling bad for her parents for having to deal with teenage her, and what was surely a daily struggle to get her to school on time.

The early morning air is cool, compared to the daily heat, but still warm enough not to chill us. I'm sure it'll warm up quick enough.

I try to think of everything we packed up while we walk the way to the pick-up zone.

- Key cards
- Special sunscreen on us, and in the bag
- Bathing suits under our clothes
- Towels
- Money
- Underwear and bra
- Hairbrush
- Shampoo, conditioner, and body wash
- Camera

Am I forgetting anything?

I hope not. And, if we did, I hope it's not too important.

Bree and I arrive at a white shuttle van in the front of the resort; right where the bus dropped us off.

"Hola. Buenos días." A man with a clip board greets us.

"Buenos días." I greet back. "Is this the shuttle going to Tulum, and Xel-Há?"

"Yes. Names?" He asks as he looks down to his list.

"Skylar and Bree." I say. Nervous for a second. I reassure myself that I booked in our names, so there shouldn't be confusion. He checks his list, and seemingly finds us quickly; checking us off.

"Ah, yes. We're just waiting on a couple more people, and then we will be off." He explains.

"Perfect. Gracias." I usher Bree onto the bus in front of me.

"Hey look, it's Hottie." She points out the sandy blonde scrunched up against the side of the van.

"Bree!" I scold quietly.

"It's fine. He's sleeping." She flicks her hand to wave me off.

"He's trying to." Will's voice sounds so unlike his own regular one; scratchy, groggy, and deeper. He sounds awfully like he's having a rough morning after an eventful night. Free booze and no self-control will do that to you.

I'm amazed I feel as good as I do, after drinking so much yesterday. But, I guess everything was paced out through the day, and we didn't increase drinks into the evening.

I wonder how much alcohol really goes into their drinks. Or if the rest of the slushy part of the drink balances out the dehydration normally experienced.

"Sorry." She apologizes.

Bree pulls into the seats across from Will. I sit in the aisle seat, and place the back pack between my legs on the floor.

Bree leans over to me, and makes herself comfortable against my side and shoulder. I know she'll be asleep in only moments; she can sleep anywhere. Keeping as still as possible I glance over to Will, who hasn't moved this whole time.

I make sure to look away. His sunglasses could hide open eyes. I wouldn't want to be caught staring.

I wonder if he's managed to get himself to sleep. I have no history to speak of. No knowing if he easily falls asleep or takes a while, or if he's a light or deep sleeper.

I wonder why he's here. I thought they were going to do the pirate ship today. The bus doesn't look like it's got anyone else on it from his group. This excursion was an all day trip. I doubt he'd be able to do both trips in one day.

An older couple smiles warmly as they spot us. The wife gives me a short wave, and a smile. Stuck under Bree, I smile back, and wave cautiously with my free arm. They take spots closer to the front before I realize she probably couldn't see my wave from where she was, and where I had waved. It's too late now to do anything.

Three more people arrive with the tour guide in toe. He sits down next to the driver, and we set off on our adventure.

It doesn't take long before I hear soft snoring from Will, and Bree gets breathy. I imagine I'll be drooled on before the end of this drive.

I watch out of the windows I can see without big movements, but can't see much. There are either trees, buildings tops, or sky.

The sun is up fully before we finally reach a parking lot. Our shuttle van parks in a long line of vans and busses.

"Hola." Our guide calls loudly.

"Hola." The van calls back. I nudge Bree awake, so she can get ready to leave. Once she's off my shoulder in a fading confusion, I reach over, and nudge Will awake. I'm amazed neither woke up to the loud greetings. He must be a deep sleeper.

Eyes furrow under his sunglasses, and he frowns at my intrusion. I point at the guide, and whisper, "we're here.' His haze drops, and he perks up to listen to the guide.

"You will follow Juana for the tour, then will be given time to explore on your own. You will be responsible for getting back here on time before we leave for Xel-Há.

We will leave without you if you are not here at a reasonable time; departure is at 11.

Remember the shuttle number; 104. Look for our logo. We will try to stay parked here, but sometimes we have to move along elsewhere in the lineup." He sends off the group with a nod to Juana, and sits down in the seat behind the driver.

"Hola, are we going to have a good time this morning?" She greets us with enthusiasm.

"Yes!" We all shout together.

"Great! Follow me." She goes to leave, but seem to think second of it. "Do not get distracted by anyone holding an animal. They will ask if you wish to hold it, then take a picture, and expect payment for the picture, and a tip for holding the animal." Juana exits off the bus, and like little ducklings, we all follow her out of the bus, and to the ruins.

A crowd of tourists crowd the entrance, but everything moves fast, and efficient. Juana passes along the tickets for us. We each get a stamp on our hand, and the remaining ticket stub.

It's a blue backgrounded card, with a picture of a ruin on it; El Castillo if the wording at the bottom is supposed to be the name of it.

Apparently, the ticket cost fifty-seven dollars, but there is no indication of which currency is printed on the ticket. Just because I paid in U.S. dollars doesn't mean the ticket is in U.S. dollars. But, if it's in pesos, then the tickets are extremely cheap.

But, thinking of it now, the tickets for these places might be cheap, but they also have the tour guide, and the shuttle van to account for. Everyone along the way needs to get their cut of the price I paid.

If I was more versed, and well-travelled, I might opt to rent a car, and travel on my own to these places. It might be cheaper in the end. Then again, it might be more of a head ache, and certainly less convenient.

It's not like the prices were absolutely ridiculous for a full day of fun at two separate places, with food, and drinks included. Around one hundred and fifty bucks each by the time it's converted to Canadian; for absolutely everything included.

We walk along a white dirt path. Rope blocks off where we are not allowed to walk. A whole other group seems to have been added to ours, as suddenly our group is at least doubled in size; all walking after Juana.

Bree and I get shuffled more towards the back of the group. So when the tour guide talks, I can't really hear everything she says; which is a bit disappointing.

But, Bree doesn't take any cues to move further up in the pack, so we stay where we are. I don't want to completely abandon her just because I want to learn more about this particular area.

I'd likely not be paying a hundred percent attention to her anyway; there's too much to see. I try to reason, but I don't believe myself. I'd be hanging on Juana's every word trying to soak in all the information.

The area is vast; to say the least. I cannot see an end, which was not what I was expecting at all. I had thought we were visiting a few buildings, not a full blown city of ruins.

Basking in the sun on the grass was another thing I wasn't expecting to see; an iguana. There hasn't been any sightings of wildlife so far.

The white grey rocks are carved, and stacked in various ways. Some buildings look more complete than others. Some look like only the barest bottoms of the wall remain; or maybe they were fences and dividers.

The plaster used to make everything white and pristine in the past, is in various stages of ruin. In some places it's along the whole wall, and in others there is nothing remaining.

That same plaster is theorized to have contributed to their downfall. It required immense amounts of wood burning to create their lime plaster, which contributed to deforestation, which made their droughts worse and worse.

I bet their plaster covered cities made for quite the sight back in those days, though. Would have certainly made their drawings and carvings have a significant contrast we largely miss out on these days.

If we were smarter, we'd listen more to those types of lessons from the past. Deforestation can cause issues to even the most advanced civilizations of the time.

The guide moves fast. Barely enough time to look at each building in detail, unless she specifically takes the time to point some things out; which is rare. Some of the carved decals on the buildings remain in decent condition; Gods of the past. Stories of something; I assume.

I take copious pictures so that I can go over everything later. Hopefully Google will pull up plentiful information about this site.

Juana explains at one point about how the Mayan's used to build their houses in such a way, that if not maintained, that it would collapse the doorways. I wish I could ask more about that, I've never heard such a thing before, but I suppose Google will find me an answer later.

We come across some buildings that look safe enough to enter inside, but I wouldn't suppose that would last long with these types of crowds. Even if everyone was completely respectful, accidents happen, and wear and tear happens.

They would be liable if a building collapsed on top of the tourists; would be bad for business. Might be bad for the economy as a whole, if Mexico is found not to be keeping tourist wellness and safety in mind.

Juana sounds like she finally speaks up at the very end. "Looks like this went a little longer than normal. You have to be back to your bus in one hour."

I stop listening to her at that point in my disappointment. I wish we had run off long ago. Explored on our own, but we obediently stayed with the tour despite not being able to hear what Juana was saying ninety five percent of the time.

"So, now what?" Bree asks, her boredom seeping into her voice.

"I'll set an alarm for ten thirty." Will, suddenly back in our vicinity, offers. "That should give us plenty of time to make sure we're back at the bus."

"Thanks." I try to think of what to do, but there isn't much I can think of for the next thirty minutes.

Walk aimlessly, and try to see details we couldn't while the tour was on? Try to go somewhere the tour didn't go; which is probably about half of this place.

"Could we go to the stairs down to the ocean?" Bree asks.

"Sure," I answer. I can't think of a better plan, and I can look at things along the way. Bree gets to see the ocean. Works for the both of us.

Will agrees, and we all walk towards that direction. We pass pyramids with stairs up to second levels, wells, holes in the ground, trees, and buildings that could have been for any number of uses in the past.

It's a longer walk than I expected, and I suspect we are nearing our time limit once we finally make it over. Bree heads for the wooden stairs, leading down the high cliff to the beach.

"Will, what time is it?" I ask.

Will checks his wrist watch. "We've got five minutes until the alarm." He answers.

"Bree, let's stay up here." I call over to her. She looks back at me with a frown. "We don't have time to go down there. It took almost the entire half hour to walk here; it's going to take at least that to get back, and more to get to the van."

"Stop doing math; it's a vacation." Bree complains.

"The van's not going to care about Bree time. And, do you really want to get stranded here?" I really don't want to figure out how much of a bluff it is that the van will leave without us. I don't want to try to figure out how to get back to the hotel without our escorts.

A taxi to Xel-ha would be out of the question since we don't actually have the physical tickets on us, and I'm not paying twice.

"Think about the food, and snorkeling waiting for you at Xel-Há." Will suggests. "They never did give us our breakfast, did they?"

I don't remember anything about being promised breakfast, but in the midst of everything I suppose we had forgotten to eat breakfast.

When were we supposed to be able to eat breakfast anyway? If the tour didn't provide breakfast, and the hotel doesn't set out breakfast until after we leave, where were we supposed to get food from?

"Fine. But, let's take some pictures." Bree agrees and grabs the camera from me. "You, and Will, stand over there. I'm going to take some pictures of you." She commands.

I know she'll take up the whole rest of the time with the pictures. I look at Will with a touch of defeat, and a silent apology. He, however, seems to pay no mind, and starts moving over to where Bree tells him to stand.

We stand far enough out of the way that people are respectable, and go behind Bree rather than in front of the camera. Will switches out with Bree after a couple pictures. She grabs onto me, and we hug to the sides of each other.

Will takes pictures of us, in all the various positions and spots Bree wants, until his watch alarm goes off.

He moves to hand the camera back to me, but Bree snatches it. She has to review the pictures. I can only hope that she doesn't delete any ones that she deems bad; for her self-image's sake.

She's got a nasty habit of doing just that.

We rush towards the exit. We get the option to walk through a tunnel made into the wall surrounding the city, and we take it. I can only chuckle as both Bree and Will have to duck through; Will more so than Bree. People were typically shorter back then, at an average height of five feet or so. My height would have been average or possibly on the taller side.

Bree instantly realizes why I'm laughing to myself. "Oh, shut up Shorty." Will belts a laugh out as it clicks in to why I'm laughing. I watch as he knocks the back of his head a bit on the ceiling.

We make it back to the shuttle, just in time. The van pulls out after we get seated. We were the last ones needed to be able to leave, though we still had a couple minutes to spare according to Will's watch. Others without watches may have given themselves extra buffer time to make sure they got to the shuttle in time.

"I'm starving, how long should it take to get there?" Bree breaks the silence.

"No idea."

"You booked it." She tells me.

I defend myself. "They don't tell you how long of a drive it takes to get to each place. I assume that we should be there in time for lunch." Driving time between events was not even a blip on my radar when I was booking things. Though, I wouldn't imagine they would be too far apart.

She grumbles for a moment. "Are you having lunch with us, or are you going to look for your friends?" Bree asks Will.

"I figured I'll have a quick peak around for them once we get there, but if I can't find them in about two seconds, I'll join you for lunch. Xel-Há is huge." Will explains his plan, and I find myself not minding if he hangs around for a little longer.

"Have you been there before?" Bree asks.

"Yeah, once. A couple years ago Sil, Sam, and I were there with our folks. It's massive, and has a hundred things to do. It might take a couple hours to find them." It takes me a moment, but I end up deducing that Sam might be the name of Silvia's soon-to-be husband. It would make sense, knowing they've been dating for eight years, and that he's also Will's best friend. Might make sense for them to go on a vacation between the two families.

In a lack of introduction, we missed his friend's name. And this way, I no longer have to call him Silvia's soon-to-be husband or use descriptors. At least, until I figure out whether it's actually his name or not.

"Why didn't you go with them?" Bree asks. I perk up internally. I too, wish to know this. It's something I've been asking myself since we found him on the bus. I hadn't the courage to ask him myself.

"They wanted to do the full day at Xel-Há. Sil and Sam wanted to see what it was like for a full day. We did the half day last time, but it didn't seem like quite enough time to do everything. But, I also love history, so I wanted to do the ruins again." I file away that tidbit for later. Something we may have in common.

"Oh goody; another history nerd." Bree mutters behind me. I ignore her, and it doesn't look like Will heard her.

"I thought you would have been doing the pirate ship today?" I question. Wasn't that the whole reason for him talking to me yesterday?

My heart flutters unexplainably at the possibility that he

might've just been making an excuse to speak with me.

"Tomorrow." With one word, he dashes it.

"Pirate ship?" Bree asks.

"Dinner and a show on a pirate ship." I quickly summarize for her.

Her hands fly to each air pocket over her shoulders in a grand gesture. "And you picked a boring history lesson, and swimming instead?"

I can just hear her tacking on a *what the hell Skylar*, but I quickly interject before she submits the van to a swearing outburst. "Yes. You can pick the pirate ship for your turn. Or, whatever else you want. You're the one who didn't want to get up with me to go pick the excursion for today."

"Yeah, yeah, yeah." Bree settles back in her chair, and looks out the window. She knows I'm right.

It's silent for a couple minutes. I take in my own hunger, and exhausted legs, yet I somehow also have energy.

I may be used to being on my feet all day, but there's usually not so much walking on unlevel terrain, and in the heat; this seems like a different sort of expenditure. As well as a different kind of energy that's keeping me up, and going.

"So, you like history too?" Will asks, I guess he caught on from Bree's comment.

"Yeah, I find it interesting." My short sentence doesn't seem like enough, so I scramble to say something else. "Started my hobby with reading everything I could about ancient Egypt after watching the Mummy."

"Loved that movie. I'm a bit of an amateur archeologist."

"What makes you an amateur archeologist?" I'm suspicious of anyone who calls themselves an amateur anything.

Not that they can't be incredibly intelligent or skilled in

whichever it is, but because most of the time someone uses it to mean that they spent a few hours perfecting one iota of a section of the particular subject matter, but only enough that could impress someone in a five minute conversation.

Like an amateur astronomer I met, who knew less about space than I could remember from sixth grade science class, and The Magic School Bus, however could name, not find, a bunch of constellations, and explain some of the stories behind them.

Or the amateur pianist I met, who taught themselves how to play one song really well, but couldn't do anything else on a piano.

"I went to school but never completed my degree. I know a lot, and have a bunch of contacts in the field, so I can go to some digs, and get behind the scenes in many places. I've worked in a few places, but never for too long."

He's got some experience in a school setting, and at some digs, so I give him the free pass on qualifying himself as an amateur. Although, he doesn't mention how much of the schooling he completed; could be a few days, or a couple years.

"Cool. I wish I could have done that." Will opens his mouth, I assume to ask why, so I beat him to the answer. "I was groomed to take over the family business. There were no other options for me growing up. So business school and I've only ever worked at the cafe."

"Can't you train a location manager, and call it good?" His question plucks a cord.

"Hn, apparently not. Keeping it in the family, family owned and operated, is super important." Similar conversations have taken place, to the complete refusal of my parents. They can't see the benefit to having someone around that can run things when one of us can't. They can't even see how having outside help for servicing would be of help. "One of those things you just accept because that's all you've ever known. It's been the only option since I was conceived. Probably the reason I was conceived. So any notion of something else was always brushed off as, *that's a nice hobby.*"

I don't even know if I'd've actually have liked to do archaeology as a career, but I would have liked to have been able to explore it as an option.

"That's sad. Glad my parents are sell outs. They own a huge business building houses, but we work through contractors, and have management handle the bulk of everything. They work a couple hours a day, mostly meetings with clients, and contractors, maybe some other employees like the accountant or supply manager. But otherwise, they're pretty hands off."

I nod, and hmm thoughtfully. If my parents had been willing, that could have been them, or working respectable hours while being able to take time off when they want to. Time off as a whole entire family, together, at the same time.

"I had the opposite problem of you, it seems." He muses as he stares off towards the front of the van. "I was always told to do whatever I want, because I could literally do whatever I wanted. So I've been everything; dishwasher, wine taster, food critic, carpenter, model, dog walker, pet groomer, video game tester, trail guide, storm chaser, BMW car salesman, barista…" His trailing off has me assuming there are far more titles he could be adding to his list.

"Hard to narrow down job prospects when your parents say *there's a million jobs out there, and you can do any of them.*"

At his pause, I comment passively when I can think of nothing else useful to say out of politeness. "That is definitely on the other end of the spectrum." I would have rather had his issue, than to have my life set out before me. "So, do you think you'll stick with archeology?"

"My track record says no. I am well aware, and I've been made very well aware that I have issues settling into a career."

I recall his words from earlier; at least he's honest.

"I think I'd like to stick with it." He continues. "The problem with being official is that you tend to have to settle down to one area, stick to one dig for years. A buddy's dad has worked his dig for fifteen years. I just- I don't think I could do that."

A rich kid with commitment issues, I scoff internally. To have his problems...

Yet, part of me pities him. It's how he was raised that likely influenced how he turned out. Hard to get away from your roots. Hard to untrain what you were taught for ninety percent of your life; especially when those that influenced, and raised you are still in your life.

"Sounds like you need a job that brings you something new every day, or month, or whichever. Something flexible, but steady in some aspect."

Chapter 5

The bus drops us off, and this time our guide is the guy on the bus. He checks us into Xel-Há after the general run through, and warning; meet back at the bus in four, and a half hours or you will be left behind.

We each go into our designated bathroom areas to change, and lock our stuff up. We meet Will in an area after the showers, and collect snorkels, goggles, life jackets, and flippers.

When they finally release us into the park, we find out we still have a little ways to go. The place has a couple areas to swim with some dolphins, and some other sea creatures; for an extra fee.

The path opens up after this, and we finally get to see exactly how expansive this park really is.

A floating bridge blocks the way out to the ocean on the left, but there is no end to what I can see on the right.

Hunger gone with the anticipation of exploration, I walk closer to the bay area.

People flood the water, and what surrounds. There are rocks making up a small island which people are climbing, and resting on in the center, quite the distance away. By the time anyone would reach that, they would need a rest.

The jungle surrounds the water, and hides much of the park. They have a map of the whole park displayed on a huge billboard, and I am in awe of the expansive place.

"How are you going to find your friends?" I ask in wonder. It might take the whole four hours just to make one lap around the park.

Will shrugs, the daunting task doesn't seem to bother him. "That's a question for a full stomach."

"God yes!" Bree cheers. "I'm starving."

Will takes the lead with Bree to the large building on the right. A buffet, larger than I've ever seen before, is laid out to the side of hundreds of tables, and chairs. There even appears to be an upstairs portion with more seating room.

Despite it being lunch time, it's not too busy, but I get the idea that many people haven't discovered it's lunch yet. People don't wear watches much anymore, so unless they find a clock randomly around, they are hopeless for time telling.

That would be something to note if we stay with Will; at least he wears a watch, and it appears to be waterproof since he didn't take it off. He would be handy to keep around so we don't miss our bus.

We grab up plates at the beginning of the shuffle. I quickly realize that they serve everything familiar and otherwise. Salads, burgers, fries, hotdogs, pastas, and everything else that I would expect to get back home. Fruits and raw vegetables hold their own sections.

Above the food, scattered around, are intricately carved watermelons and flower arrangements.

Bree loads up on what she finds familiar, and comforting; starting with fries. I'm hesitant to grab at the first things I see. Much more interesting items could be further down the line, and I don't want my plate filled up before I can get to them.

I follow Will beyond to the local dishes. I would be remiss to go to another country, and not take advantage of the more local cuisine.

There are all sorts of dishes, most of which I could not name without looking at the name placards, and even then the name doesn't stick in my mind for long.

I end up just picking up whatever looks like it would be good, and fill my plate that way. There's taco chips covered in a green sauce that Will takes, so I grab some too. A chicken in a brown sauce is next; I think it's some sort of chocolate derivative sauce. I plate up a spicy shelled shrimp that looks fresh and interesting. Some mixed cooked vegetables and a fruit salad make their way onto my plate too.

We pass by the desserts, and I'm ecstatic to learn they have an ice cream machine.

Will, and I sit down at an empty blue table, and chairs; depositing both food, and all the gear we have to haul around. A patterned tile lies in a grid on top, and yellow napkins hold the cutlery.

That's truly something I appreciate about my short time here; everything is so colourful, and vibrant. At home, most colour comes from accents placed on white, black or brown.

It makes everything so much more vibrant and cheery when the main colour is an actual colour.

I can't wait to dig into my food, so I don't. I try the taco chips with some sort of green sauce on it. Like a green warm salsa, delicious.

Bree finds us quickly enough. She's managed to pile desserts onto her plate as well.

"I hope there aren't sharks or alligators in the water." Bree announces as she sits down.

"I don't think they'd have an attraction like this open for long, if that was an issue." I use logic to debate the question, though now I hope the same. One would hope that they wouldn't cover up a bunch of tourists being eaten just to make a few bucks; then again money is greedy.

"There's a shark net if any venture close enough." Bree's eyes widen. Will works quickly to help ease her fears. "We were told last time, that they don't like the two waters mixing so they don't come in here."

"Right, you've been here before." Bree shovels some fries into her mouth. "So what did you see last time?" She asks between bites.

He thinks for a moment. "Probably the coolest thing was the snuba diving."

"What the hell is snuba diving?" Bree asks before I can.

"They put a clunky helmet on you that has a hose to the surface, and you walk a path on the ocean floor as the staff lures fish to you." Will explains.

"Well, that sounds safe." I mutter.

"That's why the staff are there; to make sure you stay safe. They do it out on the other side of the bridge, where the water is clearer, and more salt water."

I almost echo myself. It doesn't sound the safest to have people luring fish to you in the ocean part of this place.

Will continues after a moment of silence. "And, I don't know what exactly it was, I think maybe a grouper or barracuda but I'm not sure, but there was a, had to be, six foot long fish that came to us. Long, dark brown, and the diver guy a few feet from me opened up the fish's mouth. A hand on each side as it grew as big as the guy's head. It swam off after that, but it was awesome."

"I'm not going in the water." Bree declares.

"That's why they have the shark net, and those guys don't like the fresh water inside the lagoon; so you're safe. They don't come in here, because they can't physically breathe in the fresh water." Will explains.

It sounds right but I wish I had my phone to fact check him. I seem to remember inklings of some sharks being able to switch between the salt, and fresh water.

"Okay." Bree drags out in her unconvinced suspicion.

Will glances around the large room; probably looking out for his friends. It would be quite the convenience if they would come in for lunch while we're here.

Will, and Bree discuss his previous trip to Xel-ha, and to Mexico, as I go off in my head, and dig more into my food, and only half listen to the conversation.

His mom prefers to stick around the resort, while his dad is up for adventures; he sounds like he takes after his dad.

Bree bursts out laughing when his story turns to when his sister punched his shoulder, when he ran his fingers up her back to pretend she had a poisonous spider on her; it sounds like he deserved it.

The whole park is huge. If the party keeps moving around the park, as he does, he could possibly never find them. It doesn't sound like they had any plans to meet up at a specific spot.

Having no plan, is not a good plan strategy.

Since he's been with us all morning, I feel obligated to ensure he makes it back to them safely.

When they reach a natural pause, and not just in order to eat food, I take my turn to talk. "We should help him look a bit. That way he's not alone the whole time if he never finds them."

Will negates my suggestion. "No use in letting you waste your visit."

Bree suggests instead, "we could stay in one spot for a while, and if he doesn't find them in a half hour, then he can come back, and find us, if he finds them then we'll just move along."

"I don't want you having to wait on me. I'll be fine, even if I don't find them. I know how to have fun by myself." Will sticks out his chest, and puffs out; like we questioned him on his abilities.

I have no doubts that he can find things to do, and people to hang out with, but I kind of want those people to be us. Especially, if the alternative is strangers; not that we're anything but one step above strangers.

"Relax," Bree puts a hand on his shoulder to deflate him. "Sky probably has already thought this through, and has her mind made up. And I agree, so you have no chance of shaking us now."

"You're not going to let this go?" He asks between the two of us. Bree smiles wickedly, and shakes her head. I tighten my smile, and hope he doesn't get ticked off at us. "Alright," he laughs in a huff of resignation. He gives in a bit too easily for any ill will. "But, we do things along the way. That way, if we don't find them, I'm not wasting your first trip here. Deal?"

"Deal." Bree and I agree together. It sounds reasonable.

We finish eating our meals. I'm disappointed when Bree, and Will deem it time to go before I can grab any dessert. But, I don't fight it and don't mention it. Maybe I can convince them to come back before we leave.

Will suggests snorkeling first. "We can swim out into the lake to get some distance, while we see some fish. You'll want to do it now, before you get too tired from walking around the place."

Bree agrees. She sticks close to him, and I start to wonder if she thinks she might be able to get a good rebound in, before returning to real life. Doubtful, but still…

A pit forms in my chest when I think about it. I shake it off. If she wants to rebound with Will, then it's my job to back off, and let her. It's not like anything would even happen between us anyway. I'm not the type to have a vacation hookup. Neither was Bree, but after what's happened, who knows.

As we approach the stairs, I notice something that looks very out of place; a faucet spout on the rocks seemingly suspended in the air. A water feature some are taking advantage of. It's odd that I hadn't noticed it before, since it really looks so out of place.

A sign before the water explains what Will had. Stating that the water is murky because of the fresh and salt water mixing. I hope we'll still be able to see enough despite this.

The water is cool, but not cold; nothing like the glacier water in Banff. It's certainly more than tolerable and doesn't cause goosebumps. After just a few moments, the water even seems warm around me.

After the stairs there is a very brief ledge in which you can get your bearings, and your flippers on, before you jump off. After that, the lagoon floor is meters away.

Now I know why they give everyone life jackets. Grasping ledges are too far away, and there's nowhere to put your feet to catch your breath. Only experienced swimmers would be able to last long enough to get a good view otherwise.

Adjusting my gear, I put the goggles over my eyes and the snorkel in my mouth. Immediately, I don't like the feel of the plastic mouthpiece.

I try not to think about how many people have used this before me. All I can hope is that they've got a great sanitary wash system.

Dunking my head in the water I try out the breathing tube but water rushes into my mouth. By some miracle I don't breathe any of the water in but the salty taste isn't pleasant. I spit the water out, and then try again.

The mouthpiece is still unpleasant, and now I have the ocean in my mouth to add to the experience. It doesn't change no matter how many times I attempt to use the snorkel. Instead of being able to breathe air, I just get a mouth full of water. The longest I'm able to go is just three breaths of fresh air.

Neither Will nor Bree seem to be having the same issues as I am. Maybe my snorkel is broken. Maybe it's user error. I don't know enough about them to know.

Once annoyed enough, I decide to give up on the snorkel, and just hold my breath instead. By doing this I'm able to finally get a good look around, and catch up to the others.

"I've given up on the snorkel, I keep breathing in water." I announce once both their heads come up at my approach.

Will tells me, "it's easy once you get the hang of it."

"Before or after I drown?" I wonder in all seriousness.

"Hopefully before."

"I think I'll stick to holding my breath. It seems safer that way."

Will shrugs, and leaves me be. We decide to head off to the right, to make a loop around the park, starting out with swimming along the pathway.

Though we swim together, we each go off in our own little world divided by water. There's no point to try to catch another's attention when ears are under the water, and plugging up noise from above.

When I spot a large turtle swim up a few feet from me, I wish to alert Will and Bree so they can see too. But, I know there would be a slim chance of them hearing me, and a large chance I lose the turtle.

I swim along slightly behind it, so as to give it its own space, and not disturb it. A respectful distance between me and a wild animal. It's at this moment that I have no idea whether or not a turtle could actually be a danger to me. I've heard snapping turtles have a nasty bite, but that's about it.

Swimming a little faster, I keep good pace with the turtle, but I know that I'm veering a little bit off the path we were going.

Will manages to come up beside me, and I point at the turtle. With a little expression that goggles give way to, I realize he's excited, and has already noticed the large animal.

It has to be almost as big as me, though the size estimate might be off.

If a turtle as big as this could get in here, who's saying a shark couldn't? Those shark nets must have some large holes in them if a five foot turtle can get inside.

We follow the turtle for a bit before it decides to pick up speed, and turn about.

Surfacing for desperately required air has me losing sight of it altogether.

Will follows me up. "That was awesome!"

"Yeah, Bree's going to be sad she missed it." I air my regret. At my own mention, I look to find her. She's a little ways away at this point. Her head bobbing up and down and she still swims along our original path.

"I tried splashing some water her way to catch her attention, but that obviously didn't work."

"Thanks for trying." At least he tried, I didn't.

"No problem." He smiles before sticking the tube back in his mouth. We head over to catch up to Bree, who hadn't noticed our absence or approach at all. She's in her own world.

I grab onto her arm, and she surfaces to talk. "We saw a turtle."

"Where?" She dips under water to look around.

I pull her back up. "Swam off."

"Awe." Bree sinks her shoulders.

"It was awesome. As big as Sky." Will holds out his arms to demonstrate.

"Awe." Her second iteration is held longer than the first. She's disappointed that she didn't get the chance to see it.

"I'm sorry." I apologize, wishing I would have tried to grab her attention; even if it meant I would have lost the turtle. "I wish we would've had a waterproof camera, so I could've taken a picture of it."

"Next time." She declares. I don't wish to break her heart more by telling her it'll likely never happen again; what would the chances be? We could come here every day for a whole summer, and likely not have the same experience. "I'm starting to cramp up." Bree complains as her hand goes to her side.

"We should get to land then. We don't want you to get bad enough, we have to drag you back to shore. We can walk for a bit." Will jokes. But, if it got bad enough, that certainly could be a possibility.

I think back to our lunch, maybe we should have waited a bit before swimming. Would have been the smart thing to do.

We come upon the land at the next opportunity, and adjust ourselves to walk from there.

I quickly decide that if I were to do this again, I would skip the flippers, and snorkel. The flippers are a lot to carry around when out of the water, and I don't wish to drown myself with the snorkel. I could do well enough without either. If I didn't have to return them for a deposit back, I'd ditch them.

I watch around me, as I look to all the trees along the path. There are signs in some places, letting you know which paths to follow for what activity.

We walk a long ways between the different sections and activities. Nothing appears to catch any of our interest along the way. Though, I might've been good for a nap in some of the hammocks if we had more time.

My arm yanks my whole body back through a heavy grip around it. I stumble a bit. Grasping for balance from the same

54

force that dragged me back, I grab onto Will's torso with flailing arms.

Before I can shout my shock at him, he beats me to it. "Watch where you're walking." Pointing down to the ground.

I frown in confusion, before looking along where I had been walking. A fat dull green iguana eyes me up. Two more steps and I would have walked right into him.

"Thanks." I gasp, regaining my composure.

"Why is that here?" Bree shrieks.

We cautiously walk around the iguana, and then speed away from it as Will explains. "Xel-ha is a nature preserve, of course there's all sorts of creatures here, and not just sea-life. Poisonous spiders, venomous snakes, scorpions-"

"Stop talking." Bree covers her ears with her hands. More of a gesture than anything that actually would help. "Why the hell would you tell me that?"

"You didn't check before you came?" He seems surprised.

"No! Why the fuck would I want to know all the things that would kill me while I'm here?" Bree decries.

"Ignorance is bliss. Now I'll never get her to leave the resort." I speak low, mostly to myself, yet hoping Will hears the damage he's done.

"Why would you go to a whole other country, and not research the dangerous wildlife you might come across? You need to know what to do to avoid them, and how to lessen your risks. How not to get bitten or killed." Will's reasoning is sound, but I know plenty of people who don't know what kinds of dangerous animals are lurking in their own back yard, let alone in another country.

I only learned last year that we have a local-ish poisonous spider species called a brown recluse spider. That only took twenty four years to learn.

I decide to catch Bree up to speed, and show Will that at least one of us did our research. "Black widows, brown recluse, and bright colour spiders are poisonous. In many creatures a bright colour means poisonous. Arrow head snakes usually mean venomous and no arrow head may mean not venomous; you might still get bitten but the bite probably won't kill you. Scorpions don't generally sting unless provoked. If you get bitten or stung, and can't bring a body with you, then be able to describe the animal so they can give you the right anti-venom. They have big and little wild cats; like jaguars, mountain lions, and ocelot. Wolves. Oh, and don't forget the sea urchins we came across the first day. And jelly fish."

"And iguanas that will bite you with serrated teeth, and infect you with non deadly venom if you step on them. Probably get an infection from the bacteria, maybe lose some toes." The admonishment in his fact is well deserved.

"Yes, I should definitely watch where I'm walking better. I was too busy gawking at everything else." It's a lame excuse, and I know it. If he hadn't been paying attention, then I would likely be paying the painful consequences of stepping on a wild reptile.

"At least one of you did your research." Will looks to Bree.

"Yes, yay her. Sky knows all the things that could kill us. Is it going to help if they decide to kill us; no, so why bother?" Bree freaks a little.

I think she's a bit freaked out from the talk of all the dangerous creatures that could be hiding around the next corner. I didn't look up the individual chances of likelihood of bites and stings, but most state that chances were low of coming across the creatures, let alone having them attack you.

We should probably stop and divert the conversation anyway.

"They've got the cliff jump that way." Will smartly distracts with sight of the sign. "Anyone up for a brief swim?"

"Yes, thank God. Anything that gets me out of this jungle, and all the things I now know can kill me. Thanks for that." Bree breezes by the both of us, in her bid to get to the cliff.

As we round the corner, Bree's already taken off and deposited all her gear, and is making a break for the edge. Her body jumps slightly up before dropping out of sight.

I walk cautiously to the edge. It's a dizzying height down to the water. They have a rectangle you need to land in, likely so you don't hit any rocks, and seriously injure yourself.

Bree comes up, and swims back to the shore line. Disappearing for a minute, before she comes up from a path.

I see the little hitchhiker immediately. The smallest crab I've ever seen has hitched a ride in her hair.

Walking calmly to her, I scoop the little guy up. She shrieks when I pull my hand back, and she spots the little guy in my hand.

"It's just a baby crab." The little pale brown guy does look very much like a spider, at a passing glance. It tickles my hand as it tries to run away.

Her scream stops immediately, and is replaced by cooing. "I thought it was a spider."

"I wouldn't have grabbed a spider out of your hair." The suggestion otherwise is absolutely ridiculous. "I would have suggested you take another dive, and hoped that would have gotten rid of it without biting either of us."

Bree looks slightly betrayed, but gets over it quickly, and nods in the fairness of it all. "Oh, go jump off the cliff." She tells to Will, who's laughing at the both of us. He salutes her command, and jumps off. She turns her attention to me. "You too."

"I think I'm good staying up here." I get a flash of dizziness remembering the height.

"What happened to you being spontaneous for this week only?

Please, I did it, and Will did it. So you have to do it or he'll think you're a wimp." Bree goads.

"I am a wimp." I state.

She gives me a glare, and against my better judgement, I let her talk me into it.

With all my gear to the side, I look down to make sure Will is clear. I don't see him anywhere, but I know he's not in the semi clear water.

Going now would be best, before Will witnesses a pitiful fall, and before Bree starts heckling.

A simple jump won't do. I need to take a run at it. I wouldn't want to risk not jumping far enough to clear the cliff.

Two meters back, I charge, and run. When I get to the edge, I nearly miss my footing. A heel hits the edge, and I can push off from it. A fleeting thought realizes exactly how bad of a fall that could have been.

Leaving my stomach at the top of the cliff, my breath catches in my throat. I plug my nose shut with my fingers, and close my eyes.

When I hit the water, I quickly sink to the bottom. I kick, and push up. The distance to the top is nearly too much for the small breath I took. I gasp at the air when I finally get to it.

A small victory allows for an excitement to build; I would do that again. It wasn't bad at all; fun even.

I turn around, and swim towards shore. Will puts his hand out, and I take the offer of a boost out.

The river edge is a little steeper than the gradual entrances some pools have. But it is angled rather than a straight edge.

Will's yank pulls me faster than I was expecting, and I'm out, and on my feet in a split second.

"Thanks." I say. His eyes catch me in a moment, with my hand still in his. Comfortable warmth blooms in my chest.

I realize I've been staring too long, and holding his hand too long; despite only a moment passing.

Seemingly to make up for that, I release him, and quickly turn away to meet back up at the top with Bree.

I have to consciously slow my pace to keep in mind to wait a bit for him, as he did for me.

The moment gone, and with it my embarrassment, I mentally check to make sure my top is in the right place and covering the right things. Fleetingly hoping that wasn't what his look was about; all seems well.

Chapter 6

Will calls out, "SILVIA!"

Nothing.

"SAM!"

Nothing.

"MEL!"

Nothing.

"BOGTROTTER!"

"Bogtrotter?" Bree asks.

"It's my last name." Will explains. Will Bogtrotter. It's certainly an interesting last name.

"What kind of name is Bogtrotter?" Bree asks.

"Irish, basically means exactly what you'd think it would. Dad blames our last name on me being a wanderer." Will doesn't bat an eyelash, as he tries to get back to his friends.

He's probably heard all that could be said about his last name, by this point in his life. School children can be cruel, whether they mean to be or not.

"I don't think they can hear you." Bree tells him.

So close yet, still, very far away. The larger group disappears into a river pathway covered by foliage. They are on bright inner tubes floating down the river.

"They've gone down the lazy river. We can catch up if we

hurry." Will says. He picks up quicker than his previous pace. It seems that striking the unlikelihood of finding them, has created a sense of urgency. We are so close; it would suck to lose them now.

Bree and he take the lead to the lazy river entrance. When Bree takes hold of the inner tube, I guess that we're making sure we deliver Will straight to his people; finding them isn't enough.

I hope they don't mind the intrusion. It's not like there will be a path we can divulge to, to part ways with them in the middle of the ride. I don't want to make them feel obligated to take us with them from there.

We get inside the tubes, I rearrange my carry-ons to be a bit more comfortable, and the staff pushes us off.

Very quickly our speed lulls to a dull crawl.

Bree takes the lead by pushing her hands through the water. Will looks content just to float along; though we'd likely not catch up to his friends that way, not unless they stop randomly.

Between the life jacket, and the tube, I barely make a difference in my speed when I try to brush my hands in the water.

The water carries me into the thicket. I push away with my foot to get away, but I keep bouncing back.

Will's hand grasps onto my handle to stopping my yo-yoing. "Looks like you need a bit of help."

"Thanks." I hadn't noticed when he got off his tube. He walks, and pulls me away from the trees. Quickly, we catch up to Bree.

"I didn't realize this river would be so lazy." Will says.

I can't help but to call him on his erroneous thinking, as a joke. "Pretty sure it's right in the name."

"I've been on lazy river runs before, all with more zip and pep than this one. Wouldn't be so slow with a beer in hand, and all day to waste. But *we* are on a mission." He emphasizes the we, like he wishes to include us in on it. I suppose that's been true thus far.

I grab onto Bree's hand, and Will pulls us both along until we find a man. At first, he appears to be sleeping in his tube, but a quick splash from Will, pulls him back to the living.

"What the hell!? Bogtrotter!" He clamours out of his tube clumsily, and tackles Will. The cool water splashes onto us.

We leave Will wrestling with his friend as we are pulled along.

Bree and I look at each other. Stuck on the lazy river with our companion delivered to his friends, or at least one of them.

Out of nowhere a couple staff members peak out from the woods.

"A picture ladies? You can preview them in the lobby when done, and decide then if you wish to purchase them." One of the men says.

"Sure." Bree agrees.

We link our hands together, and grasp onto each side of the pathway. We smile, and the one man takes a couple pictures.

"Lovely ladies. Enjoy the rest of your float." He wishes.

"Thank you," I respond.

Bree and I unlatch and push off to continue down the stream.

"So what do you want to do after this?" I ask in the pensive silence.

"I don't know. Continue down whatever path, and see what we come across? Don't suppose you paid attention to the map enough to remember where the river run ended?" She asks.

"Nope." And, I take it she didn't either.

I wonder what time it is. We have to be nearing the half way mark; at least. We ate lunch, and travelled at least half way around the park; if I were to guess.

We float a ways in silence until Will, and his friend catch up to us, now tubeless. "Let move this along, shall we?" Will asks rhetorically as he takes a hold of the handle on my tube. His friend helps drag Bree along.

He introduces himself to Bree as Ryan.

The ground gets steeper, and the boys start swimming us along. I almost feel bad that they are doing all the work, but not bad enough to get out of the tube to help.

The boys catch us up to the larger group quick enough. They greet us with a big cheer.

"Hey look, Ryan found Will!" One shouts. The group pushes towards the beach, so we follow them.

I get out as soon as I figure the water would be at my waist, while Bree lets Ryan push her right up to the beach.

A girl comes over as we make landing, so Will introduces us. "This is Silvia. Silvia, this is Skylar, and Bree. I'm not going to bother with anyone else, because there's way too many of us, and you'll never remember their names anyway." The familial resemblance between her, and Will is nearly nothing; except for the eyes. She's much shorter than he is, and has brown hair and eyes.

On one hand it seems rude to nix the introductions, but on the other hand what he says is very true. Learning ten names on a once over, is difficult, and nearly impossible for me. I'd maybe be able to remember one name, possibly two.

Bree on the other hand, might have a better chance. She's always had a knack for names. Remembering the full names of people we knew in high school, when I can only remember a face; let alone their first name.

Silvia takes my hand is a shake. "Hi, nice to meet you. Mel says you're the person I have to thank for keeping Will on track until she got there."

"Oh, it was nothing. He asked for a suggestion, and I gave him a couple." I get the idea that Will is a handful. Each person we've come across has always got some passive aggressive comment about his behaviour.

I wonder who Will is when he's not on vacation, or if he's exactly who he's presented himself to be, but there is much more to uncover.

Or, if his friends may be stuck on his past numerous behaviours and actions, and have painted him with that brush; despite countering circumstances and growing up since then.

But, then again, people don't usually change; they just naturally or mindfully shift a bit. It takes life altering situations to force remarkable change.

"Ryan says you're going to the cave next, mind if we join?" Bree asks as she comes closer.

"Of course, the more the merrier." Silvia smiles. Bree turns around and joins with Ryan, who wraps an arm around her shoulders as they go off to the large group.

I can only stare for a moment, exasperated at Bree. "I'm sorry, she forgets her manners sometimes. Thank you." There goes my bid to not intrude on the party. Can always count on Bree to insert herself.

"No problem, I'm used to the type. She's excited." Silvia smiles after Bree as she assimilates with the larger group nicely. "Did you enjoy the ruins? Sorry, you got pegged with this disaster." She pushes lightly at Will's chest. "Hope he didn't bore you."

"Not at all. He actually didn't reveal his history nerdiness until we were on the bus coming here." I feel an unexpected need to defend him a little. "If he had, Bree wouldn't have survived the tour. I actually have a thing for ancient history as well."

"Oh goody. You can talk amoungst yourselves, and he doesn't have to bore me to sleep."

At a shriek of her name, Silvia is off and yelling at a guy pulling one of the girls into the water.

Silvia quickly arranges her ducklings in an orderly fashion long enough to direct them to put their tubes in the cordoned off section, and go up the path.

She successfully gets us all moving on our way up the path, and on the way to, what I assume is, the cave.

I watch my steps carefully as we walk through another section of the jungle. There is no other wildlife on the path, but I won't let that stop my vigilance.

Will seems content to walk beside me in silence; but he's hard to get a reading on. I don't dare look at his face.

I itch to start up a conversation. While silence is normally comforting, it's nerve wracking with him; for some reason. He seems like one of those people who need to talk, so silence for him could be a sign of something bad. Perhaps, I'm boring him, or he thinks he's saddled with me now.

The slightest chance that he might be okay with our silence, keeps me from saying anything until he does.

When we get to the cave, it's different then I thought it would be. We put our flippers back on, and swim a little inside.

We come around a bend and under a ceiling that gets larger, and deeper going back. It's chilly the further we go.

There is a uniformed man sitting with a camera in hand, instructing the group where to go for the picture.

Bree and I separate from the group as the wedding party sits, and stands around the back of the cave while a photographer takes a few shots of them. Bree and I stand waiting for our turn when Silvia invites us in for a couple shots.

We join in on the side but Ryan pulls Bree towards the center. Will comes around, and places his arm around my shoulders.

I look up to him just as a flash goes off. Looking back to the photographer, I'm ready for the second picture.

The photographer hurries us out to get to the next group, a couple waiting patiently for their turn.

I instantly regret that I won't get a picture with just Bree and I, but I don't want to take up more of the man's time for a shot I'm not sure I'd purchase anyway.

The flippers don't last long as we circle around to the bridge and remove them to walk across. As the waves go up, and down, the bridge sways every direction.

The bridge feels like a fun house ride. I use the bars to help myself get along. Without them, I'm certain I would have been tossed into the ocean on one of the sides.

Some of the wedding party starts tossing each other in. I'm unsure who started it, but become aware as Bree shouts my name. She's suddenly missing from the bridge, but pops up quickly in the water thanks to her life vest. Others are tossed in after, while some bob in the water from their trips prior to my watching.

A few of the guys try to get back up on the bridge, but the sway makes it near impossible, and they appear more likely to get knocked out in the attempt.

I jump in so that I can join Bree, and swim the rest of the way to shore.

Someone announces that it's nearing three thirty, and that we should go before the rush; I like their thinking and link eyes with Bree for the same.

We return our extra rented gear, and get our deposits back. Then, split off into our respective change rooms.

Bree and I leave through the only exit, right through the gift shop; a clever way to get people to purchase something. We peek at the assortments, but quickly balk at the prices, and decide against mementos.

We get back to the bus, and discover that we aren't the first back; the older couple is already settled into their seats. We are however, the second to get back here.

We find out that we have twenty five minutes until the bus wants to leave, which is better timing than I thought we'd have. Others arrive in the time expanse between.

Bree and I are overcome with a sudden exhaustion. It's not enough to have us fall asleep, but enough to sink us comfortably into our seats and weigh us down. A force holding us in place, unable to get up if we wanted to.

Will arrives last and out of breath. I had almost thought he was going to hitch a ride back with the wedding party.

"You almost missed the bus." I joke.

"Here." He hands over a large picture frame, and some loose pictures in his hand. "I grabbed these for you." Will settles in his seat across from us.

"Oh, you didn't have to get these for us." I know how much this must've cost him. He doesn't appear to have any left for him. The guilt churns me. I wonder if I miss heard, or misunderstood. All of these can't be for me. Maybe, he wants me to pick one from these and give the rest back. "Did you pick out some for yourself?"

He holds up a silver rectangle around his neck; something hanging from a necklace. "When you buy the pictures you get a memory stick of them. Sil took some, I grabbed some for you, and I get the digital copies."

"Thank you." I smile appreciatively. While glad to have cleared that up, the guilt remains; he shouldn't have spent that kind of money on me, on us.

Bree takes the picture to run through them. I look from the side, but a sun glare stops me from seeing some, while Bree shuffles through them too quick to see the rest well enough.

I'll look at them later.

Settling impossibly deeper into my seat, I find that I could possibly sleep here. I won't, but I think I could if I let myself. Especially as the van starts moving. The rocking is lulling.

Drained from our entire day's journey. My entire body sinks in, and becomes one with the cushion until we return back to our hotel.

Chapter 7

Bree finally emerges from the bathroom.

Food had been our number one priority when we had returned, and getting clean was number two.

The black of the night has a way of making our room feel isolated from the outside; though I know it isn't too terribly late in the evening. The sun here seems to disappear in a matter of minutes.

"God, took you long enough." I exclaim dramatically.

"Yeah, yeah. You know it takes me forever to get ready. You should expect it by now." She's unapologetic about it, but it's also why she took up the bathroom second.

"Did you really need the make up, and to do your hair?" I ask.

"Yes. Not everyone pulls off natural." I force myself not to visibly cringe with her words.

Her low self esteem strikes again. I don't know where she got it from. We've known each other since before all the glam. It felt like, just suddenly, one day she started the snowball rolling, and it's escalated gradually since.

She's so down on herself, yet will be the first to lift someone else up.

"You're beautiful with or without it all done up. I don't know why you don't see that, and think you need it to look good." The conversation will end here; it always does. Bree doesn't say more, as she puts on her shoes.

The hair, and make up thing started in grade nine. First, her hair always needed to be straightened even if it was going into some sort of updo. She literally would pull out any hairs that wouldn't cooperate or that flew out of order.

Then, came the make up. Variations between needing to do a full face of make up, or a minimum of foundation, and mascara at the start of the day.

She would actually refuse to leave her house if she didn't have her hair straightened or her minimum make up on; no matter if it was to just go to my house or out shopping or even the pool.

Just in case, because you never know who might see her... I mock her in my head.

Bree leads the way out of the room. Our overheard invitation gave vague instructions on where to go. The resort lady was informing a couple of girls where to go tonight for a party held by the resort.

The promise of a discotheque called to Bree; once she figured out it meant dance party.

I went for jean shorts, black tank top, and a red plaid; with no make up, and hair just combed after my shower. She went for a flowing yellow summer dress, full make up, and straightened hair. Pretty much our staple summer looks.

We follow the sound of the loud music once we get to the lobby. Around the corner, a set of doors has opened up to a large and open room.

Light flashes in red, blue, and green. The music is loud, but I'll adjust. Base is booming in my chest, and along the floor. This isn't really my normal scene, but it can be fun.

Bree pulls me over to the bartender. She orders us, something I can't hear over the music, but I see her throw up two fingers, so I figure she's ordering for us both.

I try not to baulk when he pours us liquid drinks, but then I notice there is no blender in sight. People likely don't want a loud blender interrupting their music.

He pours tequila and something else, and the tequila seems excessively poured.

Bree hands me one when she gets them, and cheers me. When I sip the drink, all I taste is the tequila, and nothing more. I have a feeling this will be a one and done drink for the rest of the night.

Bree takes down half of hers. A big smile breaks out, and she waves at someone. I look over to see Ryan beckoning her over.

I can't help but feel like the wedding party is going to get sick of us for tagging along to everything. I don't think I'd enjoy random people joining in on what I feel should be more intimate.

Bree walks by me to go to him, and I guess this is happening now. I curse Bree silently.

I wander off to the side. Dances and the bar scene, have never been my thing. If not for Bree, I wouldn't be here. And now, she's gone and abandoned me.

I have to admit to myself, that that last part is slightly my fault too. I could have followed if I had wanted to.

I long for some seats that I could sit at, enjoy the music and drinks, and not look like the weirdo leaning against the wall and not participating.

Bree catches me as my gaze goes to her. She tries to wave me over, but I hold up my drink. Her eyebrow raises, and her head tilts; she doesn't believe my excuse.

I take another sip.

She calls me out, and walks over to me. Taking my drink from me, I have no idea where hers went, she downs it. Bree tosses my empty cup in the garbage nearby, and pulls me over to the group.

Bree seems content with my being closer, and leaves me alone again to go over to Ryan.

I don't know what her point was in bringing me over, if she was just going to leave me.

Mel waves a welcome to me, so I wave back. But, she seems more interested in dancing with the girls group to do much more. I wonder if I should go over and be social able.

Warm hands grab onto my hips. A body latches into mine with some force just a moment later.

I turn to find that some random guy is trying to get me to dance with him. I try to get into it, to be more sociable, but last all of two seconds before his crotch starts to rub into my butt.

I turn around to motion to him that I'm done. I shake my head, and mouth 'no thanks'. But, he just rearranges his hands on my hips, and thrusts closer.

A hard grip makes an easy break away hard to do, but I manage by pushing against his chest with both hands. The alcohol assists as he loses grips. I shake my head again, but he reaches out to grasp at me again.

A large body cut between his and mine. I stare at a dark t-shirt for a moment before I realize what happened. Looking up, Will's back is to me, and he's an acting guardian statue against the other guy.

Will and the other guy say things to each other that I can't hear. It takes a moment of persuading, but the man relents to finding another dance partner.

Will turns and faces me once the other guy slinks into another girl's personal space. He smiles, and asks me something, but I can't make out what it was. I point to my ear and shake my head.

He thumbs up with both hands and raises a question eyebrow instead. I copy the movement, and shout, "thank you!"

Will points over to where he had come from. I don't feel like dancing much, so I motion cupping a hand around an invisible cup, and taking a drink. I'd feel more comfortable with a bit more alcohol and a reason to cling to the sides.

He thumbs up again, and walks by to join his friends again.

I go back to the bartender. As I wait for my turn, I see the drink options are limited to all non-blended drinks. I'm not familiar with most of the drinks, though I've heard some of the names before.

I split the decision between a Mai Tai, which I've heard of but have no idea what it might taste like, and a familiar minty Mojito.

The line moves too fast. Suddenly it's my turn. With my mind not made up yet, I go with what I know should taste good, and ask for a Mojito.

Taking up a spot against the wall again, I sip the minty drink. The mint, and rum are in equal parts of the taste, and I feel like I can enjoy this more that the all tequila thing Bree had chosen.

I'm quite certain, this bartender is excessively over pouring on every cup by design. Perhaps trying to get the partying tourists a little more drunk now that the sun has gone down.

I watch the fun, and sip my drink, until Will catches my eye. The lights make it seem like he's walking in slow motion towards me; the alcohol might be helping a little too.

I can't help but think this is the moment in those cheesy romance movies where time slows, and the person does some ridiculous sexy head shake. His blonde surfer hair even sways back, and forth, and I can almost picture him flipping it out of his face dramatically sexy. Maybe next he buttons down his shirt, or removes it altogether.

Will comes in for a jovial hug I'm not ready for. Ulterior motives made clear as he talks in my ear. "Go check on Bree. She's not looking too good."

He pulls away, I nod to him before he goes in another direction.

On his cue, I locate and walk over to Bree. Getting to a good angle, I take a look at her. She looks a little flush, yet pale at the same time. The colours of the lights are replicated on her face a little too well.

She's either sick, or going to be.

"Hey," I interrupt between her and Ryan. Loud enough, for Ryan to possibly hear, I shout. "Bree, we need to go pee." She nods appreciatively. Ryan nods and lets us go.

Instead of finding a bathroom nearby, I lead her away from the discotheque, and from everyone else.

"Are you okay, you don't look okay?" I ask her quietly.

A burst of tears, and a sob were the least of which I thought could happen. "No." She tries to say, but it comes out weak.

"Let's go back to the room." I lead her back, hand in hand. I have a feeling this is something huge; a breakdown in the making.

Her thoughts come out just as fast as she can say them, as soon as we get into the privacy of our room.

I let her talk, nodding where appropriate. Letting her finally get things out in the open. The alcohol loosening her lips more than what she spoke of while sober and devastated.

I brace myself for the long talk, getting comfortably settled on the bed. She takes a cue, and sits on the bed too.

"How could he? Why wasn't I good enough for him? Why would he drag me on? He cheated on me for pretty much our entire relationship, five years, with her. How could I not know?

And, we got married.

I was stupid enough to marry him.

We had sex, and he thought a good pillow talk was to tell me that he wanted a divorce; that he loved her more than me; that he knew it now because the sex didn't feel the same.

How fucked up is that? He based his relationship on how the sex felt rather than everything else; if he hadn't, we'd of never been married.

Hell, he said he wasn't sure starting at six months. SIX MONTHS! Why the fuck would he stay, if he wasn't sure who he loved at six months in? He thought it would be fine, but obviously it wasn't.

But, somehow ruining my life is fine, because he's leaving anything that isn't a personal possession to me.

Why would he do it? It doesn't make sense. He had two relationships side by side. He decided to propose to me, and marry me. Why would he do that if he wasn't sure?

Why would he propose if he wasn't sure?

It doesn't make sense."

She pauses. I wait a moment to see if she's just taking a breath, or if she's looking for an answer. Her eyes search mine. When she doesn't continue, I take the chance to talk; trying to hit back at all the points blurted out so quickly.

"Nothing is wrong with you, it's all him. Somewhere along the way, he got the idea that cheating was okay. That having two serious relationships at the same time was okay.

It sounds like he gambled with his choices, and picked the wrong one; in every scenario, and step along the way. And you got caught in the repercussions.

He might regret losing you, and what you did had, because you obviously had something that she didn't that kept him staying.

Either that, or he's a complete idiot. More so than he obviously already is.

But, you know what they say, once a cheater, always a cheater so he's probably going to cheat on her too.

I don't understand cheaters either. Never did. If you can't be faithful in a monogamous relationship, then you shouldn't be in a monogamous relationship. Whatever the reason for cheating may be, it's wrong on his part, and it's wrong on her part.

She knew that he had you. Not once did she ever say anything to you. That shows a lot of her character as well.

Beside, for all he knows, maybe she's been cheating on him too. Or, she doesn't want something serious with him. Maybe his life is going to explode because he screwed things up with you, and maybe she dumps him now too.

Who knows?" All my pieces sound disjointed to me. I've never been good with consoling, or making big flashy speeches to make everything better.

I just say what comes to mind as it comes to mind, and try to hit all the main points of her own thoughts.

Bree tilts her head down and her hands come up to wipe away her unending tears.

"But, I do know this. There is nothing wrong with you." I have to say that. I need to say it over, and over, if that is what she's thinking of herself; I can't say it enough.

"Okay, you might be a bit bossy and unpredictable sometimes." She snorts at my nudge of a joke. "But, who doesn't need a little of that sometimes."

Bree gasps for a deep breath, renewing her tears. I watch are her face scrunches in anguish. Placing a hand at her back, I rub up and down in a soothing motion.

There is more to say, and she needs to hear it. "There is nothing you could have done differently in the last five years, that wouldn't have been a betrayal to yourself.

If someone truly wants to hide something from someone, they

can.

You trusted him, so of course nothing looked suspicious.

We all know, if you thought something suspicious was going on, that super detective Bree would have unraveled the whole thing in under a day."

She laughs through her quiet sobs. "Yeah." I finally get a peak of a smile.

Bree flops her back down on the bed, but just a quickly, she's back up and sprinting by me.

A second later, I find my confusion is unfounded when I hear her retching.

Great, alcohol poisoning on top of the breakdown. It's going to be a long night.

I place my mojito down on the dresser, it's mostly empty now anyway.

I open up the mini fridge, and pull out a water bottle. She's going to need the water to help her throw up, then to help her replenish fluids.

On the side table is a ponytail, I grab it to wrap her hair up. I pull out a change of clothes for her; pjs for her comfort.

Taking my supplies into the bathroom, I deliver them to her, and help her put her hair up. The bathroom smells acidic from the vomit. It bothers my senses, and stomach.

"Go, I have to shit." Bree announces suddenly.

She's standing, and hiking up her dress before I get turned around, I double the effort to get out of there fast, and close the door behind me.

I let a big breath out.

It's going to be a really long night.

Chapter 8

My ears register the faint sound of puking.

She's at it again. She's been at it all night. I got to get up.

The light through my eye lids tell me that it's finally morning.

It might be too much to hope that she at least got a couple hours between the last stomach purging, and this one.

I hope she's gotten that much, it would mean she's going longer between throwing up, and might be on the mending side of things.

She's done this before; a few times. Her worst alcohol poisoning, her puking lasted her until four in the afternoon; she should've gone to the hospital to get her stomach pumped.

I don't expect her to be fully mobile until tomorrow, since she's still going at it. Probably wasn't such a good idea to let her down both of our drinks at the party.

Opening my sand bagged eyes to a view the ceiling and lifting my arm to swipe over blankets that aren't there. Somewhere in my mind, I remind myself that I was too tired to sort out the blankets the last time I went to check on Bree.

The clock says it's nearing eight, which means breakfast is open. I'm ravenous after such a long night of trying, and failing to do anything more useful than rubbing Bree's back, and providing some comfort. Trying to get up each time she did, just in case things got dangerous.

I pad over to the bathroom to go check on her.

Bree hangs onto the toilet like a teddy bear. Any thoughts of germs have gone wayside in the desperation of constant hurling.

"Morning."

"Morning." Her voice is hoarse, and sounds like she's talking around razors in her throat.

"Should I even ask how you're feeling?"

She groans her response.

I didn't have to ask. I can see she's doing horribly. Bree is pale. Her eyes have dark bags under, and she's closed her them. She looks like she could fall asleep where she's at.

At some point she may have done just that during the night.

I know her answer, but I figure I should ask anyway. "Don't suppose you're up for getting food."

"No." She moans.

I brush my teeth, and quickly put a brush through my hair. Grabbing another water from the fridge, and placing it within an arm's reach of Bree.

She hasn't thrown up since I got up, which I take a neutral sign; not horrible, but might not be anything worth cheering about. "Do you need help getting back to bed?"

"No. I'm going to drink some water, and see if it'll stay down for a bit." Bree is untrusting of her stomach still. The unpredictability of a little bit of water keeps her vigil at the toilet, but at least she's still attempting to get some hydration back.

I wonder if I should stay, but there isn't much that I can do at this point. If I eat quickly, I can help her back into bed. "I'm going to go eat, and come back after. Feel better. Don't die before I come back."

"No promises."

I change into a different shirt and plaid covering. In all the bits of last night, I hadn't managed to think to change myself. I grab my card, and slide it into my pocket before I leave.

The fresh air is unexpectedly appreciated. Maybe I should crack the patio door open for a few minutes to air out the room.

Might be good for Bree to get fresh air in her too.

I get to the buffet as one of only a few guests that seem to be up so early.

Feeling lighter on breakfast taste, I dish up yogurt, and all the assorted fruits. I get fruit juice to accompany it, and sit down at a table for two.

The fruit is fresh, and pleasing, while the yogurt helps to cut down on the acidity.

I try to keep to myself, but a rowdy laughter peaks my attention at the omelette station. Mel, Will, and a couple others from the wedding party have made their way down for breakfast.

Mel spots me sitting alone, and waves. She finishes gathering her food, and comes over. "Where's your friend?"

"Hopefully sleeping." Bed or toilet, I don't care at this point; sleep is sleep. "Alcohol poisoning, and maybe a touch of heat stroke." I give her my two diagnoses I flipped between all through the night. I've been tossing around the idea that maybe it's more than just the alcohol that has made her this sick. It's a different sort of heat here, so maybe she got too much yesterday. Possibly join that with alcohol poisoning, and it could explain how sick she is. "She's been throwing up the whole night."

Mel seethes and grits her teeth. "Oh no." She helps herself to the seat across from me. Her plate down, and she's unravelling the cutlery.

I guess she's staying for the company.

"What's your plans for the day?" She asks.

"Go back, and check on her. But, most likely just going to be a very relaxing day." I add a second thought. "If she's up for anything, it might be lounging poolside or at the beach."

"Did you have to miss out on any excursions?" She asks after she takes a bite of her omelette. At her example, I continue on with eating my own breakfast at an eased pace.

"No." Thankfully, that would have been money down the drain. I probably would have forced Bree to go even if she was dying. "We only booked the one so far. We were supposed to book another for tomorrow, but I think we'll see how she's feeling by the end of the day. I have a feeling she's going to have a touch of the second day hangover." We don't bounce back from hangovers like we did in our teenage years; oh, the difference just a few years does to your body. "What about you? You have the pirate thing, right?"

"Yes, but that's not until after lunch. We were thinking about going to 5th Ave this morning." She reveals like I should know what she's talking about.

"What's 5th Ave?" I ask.

Mel's eyes light up. "Shopping. It's like a long street full of touristy shops."

"And the tequila museum!" Will barges in, pulling up a seat from another table to join us. He has his own omelette, piping hot and straight off the grill. His made to order dish looks loaded compared to Mel's omelette.

Mel rolls her eyes. "And apparently a tequila museum. They have a shuttle that leaves every hour; starting at 9."

"Come with us!" He urges.

It sounds like it could be fun. A museum about the history of tequila might be interesting to go to. "I should check on Bree, and see how she is. I don't really want to abandon her in her misery. But, if she's going to try to sleep away the day, then I could join in. When were you thinking of going?"

"Sometime this morning, probably right after breakfast." Mel thinks for a moment. "I could come back to your room, and check on Bree with you. See how she's feeling, and if we get the go ahead, we'll head out after that."

"That sounds great." I smile.

"So Bree did get sick?" Will asks for more information just as I stuff a large pineapple into my mouth. I smile around the food and continue chewing as he chuckles, realizing what the delay in answer is. We wait in humourous awkwardness as I finish my bite.

"Yeah, real bad. Alcohol poisoning, and maybe a touch of heat stroke. She was still throwing up when I came for breakfast."

"That's not good. She looked awful when I went to grab you, but I didn't think it was that bad."

"Yeah, thanks for that." I remember my appreciation. Will hadn't had to get me like he had. Many wouldn't have noticed Bree in her state, not until she would have been throwing up then and there; Ryan hadn't and he was in her main purview. "I grabbed her and took her back to the room, and as soon as we got there, she started throwing up. Glad we got her before she was puking on the dance floor."

I leave out the heart break and breakdown as it's really none of their business. Between everything that was happening last night, I wonder if part of it was said in a sick decry. Bree may not even completely remember what she told me. Time will tell if she does.

Chapter 9

With food finished Mel and I leave to check on Bree. Will decides to tag along, discarding his half eaten gargantuan omelette.

I know Bree isn't doing well the moment we get through the door, and I hear heaving.

"Bree?" I question.

"Toilet." Her location was obvious, but I guess that's how she interpreted my question.

"You okay?"

"What do you think?" She bites in exhaustion and frustration. A weak arm reaches up to flush the toilet.

"Bad question." I help Bree up off the floor once she's had a moment of calm, and she signals for up. "We have guests." She glares at me. "Mel and Will invited me to go to 5th Ave; it's a shopping district. But, I'll leave the decision up to you. If you want me to stay, I'll stay."

"Hi." She says weakly as we walk out of the small room. The two return a greeting. "Go. You might as well do something today."

"Are you sure?" Obligation and concern forces my question. Is she well enough to make this decision. "I don't know if I should leave you like this."

"I'm sleeping, and throwing up. Go." I don't want to argue with her, every word sounds painful for her to get out.

"Okay. I'll come check on you when I get back. If you manage to get out of the room, leave me a note."

I grab from our mini fridge supplied water. Will holds out a little pastry. "Bree should try to eat."

"Thank you. I should have thought of doing that." I put the pastry and water on Bree's side table. "Take nibbles of this now and then. Hopefully we can get something to stay down. Start slow until you know it'll keep."

"Yes, Mom. Go, have fun." She's instantly drowsy as she reaches a comfortable position on her side.

"Sweet dreams."

I back away, then go over to my bag. Grabbing what I quickly figure out is about a hundred dollars Canadian in pesos, I stash it in my pocket.

I make sure I still have my key card, though I just put it back inside my pocket, and we leave the room.

Mel turns back to me wide eyed. "I forgot about money. I have to our rooms."

"Mel, Mel, Mel. Unprepared. Shame on you." Will teases.

"Oh right, and you brought money?" Will pulls out a wallet from his back pocket with a grin. "I hate you." She lightens her tone to talk to me. "I've got to dash to my room. I'll meet you up front."

"See you soon." I respond.

"See you."

We all leave in the same direction, with Mel travelling at a quicker pace. We go down the stairs at a close range, but Mel splits off to go towards the beach.

As soon as Mel is out of earshot, Will admits, "Don't tell Mel, but I put on the first pair of pants I saw. They turned out to be the same ones I wore to Xel-ha, and I didn't figure that out until

84

I was already on my way to breakfast, or else I wouldn't've had my wallet."

I laugh a little. Partially disgusted from the reuse of dirty clothing, but I'm willing to keep the secret. "How long have you known Mel? You seem to bicker about as much as you and Silvia do."

"I've known her for nearly as long as Silvia's been alive." He takes it back as he goes into more detail. "Well, since she was in pre-school with Silvia. Mom thought Silvia needed friends, so she put her in pre-school, and started inviting random girls and their moms over from the class. Mel's the one that stuck."

It seems like an odd thing to do, but perhaps normal in parenting; I wouldn't know.

My parent's certainly didn't do anything like that with me. I barely had prolonged child interaction before I went to kindergarten. Before that, my kid interactions came from when I would be at the café with mom or the odd time we'd go to the park. I was a joke growing up that I got along better with the adults than I did with children, but that was really just because I had no idea how to interact with someone my own age.

"Did your mom do that with you too?"

"No, thank God, I made my own friends, and had no problem making friends wherever I went." He pauses thoughtfully. "That's probably why she did it. Sil wasn't as social when she was a kid, Mel's really brought that out in her. So, when faced with one kid that made friends everywhere, like I would go and hug strangers, and strike up a conversation no matter how old they were, and then the next one was happier playing by herself; what do you do?" Will's explanation does well to explain why his mom might go to those types of lengths, but it brings up more questions than answers.

"You just went up, and hugged strangers?" I would have never dreamed of doing that as a kid. Stranger danger.

Will goes up to a hotel staff greeter standing near an awaiting white van. "Is this the shuttle for 5th Ave?"

"Yes Sir. Just arrived."

"Gracias." Will and I both say. We enter onto the nearly empty shuttle; only a driver sits in his seat eating an apple. I can only imagine he's trying to get in a quick bite before a long day of work.

We settle into deep blue seats, with shape patterns on them.

"Mom, hated it." Will continues. I mentally trek back to what we were talking about before. Will hugging strangers as a kid. "She always thought I was going to get kidnapped because I was that kid who just had no boundaries or fear of these people doing anything. Oh, you've got candy in your van, great, can I have some? A puppy, even better."

"I think I'm starting to understand all the warning labels that come with you." I joke.

Will pulls back the slightest bit. "Warning labels?"

"Everyone- do you not notice it?" He shakes his head. "Everyone has comments about typical Will behaviour. You were a terror as a kid, and gave your mom heart attacks; didn't you?" I accuse.

"Yup, and trouble as a teenager." He almost seems proud of it. A smile appears as he's sure to be remembering some things he's done, and his mom's reactions.

"And everyone that's known you since you were a kid," which seems to be half of everyone that came for the wedding, "remembers all the pain you put them through. You've grown, and changed, maybe a little or maybe a lot, but they remember all the pain." I figure it's not too much to assume that all based on what he's told me thus far.

His mouth opens in a wicked smile. "Not too much, I still go up to strangers, and strike up conversations."

I giggle. That is how we met, wasn't it. "Yeah, but you're, what, six feet taller, and much harder to kidnap now."

Will laughs. "That's true."

All smiles and joy disappear when we notice the rumbling of the engine. There are only a couple others on board; none of which are known to us.

"Are we leaving?" I look out the window beyond Will. "I don't see Mel or anyone else."

"Maybe she got caught up with something?" Will shrugs.

"Should we wait for them? Catch the next bus?" It's too late anyway, the van takes off.

"She can catch the next bus, and catch up with us. It's a long stretch of shops, they should be able to find us easily." He seems more confident than I am. Maybe he's been there before, and it really would be easy to find us.

Chapter 10

The drive takes longer than I thought it would have. I assumed a trip to shopping in 5th Ave would have been somewhere in the closest town, not an hour trip to Playa Del Carmen.

The driver lets us off, and tells us to come to this exact spot to get picked up. A van will be here each hour to shuttle us back. The spot it staked out with a sign for the van service.

Will and I stake out our largest landmarks, a few shops in the area, and walk down the straight line of shops. We weave in and out of shops to get a sense of things.

Immediately, I notice that many of the shops carry the same items or similar, but not all are priced equally.

A few things catch my eye, both in my price range, and out. But, I hold off, and keep in mind the prices. If I find it again for a better price, I'll buy it, if only higher prices come, then I'll come back.

Will sees a cigar shop, and wants to go inside. I want nothing to do with it, so we part ways for a few minutes, while he buys a cigar, and I go into the next shop.

A display of carved temples, Mayan calendars, and jaguar heads catches my eye. I've seen the temples before, and they are on my wish list. The price tag on the bottoms are about equal to the couple other shops we've visited thus far. With time to kill, I decide to purchase one here.

I choose one of the smallest size and the next size up, in a white wash with some black in the creases for contrast. Weighing the decision between the two sides and the two prices.

The small one is more around what I'd like for price, but the bigger one grabs more attention for the spot I can imagine for it on my shelf.

An arm reaches beside me, and grabs up an identical temple one size up from my two. I look, and spot Will. "You've been eyeing these for a while now. Get this one."

"It's a bit out of my price range." I tell him quietly, not wanting anyone else to hear while also not wishing to lie. It's embarrassing to have to admit that. "I'm good with the smaller one."

"I'm getting it for you."

My cheeks turn hot. That's not at all what I wanted to happen. Rich or not, I don't feel right to have him buy me these things. It makes me uncomfortable. If I can't buy it for myself, then no one else should be buying it for me. "No, you don't have to do that."

"I want to. It's nothing."

He tries to wave me off, but I keep arguing. I can't let him buy me this. "I can just buy the smaller one, I'm fine with it."

"It's the first time you've been anywhere. You like it. You need something significant to remind you of the adventure of your lifetime. It's barely the change in my wallet. Just say thank you, because I'm getting it for you. And if I have to give it to Bree, to make sure it goes home with you, so be it."

Will's stubbornness wins him the argument, but loses him some respect points. He's going to do this whether I want him to or not. "Thank you." I tell him, already making plans to repay him on way or another.

"Let's look around some more." Will says as he grabs a tiny basket, and places the temple inside. He walks over to wooden carved fierce looking jaguar heads.

I put back both of the small pyramids, and walk around like he suggested.

The shop has some intricately decorated wooden jewelry boxes; one of the carved ones has a purple tinge to the wood. I grab one for Bree. It's a bit more than what I wanted to spend, but I'll count it partially as her Christmas present as well.

I pass skeletons, hats, and shirts, maracas, and other brightly coloured trinkets.

A display of Mexican chocolate catches the attention of my taste buds. When one goes to the birthplace of chocolate, one needs to taste the local chocolate; I justify.

I hope it's actually authentic local chocolate, and not just a gimmick. I snag two discs of different flavours; pure cacao, and a dark vanilla.

Shiny coins glimmer in a couple baskets nearby. On closer inspection, they are gold, and silver plated Mayan replica coins. They would only be a couple dollars, so I grab one of each. I decide to keep the silver for myself, and I'll give Will the gold one. By no means, does it make up for what he's spending on me, but it's a start.

I tally my total, and think I should be done for now. There may be other souvenirs in other shops that I might like.

I go to the tills, and purchase my things. Will comes up to a till beside mine, and pays for his things. He's gathered up quite a few assorted things.

We walk further down the road. Passing by a way to the beach under an arched carving. It looks like two mermaids at first glance, but then there's no tails, and I can see leg definition, so I'm not sure what the statues are.

"Hey, that's it. The Tequila Museum." Will steers us inside a large yellow building.

Tequila bottles are everywhere, but I get the feeling instantly that museum is less of a description, and more of a name for a retail store.

Near the back is a blocked off area with what looks like it could be old equipment to make tequila, and some barrels, but the majority of the store is designated to thousands of alcohol bottles for sale.

A man in store uniform stops us, and asks if we would like to sample some tequila before we buy.

Will replies, "yes gracias."

The man takes us to a cart with four levels of different alcohols. Without saying another word, he fills up a long line of little plastic taster cups with all sorts of tequilas, and gets us to try each one.

He has a description for each of them, laying out hints and notes that we should taste in each.

Only after we try them all, does he ask how we liked them, and what we liked about them. I get the feeling he's trying to narrow down our preferences.

I don't have the heart to tell the guy that most of the tequilas taste the same, though there is a more or less burn to some. But, I also can't identify, at this point, which ones I liked.

He pulls out tequila liqueurs after another row of straight tequilas. I like them more and finally feel ready to make a decision for purchase. I have my eye on a chocolate tequila liquor.

If hot chocolate could have a feeling of heat, without being heated, this tequila would be it. The chocolate does well to hide the tequila flavour, that, or I've already been desensitized with all the rest of the tequila, and just can't taste the flavour anymore.

Will decides on a pomegranate tequila. Telling the man, he's never come across anything like it at home. That's what he'd be looking at getting rather than something he could pick up back home.

It makes sense.

With both of us picking from the liqueur section, I feel a bit bad for all the effort the man put in at the beginning. His run down of the finer points of the tequilas was completely wasted on us.

The rest plays with a fog over my head. Even after we decide on our tequila, and tell the man such, he still has us taste a few things for the road; breaking out some other liqueurs and some rum.

We pay for our two bottles of alcohol, and leave the store.

Realizing in the after math of the too bright sun, that we basically just did a bunch of shots of tequila, and some rum, pretty quickly.

"Well that was different than expected." Will blurts.

"It wasn't an actual museum?" That was my assumption.

"Not like any museum I've been too before." He agrees. "Who needs to go to a bar, when you could go there, get drunk, and you get to leave with a bottle of something."

"Well, we did have to still pay for our tequila." I look up, and down the street. Which way to go? Do we keep going the way we were headed, or back the way we came? There's probably some other things we could grab along the way. A trinket or two that might seem more reasonable now that we're drunk.

"I think we did well. One bottle each. Won't get screwed on duty, and taxes. Got drunk on top of it. Probably drank a whole bottles worth between the two of us."

"True."

His wrist pulls up and he takes a glance at his watch. "Arms are getting a bit full, should we head back to the meeting place. We can probably make it in time for the next van." Will decides.

"Sure." I agree. Who needs drunken purchases anyway? Will

surely lead to overspending, and I'll end up with things I didn't truly want in the first place.

We walk the long path back. I avoid a man that says he knows me from the hotel I'm staying at. He uses it as an opening to asking me into his shop. I don't recognize him at all, and I'm almost certain he wasn't at the hotel.

Out of a church bursts a bride and groom, and their guests, straight out of getting married. It's an odd scene that makes me wonder how drunk I really got.

I don't feel stumbly, but the haze tingles all through my senses.

We get back to the area for the van, but it's not there yet. Will says it should get there in about ten or fifteen minutes.

We swing back around for ice cream, and I spend about ten dollars each for a cone. More than I'd ever spend back home, but the mint chocolate ice cream is smooth, and icy, and the best I've ever had. And, it helps in my pay back.

We take it back to the meeting spot, and eat while we wait for the van.

It's silent for conversation, but not uncomfortably so.

With alcohol maybe fading out of my system, I'm glad we're no longer shopping, or I might have spent all the rest of my money.

The van finally arrives, and we pile inside.

A blast of cold from the air conditioning, combined with my ice cream unexpectedly gives me goosebumps.

We sit in a huff with all our stuff, but still manage to just take up one double seat. A moments rest after a long walk combined with the tequila, drags down my eye lids.

Knowing I don't want to fall asleep, I try to shake my head awake. Finding any excuse to keep me awake, I decide to give Will his present. Digging through my bag helps keep me in motion. I find the gold coins and grab out the gold one.

"Here." I say, handing it to Will. "It's not much. But, I thought you might like it."

He takes it in, and looks it over. "Where'd you find this?"

"In the shop. I got it for you. I also have some chocolate we can try later." I'm too lazy to try to bring it out now.

"You didn't have to get me something too. But, I'm glad you did. This is awesome. Thank you."

"You're welcome." I realize I didn't specify which shop, but it's too late to go back, and mention it now. Maybe he figured it out, since we only really shopped at two places.

"It should be lunch by the time we get back. Did you want to meet up for lunch? Try to convince Bree she should eat something whether she throws it back up or not?" I find it sweet that he seems concerned for Bree.

"Sure." He also has his own friends he may needs to be concerned about. "Maybe, you should go check on Mel, and the others. Find out if they made it out, or what happened."

"I'm sure there'll be story to tell." He sighs.

I wonder if they do this to him frequently. If they often ditch him and their plans. He hadn't been too concerned when we left the hotel, maybe because it's to be expected.

Exhausted, and spent after a long walk, shopping, and the alcohol. My long night certainly not helping with the situation.

Crashing from the whole lot of it fuels heavy eye lids. Vaguely I know that I'm sinking in deeper as my head pulls down out of my control.

It'll be fine.

Will is here.

Chapter 11

A bit weary, I help Bree grab what little bits of food she thinks she can handle, and help her take a seat beside Mel. Taking the brunt of her weight, I slowly lower her to the chair.

Mel panics when she sees the grimace on Bree's face. "Are you okay?"

"You look like death." Will comments.

"Will!" Mel reprimands. She leans back in her seat as her leg swings out to kick Will under the table. If she connects, Will doesn't let it show.

"I feel like death." Never minding Mel's outburst or Will's insult, Bree cracks a smile. "Throwing up all night, somehow, I managed to pull a muscle in my back. I also managed to keep the pastry thing down so I'm hoping that's a good sign."

"Should you be lying down?" Mel asks.

"I came for food. I'm going back into hiding after this." Bree explains our plan succinctly.

Upon finding out she managed to keep the pastry and some water down, I convinced her she needed to try to eat lunch and get some fresh air. Both will hopefully help her heal and feel better.

Whatever is going on with her back, will likely benefit from rest and lack of use, but we can deal with that after food.

Perhaps a lay down in a cabana would suit her well, if lunch stays where it belongs.

"I'm going to go dish up." I excuse myself quietly.

I grab some of the tortilla chips with green sauce; quickly becoming a favourite of mine. And, I make a croissant sandwich out of the assorted meats, and cheeses; ham, and a soft white cheese. I add some watermelon to my plate, and go back to sit down next to Will; across from Bree.

"Here." He mumbles the word around his food, pulls out the pyramid temple, and passes it along to me on the table.

I had forgotten to grab it from him. "Oh, thank you." I move the pyramid to the other side of my plate.

Taking up my sandwich, I eat a bite.

Bree stares at me intently when I look up. I know that look. I'm in trouble. Bree is certain there's a deeper story to tell, and she knows I didn't tell her. What she won't accept, is that there really isn't anything to tell her, and that's why I didn't say anything. She will insist there's more to it.

Ignoring her further scrutinization, I take a bite from my sandwich, and look elsewhere.

Next too us, I see Mel giving Will a stare down of her own. I recognize the silent conversation between Mel and Will, as the same one going on between Bree and me.

At least I'm not the only one suffering in our forgetfulness. I resist acknowledging it, despite a nervous bubbling giggle ready to burst out, and refuse it into a conversation. I don't want to see Mel and Bree team up against us to discover an unfounded truth.

Bree hasn't touched any of her food. I wonder if she's feeling nauseous again. Maybe it was a bad idea to emerge for lunch. I could have grabbed her something and taken it back to the room.

Silvia bursts in like a freak thunderstorm. Her hands clap down on the table demanding attention. "Would you two like to join us for the pirate ship show tonight? I have two free tickets." It takes me a split second to realize she's talking to Bree and me.

"They're really not coming? Do I need to go talk to them?" Will just about jumps up, but he catches himself.

What happened?

"No, and I honestly don't care about them right now. If they're going to act like this, I don't want them there. We leave at two. What do you say?" I'm too speechless in shock to answer her. Still trying to understand what exactly is happening.

"Unfortunately, I've been throwing up since last night, I'm not even sure if this food will stay down. And, I pulled a muscle in my back from all the throwing up. I don't think a my afternoon involves anything more than sleeping, and hugging a toilet, but Sky's free, and would love to go with you." Bree throws me into the fray.

Feeling obligated to accept her offer now, thanks Bree, I ask the question between the both of them. "I mean, yes, but, are you sure?"

"Very sure." Silvia answers.

"Go, I need someone to babysit you while I sleep this off. They don't seem like the murdering type." Bree finally takes a bite of a bun as she purposely avoids my glare.

"Great. You have meat, so you aren't a vegetarian." Silvia observes and assumes correctly. "How do you feel about surf and turf?"

"Good." I'm not picky, I add in my head.

"Great, the name on your ticket is Jennifer Crowly. Will..." Silvia stops herself and turns about. "Mel, can you make sure she gets to the bus on time?" Silvia doesn't wait for a response. She walks away on a mission to grab some food.

I turn back to Mel. "I assume this has something to do with why you weren't at 5th Ave?" The question on my tongue since earlier today. With Silvia's abruption I feel comfortable finally asking for reasoning.

"God, yes, drama." Mel leans in and hushes a little. "Jennifer and Mandy are friends of Sil's from different groups. The groups never hang out together because they have nothing in common; except for Silvia. The nature and personalities of the two groups clash; which is why Silvia never brings them together.

Jennifer is wild and out there, and someone Sil goes to for a good time partying or sky diving. While Mandy is her complete opposite and more of a timid mouse, and is good for a quiet night in.

They would never be friends in real life. But Sil's got both those sides to her, so she's great friends with both of them for the different reasons, and depending on her mood.

They hadn't met until the wedding stuff started to happen, and both of them confessed to Sil that they didn't particularly like each other.

Anyway, Jennifer confronted Mandy saying that Sil said she didn't like her. Mandy flipped, and broke down and cried.

Sil told Mandy that she did say something like that, when Jennifer asked if Mandy liked her; saying that Mandy thought Jennifer was okay but a bit much. Mandy took this as a betrayal from Silvia, and hates that Jennifer would think Mandy doesn't like her even though Mandy doesn't like her.

But honestly, Jennifer put Sil in a no win situation. Either lie to one friend, reveal something Mandy may have regarded as a secret but wasn't told to keep it secret, or try to do a political answer.

Anyway, Mandy feels betrayed, and can't bring herself to join in tonight because of this, and her social anxiety. Silvia apologized but Mandy didn't accept the apology, and said she doesn't even know if she still wants to be friends with someone who would betray her like that.

Silvia flipped out on Jennifer, because she had no reason to do that except to cause an issue, the day before the wedding. So

Jennifer said she's not joining tonight because she's not sure she even wants to be in the wedding party anymore; pure dramatics but that's how she is."

"So, now, we have two free spots open. And, possibly two bridesmaids missing from the wedding tomorrow." Silvia summarizes in her return, taking over from Mel's long explanation.

I can only muster up a short response as the information sinks in. "Wow."

The whole situation sounds ridiculous. This is why I keep my friends group small. I can't handle the drama that comes with having a bunch of friends.

"So, now, I'm not even sure I want to be friends with either of them." Silvia adds. In this moment, I don't blame her. "This isn't the first stunt Jennifer has pulled; I just didn't think she'd be so selfish for my wedding.

Mandy, is a good friend, but completely on her terms, and I don't like having to tip toe around someone so I don't offend them. She's constantly cancelling on me for dumb excuses that are cover up for her anxiety or some reason she doesn't want to see me at that time. Like, if I'm going through a rough time, and she doesn't want to hear me rant about it, she'll cancel on me last minute instead of asking me not to rant about it because she can't handle it at the moment. Or she'll make double plans, and instead of saying that, she'll make up a dumb excuse, and lie about why she can't hang out. Or, if she doesn't want to do something, she'll still agree to plans with me, and then suddenly she's sick, and can't do the thing. She maybe makes it to one in ten plans we set."

"Well that's annoying." I agree. Mandy sounds a bit self-centered and flaky. Even with anxiety, you can't continually excuse some of that repetitive deceptive and disrespectful behaviour. At the very least, it would get really annoying to always have plans cancelled.

Doesn't necessarily mean that Silvia should have told Jennifer that Mandy doesn't like her, but it sounds like there were prevalent issues before this fight.

"Right? And with Jennifer, I'm so tired of drama for the sake of drama. And, I'm tired of being stood up by her as well. She picks her favourite friend of the moment, and completely focuses on them. If she's got a boyfriend, you can forget about seeing her at all, if she'll even respond to your texts." Silvia angrily dives her fork down to pick up some meat.

"You okay Bree?" Will asks. The table turns quiet, and their attention goes to Bree.

She's turned white, and sweaty. "Need to throw up." Bree winces as she stands up. I bolt over, and help her up the rest of the way. "Stay." She tells me.

"No, you look like you're going to pass out." She doesn't argue anymore. Probably trying to hold in the puke as we briskly walk out of the buffet area.

I mentally berate myself. I was so caught up in the drama of Silvia's story that I didn't notice Bree took a turn for the worst.

Once we are most of the way back to the room, Will catches up to us.

"I wasn't sure if you were coming back. You forgot your pyramid." He hands me the souvenir.

"Thanks."

I take one side of Bree to help her up the stairs, Will goes around to the other side to do the same.

"I'm getting old." Bree complains. "Who throws out their back throwing up?"

I take her humour to be a good sign. Maybe the feeling has passed, and she's back to feeling better.

"At least it's an interesting story to tell when you get back home." Will says.

"No one will know of this." Bree lightly threatens. "Especially, if I want Sky to ever have a chance of her parents letting her come on vacation with me again."

"You're an adult. You can make decisions for yourself."

I scoff. "That's a nice theory. But, it doesn't really work like that."

"Why not?" The two words grate on me. He makes it sound so simple. Nothing about it is simple.

"I'd be the disrespectful, ungrateful daughter if I did anything against what my parents want for me. They'd take it as a deep betrayal, and I'd get disowned." To say the least of it.

The bite of resentment stings me. Revealing the sentiment to Will is different than when I rant to Bree. Bree has seen things for herself and understands. Will, whether he means to or not, feels judgy. He doesn't understand the whole situation or he wouldn't ask such a question.

"Would that be so bad?"

"That's not really in any realm of possibility. I couldn't." It's difficult to explain without the entire background, and to someone who hasn't grown up the same. I couldn't just disown my parents. "It's easy to complain about my parents, and what they want for me, but they have the best intentions. And, it's not all that horrible. It's not as bad as it seems." I try to full stop by insinuating that it's not as bad as I complain about.

The top of the stairs brings a hope of reprieve. We are close to the room, and hopefully the end of this uncomfortable conversation.

"But, if you aren't happy, and can't live your life how you want, then you aren't really living."

I snap back at his insinuation. "I wouldn't say I'm not happy."

"Complacent contentment isn't the same thing as happy. It's accepting your life how it is, because that's how it is, and it's not bad enough to force you to change things." Will's argument is an interesting thought and view on it. But, it still oversimplifies things.

"I guess." I let Bree into the room. She walks over to the bed, but quickly changes her mind to go back to the bathroom. I place down my pyramid on the dresser.

I follow Bree into the bathroom when she leaves the door open. She positions herself on her knees in front of the toilet.

After a few moments of nothing more, I speak up. "Are you alright?"

"I feel like I need to throw up again, but I'm not throwing up yet." Bree explains.

Understanding that feeling, I replenish her sick supplies, and make sure she should be all set for the next few hours.

I notice Will checking his watch. It's likely getting to be time to meet with the rest, and get ready to go.

My gut has mixed feelings about this. Going means having what promises to be a magnificent night, but guilt tears at the thought of leaving Bree alone here.

"You sure, you're okay with me going?" I ask Bree.

"Yes." She answers, still in the ready position.

"You don't think you'd be able to tough it out the next few hours. You might be okay by supper." I understand it's selfish but I would feel better if she came; even if she suffered the whole time.

"I'm a bit jealous that you get to go, but we can always do the pirate ship again when it's my turn to pick." She waves me over and puts her hand out for me to help her up. A grunt and grimace reveal the pain in her movement. "For now, I don't want to test what a rocking boat might do to aggravate my stomach or my

102

back. I'd be miserable one way or another, and ruin you're good time while you spend the whole time in the infirmary with me. I promise, I'll be fine here. You go, and have fun." Her voice turns stern as she looks behind me. "Will, if she drowns, I'll drown you. Got it?"

"Loud and clear." He salutes.

"Great." She leaves my side to go back into the main room. "I'm going to sleep. Leave. And, have fun."

"Sleep well. Hope you feel better." I tell her.

Will and I leave the room, and leave Bree be.

"Let's go back to the buffet, maybe catch some of the others at breakfast still."

"Lunch?" I correct him.

"Lunch."

Chapter 12

It's shock and awe to see a massive floating ship in the sea. Like, those seen only in pictures and movies.

Takes you back to a time people meticulously etched every inch of space on a piece of wood to make a statement; all through blood, sweat, tears, and blistered hands.

The chatter from the three hour ride here has halted at the sight, and stirring anticipation.

A magnificent long wooden boat with three masts, and numerous white sails floats before us. The dark stained wood is emboldened by a stripe of red along the cannons.

Flying at the top of it all, a black flag with an hourglass held between a pirate, and a skeleton. The image is familiar, but I can't recall if I've seen it in movie or in historical images; possibly both.

We board the ship using the ramp the guide sends us to. Greeted by a couple crew members dressed up as movie pirates; one helps us find a seat amongst all the other people already on board.

The groom's side sits together, and the bride's side sits together. I manage to get stuck in the middle between a groomsman and a bridesmaid.

They talk within their smaller halves. I try to pay attention to both, but quickly find myself on the outside of both conversations, and unable to hear most of what they are saying to each other.

Looking around, I'm surprised by how many people are here. It seems like every inch, and level, except for an aisle down the center on the deck, is covered with guests.

Once we are settled in we wait, for all of a couple minutes, before a pirate takes our attention at the center of the aisle.

"Avast ye, landlubbers! Welcome to the Royal Fortune. Captain Bartholomew Roberts said ye would be joining our pillaging this night. But, I'm afraid we may not have to chance, as no ships have been spotted in the vicinity." He pauses for effect. "Never worry. It shall be an eventful, and entertaining night all the same."

The name of the captain sparks a memory compounded by the name of the ship. They pulled a piece from history to make up this show.

Black Bart, a name given to him after his death, the most prolific pirate of his time. He went from the navy to being a pirate, like so many did at the time. Better fortune and freedom to be found in piracy; whether the legal kind or the illegal kind.

"We will be taking off as soon as the Captain says we are ready. Until then, some rules. There aren't many we abide by, so I expect you to follow the very few we have."

The crewman holds up one finger. "Unless ye wish to become shark bait or lose your treasures, keep your hands, legs, and belongings inside the boat at all times."

A second finger joins the first. "Listen to the crew, we are here to ensure you have fun, and survive the night."

He looks exaggeratedly behind him directing our attention to the steering wheel behind him. "Ah looks like the Captain is ready to take off."

The Captain takes the wheel, and shouts out some orders. Crew members appear, seemingly out of nowhere, yet everywhere at the same time.

We sit, and watch as the ship comes alive, and starts to pull away from the land. Crew members ascend, and descend the ropes tied to the boat's masts. I hear the faint hum of an engine helping us along.

I notice extra netting above us, like that used by acrobats in the circus. A safety measure, I assume, in case someone should fall from the crow's nest or anywhere high up.

They don't let us become bored with the display, and quickly turn on the entertainment and the booze.

In between their ship duties, they bound back, and forth to serve us drinks, and putting on mini thirty second rehearsed sketches, flips, and swings.

As things settle with the ship out of the port, the Captain finally takes a moment to introduce himself, and begins entertaining through the inclusion of the guests.

Singling out those with birthdays, and we all wish them a happy birthday. He turns the attention to anniversaries, and has us all wish them a happy anniversary.

The music starts up, a mash up of all the nineties music, and some eighties, that would have been classic elementary school dance songs. The crew dances joyously, and they pull up volunteers to join in for a spot light dance.

Desperate to join in, Will bounds up from his place and goes to dance with the pirates. He does a decent job grooving around for the minute of time they have been letting each person dance for.

I'm in awe of his courage, I wouldn't never willingly place myself into that sort of situation. I would be mortified having to dance in front of so many people, even if I did have any sort of dancing skills; which I don't.

Just as I start to bore of the same things over, and over, the Captain calls for a sort of intermission; it's time to go to the galley for supper.

The crew shuffles us down the stairs to a grand room. Tables and chairs for all of us. They make sure to sit people in their assigned seating, a measure taken to ensure everyone receives their proper meal. It goes quick enough the line is constantly moving, even if it's just a minor shuffle.

Just as fast as we are seated, crew come around, and we are served our food and wine; a well ordered machine.

My food is the surf and turf as promised; a lobster tail, some shrimp, and steak with an assortment of steamed vegetables, and garlic mashed potatoes.

Supper is worthy of an expensive steak house. I eat the vegetables first, so that I can save the best for the end. Alternating between the steak and the shrimp from there.

The halves talk amongst themselves again, but now I can hear the ladies' conversation.

I eat my food at a slow consistent pace to avoid awkwardness in my silence. But, they couldn't be able to fault me for not joining in for more then nods and agreements here and there; their conversations revolving around their personal lives, their pasts together, and the wedding. I'd really have not much input into any of those topics.

The only time I talk is when Silvia makes a point to ask each of the girls how their food tastes, and to thank our pirate waiters.

As people about the room start finishing up their meals, we are told that we are free to move about the ship and explore.

Finished all on my plate, I look around to the others in various forms of completion. The prime talkers of the table a bit behind on eating their food; I've always found that to be the case.

I catch Will looking my way. Our eyes meet, I panic as though I've been caught doing something I shouldn't, so I smile a greeting and look away in a bid to avoid him thinking I was staring.

Purposely, in my next scan around the room, I avoid looking at his face; bouncing over his head. In what I can see, his head is turned my way again, so I flash in a bit of relief.

Once we've all finished, we ascend back up the stairs to find the sky dark, and the ship lit up.

People mosey about.

The music suddenly gets louder, and a section of the ship, near the wheel, is lit up brighter than before. The crew puts on a well-rehearsed dance meant to draw people back to the deck.

The chairs are now gone, or we might take a seat. If we get tired enough, there are benches off to the very sides. Their attempt, I assume, is to make the deck a dance floor, and to get as many people out there as possible.

A ruckus interrupts the dance, as the music stops, the Captain interrupts. Blasphemy declared. His first mate stole his place in the dance show.

Furious words happen, but most of it is unclear. At some points, I'm sure they're speaking Spanish and possibly repeating in English. In others, I'm not sure they're actually speaking anything legible in any language.

What is clear, is a shout of the word *mutiny*.

Swords clash, sides are taken between the Captain and the other crew mate.

I can't help but wonder how realistic this may be. From the research I've done on pirates, these things went down more diplomatically, and with votes. Pirate crews were usually more civil and diplomatic than they tend to be depicted.

It doesn't take away from the action show the ship is putting on. Quite the opposite, the real thing might have turned out to be a bit boring of a show.

Their spectacle is interrupted by a large bang in the sky, inducing a mini heart attack in me, then a firework follows.

While they had our attention to one side of the ship, another boat had come up the other way.

In an overwhelming display of timed fireworks and fight music, our Captain gains control and brings all the crew together to fight off the offending ship. Some of the crew on both ships swing back and forth between the two.

Then, the ship sails by faster than what would be normal for a sail boat, and our Captain shouts, "victory!"

I'm pleased to think that we won the battle with no casualties. I grin at my own joke.

The music starts up loud as ever; night club deafening level. The Captain's speaker turns up with the music, encouraging victory dancing, and singing to the quintessential victory song for the champions.

Crew help draw people to the center of the deck; now a dance floor. The lights flash in various colours, and a dry ice fog sets the mood. Just like back in Elementary school, but this time we have booze.

Mel pulls me over to the girls, and I dance with them for a bit, peer pressure, and booze fueling my boldness, until the guys come back with more drinks.

Will hands me a cup of beer. I thank him.

Not my usual choice, but it seems to be one of the easiest drinks to come across on the ship. Crew members with trays whisk them around. While anything else is requested or ordered at one of two bartenders.

In a display of unusual poise, I manage to dance without spilling. For the first time tonight I think of Bree. She would be so proud that I haven't spilt a drop. She'd be staring at me like an alien took over my body for dancing as willingly as I have been.

I wonder how she's doing. If she managed to get herself out for supper, and if she's eaten anything. I wish I had my phone with me so I could, very expensively, text her asking how she's doing.

I understand, even with her approval, that this trip may have been selfish of me. Regret swells a pit in my stomach. My smile drops a little, and I have to consciously pull it back up, and keep it there.

It may have been wrong of me to come along tonight, while Bree is sick. She paid for the trip, I came with her, and I should have stuck by her side.

I'm a horrible friend.

My bladder finally protests, after who knows how long I've been ignoring it, and I have to pee. I inform Silvia, "I'm going to find a bathroom." She nods, and continues dancing.

Bree would have made sure to come with me.

The men's bathroom and the women's bathroom I find in the galley have entrances inside a divot in the wall.

I stand in the long line, waiting patiently. Until, I realize, no man has entered or exited the men's bathroom for a few minutes. A small sharp pain in my lower abdomen suggests a bit of urgency that may not wait for the rest of these women to pee.

Waiting another minute before a decision is made up, I leave the lineup, and find the men's door unlocked, and the room empty. With the lack of a line up, I use it myself.

Coming out, I'm met with equal looks of scorn and revelation. "Damn, yes. This line is taking forever." One of the girls says as she walks by me to use the men's bathroom after me.

It's ridiculous to refuse usage of an empty bathroom just because it's labeled for men. I reason within my head to the other women, and maybe a bit to myself to justify my action.

My cheeks turn hot when I nearly walk right by Will; I've been caught. He stands up from his seat at a table along my way with a Cheshire grin. "Using the men's washroom; I'm a bit surprised."

"I had to pee. The women's washroom was full, with a ten person line up, while the men's had no one. Might as well use it." I shrug off the judgement coolly. I had to pee. It's better to use the men's washroom than to have peed myself.

"Fair enough." He holds up his hands in defeat.

"We should get back." I tell him.

"Drink first?"

"Sure." I agree.

We make our way to the bartenders. Waiting our turn based on the bartenders attention. They have the basics of a bar, with liquor, and mix. At my turn, while Will orders a rum and coke, I ask for a vodka slime. I'm glad when the bartender doesn't question it, because I'm not sure what's exactly in it.

He pours vodka, clear pop, and lime juice into a glass for me.

"What is that?" Will wonders.

"A vodka slime; it's good." Bree introduced it to me a while back, in my first ever bar experience.

"Do you mind if I try it?" He holds out his hand to take the cup.

"Sure." I hand it over with so little hesitancy, I surprise myself. I should be recoiling from the thought of mixing germs.

Will takes a sip from my straw. He makes an hmm noise, and looks pleasantly surprised. "It's pretty good."

Will hands me his cup. I take a sip in kind, then hold it back for him to take. His smile turns up devilishly. "Okay, trade back now. I like mine better." His is smoke and heat, and mine is sweet.

"Nah." He moves to turn to walk away.

"Will! Fine, keep it. I'll just order another." I call him on his bluff, and he trades drinks with me.

We make our way back up to the party to find them participating in synchronized dancing. The Captain cheers people along to motivate them.

Will and I drink a bit more from our glasses as we try to join in in an altered version; less jumping and no clapping.

I quickly give up trying to multitask. Downing my drink and depositing the cup on a bench before I snap back into placement.

Soon the music changes to this decade's club music. This encourages more freestyle dancing, which seems a bit goofy when I take a step back to watch.

Some are club dancing, while some are shuffling back and forth or jumping up and down, others pull out classic action named moves like the sprinkler. It's a complete mish mash, and an interesting social experiment.

The girls and guys have merged together, with some couples dancing, and others dancing around each other.

Will takes my hand to pull me back. He swings it up, and I realize in awkward lateness that he's trying to spin me around.

I burst out laughing as I finally spin. Settling closer, he places his thumb and finger to hold my chin.

The mood changes, and my senses tunnel in on what is happening. Frozen in place. My heart rapidly beats, taking all my body's ability to function.

His lips tentatively press against mine. Will waits a moment, but my body still doesn't function. A disconnect between mind and body has frozen the latter.

My mind uses all processes to think about whether I think this is actually okay for me or not. Would sober me let him kiss me?

He's pulling away, just the barest bit, when I decide sober me would be fine with him kissing me, at least at this exact moment.

112

My over thinking is costing me a moment I should be enjoying.

My one free hand climbs up to pull him back.

Our lips meet with a bit of a smack as I misjudge the distance required to pull him back. It stings for a moment, but we adjust, and press snugly against each other.

Like opening a door to a whirlwind, a rush blows at my heart. I know that I won't be able to take this back, not that I would want to. But, as we part, a piece of me already misses him; misses the opportunity of him.

My head rushes through the process of trying to protect myself. This isn't meant to be. We live in separate countries, and long distance never works for long. I could never leave my family, and he wouldn't ever settle down; he's not the type for monotony.

Will grips me for a hug and kisses the top of my head. We spend a frozen moment in each other's arms.

The Captain's voice booms, breaking up the moment and our hug.

I miss what he says, but it appears we are starting to come into dock; some minutes away still. The city lights are approaching.

Captain Bartholomew leads the people in a few organized group dances.

I join Will for the last couple dances before we have to leave for reality.

Chapter 13

Fresh memories plague my thoughts as I scrub clean in the shower. The pirate ship, the party, dinner, dancing, the kiss…

I've never felt a kiss like it, only a peck, but with more than just a touch feeling. A burst of emotion.

I can't work out whether if it was the moment itself, or the person, which made it different than all the other kisses.

Afraid of the answer, I shake the trail of thoughts away.

They come back too quick, with residual tingles of the coziest hug, and the sweetest kiss on top of my head.

Bang. Bang. Bang. "Sky! I have to pee!" Bree yells.

"Good morning to you too!" I shout back cheerfully.

"Good morning! I have to pee! How much longer are you going to be?" There's a hint of desperation. She must really have to pee.

"One minute." I say, as I turn off the shower. The cleaning portion of my shower was done ages ago, so there's no sense in making her suffer longer. I dress quickly, and grab my hair brush before leaving.

"Good morning." I repeat once more as she pushes by me.

A knock interrupts me for a second time, this time at the front door.

I open it up, expecting hotel staff; maybe the maid staff.

"Oh good. I got the right one." Mel and Silvia barge their way into the room. "And, you're up."

"And freshly showered." Silvia comments.

"Yes?" I question everything of the last few seconds. It's certainly a bunch of fuss with little explanation.

"We need a favour." Mel corrects herself. "She needs a favour."

Silvia looks me deeply in the eyes, and takes a breath. "I need a bridesmaid."

My mind blanks as it refuses to process the request. "What?"

"Mandy decided to duck out, and has booked an early flight home. I need a bridesmaid to make my side even with groom's side."

I hesitate. Is evenness really that important? So important that she'd rather ask a stranger to join in that let the spot go empty.

It doesn't make sense to me, but I know theoretically that there might be those in the world that actually deeply care about that sort of thing.

I want a nice way to decline. She'll regret this in a few months, when I am no longer in her life.

People will ask her who that girl is in the picture, and she'll respond with just some girl, because she won't even remember my name.

"She'll do it!" Bree shouts from the bathroom.

"Oh good." Mel says.

I open my mouth. I want to protest that I didn't agree to this. But, I also haven't made up my mind to a hundred percent negative response yet.

"Thank you, this means so much." Silvia ignores that the voice didn't come from me, and jumps to hug me.

After reactions like that, how am I to say no? Short answer, I can't.

Mel and Silvia let another girl into the room. She carts in a bridesmaid dress.

At first glance, I know it's going to be too big for me, but by how much?

I hope they've thought more on this than what I can produce on my own. There's so much prep that goes into getting fancied up, especially for a wedding.

I don't have any makeup with me, but I suppose I could borrow some things from Bree.

Bree evacuates the bathroom so I can change into a dress I ultimately have to hold to keep up.

"How is it?" Silvia asks impatiently.

"Come out. We want to see."

"Big." I answer as I open the door for them to see just exactly what I mean.

"Big we can fix. We have some sewing supplies back at the villa." I try to disappear back into the bathroom. "Let's go."

I point at the dress. "I'll just change-"

"No time. Lot's to do." Silvia interrupts. I wonder when exactly this wedding is. With Mel and Silvia having gone through hair, and makeup, but not dressed, I imagine it could just be an hour away; maybe a couple hours.

"Oh."

"Bree, you are welcome to come to the wedding. It's at ten on the beach." Silvia invites Bree quickly as she ushers me towards the door.

"I'll be there. Take care of Sky. Make her pretty." Bree jokes.

"She's already pretty." Silvia counters with all seriousness.

Silvia and Mel practically kidnap me, hurrying me off to the villa as I hold up the dress.

I feel goofy, and hope that no one sees me or realizes what's going on. One good thing about the resort is the lack of people out early. Those who are, tend to be close to the buffet breakfast.

We enter the villa's main room to a well organized chaos. Stations for each step in the process are set up. The remaining bridesmaids are going through, and appear mostly done.

"Oh dear." An older woman takes me from Silvia and Mel. "You are much smaller. We'll just have to work with it. We might have to sew you into the dress, but we will make this work. First thing's first. Bra off, put these on."

She shoves a box of peachy silicone into my arms. They remind me of chicken cutlets.

At my look of horror Silvia steps in. "You've never worn them before." My shock apparently makes that completely evident. "Pull off the backing, hold up your boob, and stick it on. Try to get them even. Washroom's this way." She pushes me that way, and closes the door behind me.

I drop the top of the dress, and try my best to replace my bra with the stick on things. They go on easier than I expected with Silvia's explanation helping. Making them even with each other, however, a near impossibility I'm willing to live with. I hope the dress hides that issue.

Folding my bra, I stick it to the side of the counter; I need somewhere to put it, and this seems to work well enough. The girls see to have taken over this area, no guys going through; it should be safe enough here.

I exit the bathroom, and am pulled into one of the bedrooms to get the dress adjusted.

The older woman makes her comments as she works, strictly about what she is doing. I am caught between wondering if she's related or if she's a hired helper. Either way, she's experienced in this sort of thing.

She adjusts the dress in every way she can, even shortening it on the bottom skirt part. True to her warning, she ends everything by sewing me into the dress. The size difference doesn't look too bad, by the time she is finished.

I don't get time to dwell. The seamstress opens the door, and Mel rushes in to pull me out.

The other girls are mostly finished. One is still getting her hair done. The other station's manicurist and makeup artist take care of my hands, feet, and face at the same time.

The hairstylist comes over once she's finished with the other bridesmaid, so I have three people attacking me at once.

Suffocation, in a new found claustrophobia, chokes at me, but I put up with it and try not to lash out to push them away. It's not about me right now. I try my best to stay still, and only move as they place me.

Nails and makeup finish pretty close together, completely easing the closed in feeling as they back off.

Hair takes a long time to affix my long hair into a braided bun on the side of the back of my head.

Silvia brings me champagne. "Cheers."

"Cheers." We clink glasses, and I take a sip. I try to be mindful of my makeup. I wouldn't want to mess it up or require touch ups. I don't even know if that could be a possibility once we leave the room.

"Thank you for doing this. I owe you."

"It's no problem. This is fun." I whisper the next part. "I'm sorry things ended up the way they did so close to the wedding."

"Me too." She leans in, and hugs me as best as she can with the hair stylist still working at my hair. Her arms hug to my own, and she crosses me a little as she leans her weight onto me.

When she pops up, Silvia gets back to flitting around the room.

Time is running out before the wedding is supposed to start. Silvia instructs Mel to move everyone to the tent.

A hundred bobby pins later, my hair is finally done. Silvia thanks the hair dresser, and pays her.

We rush to a tent that is set up on the beach. Silvia seems less concerned than I am about being late, but she's uttered the phrase a few times in the last hour, 'they can't start the wedding without the bride,' but I wonder if she believes it or wants to believe it more.

Though, I suppose while it is true, she may also be hiding jitters behind the phrase.

We are plied with a shot of tequila as soon as we enter the tent. The heat goes straight to my stomach as I realize breakfast has consisted of champagne and a shot of tequila.

The mood is rushed and electric.

The music starts.

Bouquets are gathered, and one is thrust into my arms. I'm placed in position right in front of Silvia.

One by one, the girls leave the tent in their order.

"Pace yourself. Smile. Go behind Cloe. V shape; angled beside and partially behind, but also in front." She lets out a deep breath. "Oh, I'm so nervous."

I turn, and hug her quickly. "Relax Sil. Have fun, and enjoy yourself. You are marrying the love of your life, and that's what today is about. Celebrating you both. Everything else, doesn't matter."

It's been more than enough time between me, and the last girl, so I hurry to leave the tent. Righting myself calmly at the exit; I smile and keep pace.

I take in all the eyes and frowns. No one has any idea who I am, but it only gets worse when the groomsmen spot me. Their recognition and gestures bumps to each other to make sure their all seeing the same thing, is embarrassingly worse.

Over all, I realize how confusing this might be, especially if no one was given a heads up.

My eyes meet Will's, and his awestruck adoration. If he wasn't looking at me, locking eyes, I would think Silvia is right behind me.

Sam's jaw drops, and he wipes a couple joyful tears. Silvia's obviously entered into his view. I do my best not to awe on the spot. It's adorable. He must truly be in love with her.

I pivot on the spot Cloe does in the moments before, to take my place.

I settle into a spot Cloe helps guide me to, and watch Silvia come down from half way down the aisle. She and Sam have their gazes locked, and are equally tearful. They ping off each other, unable to stop. Giggling at themselves.

It's the sweetest thing I've ever seen, and threatens to bring joyful tears to my own eyes.

Sam reaches over to wipe her tears, and she does the same for him. They share a last giggle, and the officiant starts the wedding.

A strong breeze blows, and I am thankful for the updo. It keeps the hair out of my face, all of our faces, and is best for pictures.

They keep the ceremony short and sweet, then Silvia and Sam walk through the aisle to clapping form the guests.

The wedding party joins with their partner on the mirror opposite, and follows after the dup to a receiving line.

We greet the guests with a handshake or a hug as they go through the line; I get handshakes from everyone except Bree.

The question on their tongues is who I am. I've heard a couple ask Silvia who I am. Some ask me themselves.

I respond with a couple variations including my name, then various versions of the truth; we met a few days ago, and have been hanging out so when Silvia needed an emergency fill in, I said yes. With the speed some go through, and by the end of the lineup of a singular repeated question, many get a shortened, 'Skylar, emergency fill in.'

Two warm hands grip lightly on my shoulders, squeezing once. I turn my head quickly, and see Will. "Hey."

I go back to shake hands with another stranger. This one stays silent as they glance up at Will, then back to me.

"How'd Sil rope you into this?" He asks quietly.

"She asked." I shrug. His hands slip off my shoulders. Another person goes by with silence, a look to Will, and a handshake.

"Is that code for kidnapping?"

"You're not the first person to suggest that this morning." The first person being me, but he doesn't need to know that.

"Blink twice if you feel like you're in danger."

Laughter fills my smile, and swells my chest, but I try to keep it noiseless in respect for the final people passing us by. "You can't even see my face. How would you tell if I blink twice?"

"Good point." He turns me around. "Blink twice if you feel like you're in danger."

I cock my head to the side, and raise up an eyebrow. "I'm fine. It's been fun."

The line has ended, and Silvia gathers us together saying we're going to do pictures now. Mel dismisses anyone who isn't important by telling them they can go find lunch, and hang out at the pool until the banquet starts in the à la carte restaurant.

I'm not sure if I should stay or go until she starts hustling people to leave. She doesn't tell me to go, so I guess I stay.

Those who do stick around are absolute immediate family.

Everyone gets their pictures done. Family goes first, so they can leave sooner.

The mood lightens as the wedding party remains, listening to the photographer's instructions for a variety of shots.

I try not to think about my inclusion. Silvia doesn't ask me out of any photos that include all the bridesmaids, so I get into all the shots needed of me.

Chapter 14

"Why didn't you tell me you haven't eaten yet?" Walking back into the main room, I hadn't expected the boisterous question aimed at me from across the way.

Silvia storms over.

"It's- I'm fine."

"I've been feeding you alcohol, and you haven't eaten since last night. It's not fine." She reprimands. I can only assume she talked to Bree while I was gone. I can thank her later for this, for now, I shoot her an unmet glare.

"If I wasn't okay, I would have said something. I promise." Half promise. I've had a couple light headed moments that signaled I could have used some food, but there's really been no time to do so.

"Please eat something, or people will think I kidnapped you." The siblings show their relation through their humour. I find it funnier than they likely would, that they both defaulted to jokes about my kidnapping.

"I will. Though I think you're a little late with worrying about people thinking you kidnapped me. I've had a couple comments already."

"Damn." She pulls me over to the food, and puts a plate in my hand. "Eat."

I dish up a plate of the assorted fruit, cheese, and meat from the platters.

When we had come back to the villa Silvia gushed about the

buffet set out and the package she had gotten from the hotel; saying the food, and champagne bottles were part of it.

It had been a bit of a tease to my stomach.

We chugged a glass before we were sent off to change into swimming attire, and undo all the work from an hour before.

Removing the makeup was the easy part. I thought it would be too much of a waste to pick apart my hair so soon so I left the updo in.

I had gathered a set of swim stuff, and brought it back to the villa, with Bree tagging along, so that I could change after getting cut out of the dress.

I hope it's not ruined, which is a funny thought to have now considering all the last minute alterations they did to fit me in there. The dress is not usable in its current condition. Though I suppose, most bridesmaid dresses never see the light of day after the wedding. Mandy certainly won't want it back now that she's pretty well nixed their friendship.

The wedding party, and some others trickle back in from their rooms. While others leave to meet at the pool, or go their own ways.

I sit down in one of two chairs centered in the room, and watch while I eat. Bree converses with Ryan. Silvia is playing hostess, bouncing around from person to person.

I quickly notice Jennifer is absent, though the rest have come back. I hope she's not pulling anything else; for Silvia's sake. Although, it might be best if she's decided to no-show for the rest of the time. One less thing for Silvia to worry about.

Silvia hands me a second plate after I finish the first. "Eat." She orders me in her passing.

"What's that about?" Will's garbled voice comes up behind me. I hadn't known he had made it back already. He has a plate of his own.

"I think she feels bad. In the chaos, I hadn't eaten breakfast, so now she's making sure I eat." I explain.

"Remember; blink twice." He blinks twice in exaggerated demonstration.

"William Connor Bogtrotter!" Our eyes snap up to Silvia's shouts. "Are you the one going around telling people I kidnapped her?"

I nearly choke on a pineapple in my laughter. A cough quickly dislodges it.

"The evidence does suggest you did."

"Children!" Both Will and Silvia shut down at, who I can only assume is, their mother's admonishment. "Silvia, no one actually thinks you kidnapped this poor girl. William be nice to your sister, and stop pestering her for once in your life. It's her wedding day, and she doesn't need you stressing her out."

"Sorry Silvia." Will apologizes to Silvia, and to the woman. "Sorry mom."

An apology sits on my tongue. I started this all with my reckless comments. I should be the one apologizing to them all.

Mrs. Bogtrotter sets steel eyes on me. "Now, I think proper introductions are in order." Her barking order promises chilling trouble.

I stand to greet her respectfully. Putting my plate to the spot I was occupying.

Silvia speeds over, and gets in front of Will. She wraps her arm around me. "Mom, I would like to introduce you to Skylar. She's a new friend of mine. She lives in Canada. Mandy decided to ditch at last minute, so Skylar very graciously allowed me to borrow her for the day. Skylar, this is my mother, Katherine Bogtrotter."

"It's very nice to meet you." I offer out my hand, but she doesn't put up hers. After a couple seconds, I pull it back to my side.

Smile. Remember to smile.

My heart thunders. I should leave. This isn't my place to be. I've pushed myself into a situation I should have never been involved in.

"I wish I would have heard more about you before being bombarded with questions." Katherine's eyes sweep me up and down. Examining every inch of me. Picking me apart piece by piece. The bathing suit does nothing to cover me. I'm naked under her view.

I don't know what to say back to her.

"There wasn't any time, or else I would have let you know what was going on. I'm sorry." Silvia ducks her head down in shame, missing when her mother softens her gaze slightly as she looks to her daughter.

Her frown tightens as she goes back to me. Katherine raises her head to look down on me an extra couple inches. "I refrained from taking pictures because I didn't think you'd want to remember your day, with some random girl in the party. I do wish we would have excluded her from some of the professional photos. Good thing we'll have a chance to do it properly at your real wedding."

"How many of your bridesmaids do you still talk to?" Will questions pointedly. He comes closer up behind Silvia and I. Placing a hand on my shoulder. Imposing himself on us in solidarity.

Katherine relents in a deep breath. "Yes, well, I suppose I should find your father. I believe he's beaten all of us to the wet bar." Her first smile appears as she looks to Silvia. "Hunny, you were beautiful as always." I receive another tight lip. "Skylar, it was nice to meet you."

"Nice to meet you too." I respond sweetly.

I expect her to say something to Will, but she just looks at him a moment before turning. He frowns at her back.

There's a tension released when she leaves the villa rooms.

Silvia wipes away a tear. "I am so sorry. She's a bit intense sometimes. She means well, but it doesn't come across that way. I am so glad you were able to stand in. It means a lot to me. And, I don't think you're just some random girl, or else I wouldn't have asked. And, Will, I'm sorry. I knew you were joking. I didn't realize she was in the room."

"You don't have to apologize to me, I know how she can be." They hug each other tightly. Family drama cuts deep, but at least they have each other to help deal with her.

"My dad probably would have reacted the same way, maybe a bit more casual swearing, and he definitely would have mentioned money." I try to lighten the moment with a bit of commiseration. Something to tell them I'm not offended. I won't hold it against them. We can't choose our parents.

"I'm sorry." Silvia hugs me tight.

"It's okay."

More and more people leave the room to go to the pool. Once Sam finally joins us in the villa, we all leave for the pool.

Bree comes with us in a group of five. She touches my arm as she spots something going on in the grass. "I'm gonna go limbo. I'd ask you to join, but you suck at limbo. Which is funny, because you'd think with your unfair advantage, you'd be better at it."

"Ouch." I pretend to be offended, but she's right. I'd probably be out first round. "Have fun." Bree runs away with a wave.

"We should probably go mingle with our guests. Make sure everyone knows what the plan is for the rest of the day." Sam tells Silvia.

Silvia nods then points at me. "Around supper time, fiveish, grab Bree, and go over to the à la carte restaurant. It's reserved for the banquet."

"Sure, thank you. We'll be there." Silvia smiles, and lets Sam whisk her away.

Then, there were two. I look to Will for a plan. I hadn't expected the others to all leave us, and so suddenly. Maybe I should have gone with Bree. I don't want to make Will think he needs to babysit me.

"To the bar?" Will asks.

"Sure."

We walk towards the wet bar, but Will stops suddenly to gently nudge me in another direction. "The other one. Unless you want to have another run in with my mom. Dad's there too. That could be fun."

"To the other bar." I declare.

"Good choice."

We walk around to the far side stairs that will let us into the pool near the farther wet bar.

Stopping for a minute to watch an iguana basking in the sun right nearby. I didn't think they would let them come in to the resort area, but the bartender seems well aware, and doesn't mind the extra company.

We climb into the pool. It's warmer today. Later on in the day than when we had gone in the other day, the sun must have warmed it a bit. Will, and I sit on the emerged seats.

I decide to try a Chunky Monkey; chocolate, milk, banana, ice, and some rum. The bartender pours a chocolate design on the inside of the cup before he pours the slushy drink inside.

"Sorry about my mom." Will starts.

"Don't worry about it. She was caught unaware, and probably didn't take too kindly to not knowing what was happening." The

128

real banana comes through the chocolate, and ends up making the drink silky.

"Still, she can be a bit much, even on a good day. Don't take anything she said to heart." His insistence on making sure I'm okay is endearing, but reading a bit more into the apology, I figure he's the one who's more upset than I am.

Will sips his sorrows while a little too interested in his drink.

"Harder to do that when you're her son." I deduce. "How are you? You seemed pretty shut down for a bit there."

He shrugs. "She's my mom, if I didn't forgive her, there'd be hell to pay."

There's so much to that comment that itches to be unraveled, but I'm afraid now is not the time or place to do a deep dive.

"Doesn't mean it doesn't hurt." I conclude. "Silvia was quick to jump in. Was she the favourite?"

"All parents love their kids equally. There's no such thing as a favourite child." Will mocks the common saying.

"So, yes."

"She's the girl. I was supposed to be a girl, but *definitely* not a girl." He emphasizes to make it clear he came out with a penis. It's not the first time I've heard men say their moms were told they'd be a girl, but there was an extra appendage surprise when they had come out. "A few years later, when we got Silvia… mom clearly got the girl she wanted and showed it."

"Sorry." I feel bad for him. Favouritism for one child over another makes me glad that I'm an only child.

It can be soft, like little extras here and there, even though the parents try to make an obvious point to make things even. Or, blatantly obvious when one child gets all the attention from mom, but she doesn't have the time of day for you. I have a feeling his was more the latter situation.

"Not that she was horrible. She was a good mom, she just had her moments." It sounds like he's trying to be diplomatic.

"So, what was your childhood like?" I give him a chance to paint a clearer picture.

"Other than my hobby of trying to get myself kidnapped?" Will ponders for a moment. "I hated school."

He twists the conversation broader, but I don't mind. He might not want to reveal details about his relationship with his mom while growing up, and I won't force him to.

"I loved school." I counter. "At one point I would take home homework just for fun." And, to avoid chores and work. "Like asked the teachers to actually give me homework when we had none. I was high honours all the way."

"I bullied kids like you."

"You were a bully?" The new revelation leaves a bad taste for him in my mouth. I want to give him the benefit of the doubt, but my experiences with my own bullies have me hating teenage William Bogtrotter for the pain he undoubtedly caused others.

"Not like, throw kids in the locker type of bully, but a snob bully who didn't think he was a bully, and thought everyone was laughing with him. Until, someone tried to do the same thing to Silvia, and I dealt with her crying, and the aftermath. It was too late for high school by that point though."

"So you were cool kid mean." I know the type. But, the regret is nice. Means he might hate teenage William Bogtrotter as much as his victims. Means there may have been growth and change in adulthood.

"Cool rich kid mean." He clarifies. Adding another level to the general term helps specify the type of bullying he inflicted. "Were you bullied?"

"Yeah. I was the nerd. I was so weird; no social skills. I was the fat kid." He looks at me wide eyed, and with disbelief. I nod.

"Yup. Always was the fat kid. Got called names in elementary school.

Junior high was spent with a bunch of mean girl friends that Bree liked. They liked her, not me, but took me with her because she didn't want to leave me behind.

And then they turned her against me, there was a bunch of backstabbing, and I became the social pariah for the end of grade nine, all summer, and half of grade ten.

Found out from Bree that the girl had promised to do the same to anyone who tried to be nice to me. They'd follow me to my parents' café, and did the dumb things like purposely spill things so I'd have to clean it up. Confronted me all around town, to rehash things I guess and make sure I was still miserable.

I had tried to reach out to Bree once, but apparently she had been hiding around the corner, then she gathered to troops to confront me at the library. Told me I had no reason to be talking to Bree and trying to work things out.

She eventually lost interest." Took two years. My thoughts trail to the next time I saw her. There is a sort of happy ending to the story. Something Will might relate to.

"Actually, funny enough, she actually ended up apologizing to me years later. We had a mutual friend, who invited us both to a party. She got drunk, and apologized. Said she felt bad for what she had done. That her parents were fighting, and later got divorced, and her mom finally took her for tests, and she was diagnosed with bipolar.

She said she wasn't trying to excuse it away, because it was crappy, but she needed to apologize, and let me know it wasn't necessarily about me; I was just an easy target.

Other than her, I also had random people say means things, and was spat on twice."

"That's disgusting. Why would they spit on you?"

I shrug and have to stop myself from gagging as the memories resurface; especially when I can clearly see the orange chunks I had to cleanse from my hair from the one guy's spit. "Yup, disgusting. I don't know. They did it because they could; I guess."

"Did you try to talk to anyone about it? Tell your teachers?"

"Bree did. She went to the school counselor, and tried to get them to deal with it. They pulled two of my bullies in to talk, then brought me in, and asked them to apologize. Then they asked if I accepted. And that's all they did. I told Bree to never do that again. It didn't stop anything, and certainly not everything from everyone.

The experience in itself was actually mortifying and terrifying. I was so scared that they or their friends were going to retaliate extensively. They didn't. Things just continued like normal. But, it didn't stop the fear for a month after."

"They just got them to say sorry, and that was it?"

"Yup." To which, of course, I said that I accepted. I was terrified of retaliation if I hadn't. Terrified that I'd have to talk extensively with the counselor if I didn't accept; until I would have been coerced into accepting.

"She wasn't punished or anything?" He cocks his head in disbelief.

"Not so far as I know."

"Heard you had a run in with your mother." A voice comes between Will and I. "Hi, I'm William Bogtrotter. You may call me Old Will or dad."

"Hi, I'm Skylar." I try to work out this one. Will's dad obviously, but what kind of person might he be? Is he super friendly, as suggested by the introduction? Or was it a passive aggressive jab from what he's heard or assumed about me? Old Will seems too informal, but might be necessary after the double naming with his son; makes me wonder if Will has a Junior

132

attached to his name somewhere. Dad, is a hard no in shear awkwardness.

"So where has my son been hiding you?" He tags a swig of his liquid gold drink.

"We just met a few days ago. Here. Signing up for excursions. Will asked for a suggestion for the bachelor party." I explain. No use in lying or avoiding it. He'd hear about it sooner or later, and it's better to just be honest.

"So, you met Will first?" He asks for clarifications sake.

"Yes." His digging into my words creeps fear into me. Maybe the niceties are fake. I make the point to remember to watch what I say going forward.

"Sil made a big move to show you were her friend." He says thoughtfully. I don't know how to respond to that. Old Will quickly turns to address Will. "You should thank your sister, or you mom would have reamed Skylar out more. Scared her away before I can get grandchildren."

Lack of boundaries friendly, is the vibe I'm pulling from him. He's a conundrum I can't place from one moment to the next.

"Did you miss the part where she said we've only known each other for a few days?" Will deadpans.

Old Will shrugs his mouth and shoulders. "Mel said she's your date."

"You know how she is. Why would you believe her?"

Elder Will shrugs both his mouth and shoulders again in a repeated movement. "Hopeful I guess. Between Mel, Silvia, and the way you look at her."

"Dad." Will forcefully throws out his name, trying to get him to stop.

His repeated movement is dolled out again, and I'm starting to get the idea that it's his move when he's about to say something he shouldn't. So far, he's already said a few things that would have been better suited without my presence. "She's been making you smile. And, I heard you kissed."

My face turns hot at the mention. Who told him that? Obviously between Mel, and Silvia, or I suppose any of the wedding party could have said something.

It's not something I would have wanted known to his parents. Some random girl crashing their daughter's wedding because she made out with their son a couple days after meeting him.

"Dad!" Will pronounces. "We just met, and you're making us both uncomfortable."

"Right, you'll have to forgive me. Alcohol loosens my lips." He looks around a little. "And I see my opportunity to make it up to you." I watch him turn and shout. "Katherine, I'm starving. Let's go check out that sushi bar."

He deflects an approaching Katherine. After dealing with the awkwardness of his dad, I don't think I could also handle his mom. I already just want to go back to my room, and disappear for the rest of the trip.

I swallow half my drink before registering any sort of taste. In a glance to my side, I watch Will's hand shake around his own.

"He's right, I think we do have to forgive him after such a successful diversion." I try to lighten the mood. To show to Will that I'm not offended by his dad's assumptions; more embarrassed than offended, but he doesn't need that put on him either.

Will seems agitated by them. There seems to have been more deep cuts given to scars already existing.

I wish to hug him, and let him know it's fine. But I don't think that would be welcome in the particularities of the situation. Especially, with so many possible witnesses.

So I look for a distraction instead. Snacks are out, if we want to avoid parents.

I find one in the other side of the pool. Limbo has finished, and evolved into another activity. "Volleyball?"

He looks over to where I point, smiling when he returns back to me.

"Going to have to chug our drinks."

I look at the level in my cup, willing to take the small sacrifice if only to make him feel better.

I grab the cup, and hold it up between us. "Cheers!"

"Cheers." We clink cups, and drink away what's left.

Chapter 15

Silvia announces, "for all those interested, we will be moving to the disco hall for the bouquet toss, some drinks, and some dancing after supper."

Some people return to their on goings, and some go over to talk to Silvia.

The Mediterranean buffet styled dinner was delicious. I surely over stuffed myself, but it was no wonder after not eating much for the rest of the day; I was starving.

Bree and I sit at a table for four, with two others. At first, we had some polite talk, but they quickly turned the conversation more towards each other.

They leave as soon as they finish their food, and gulp down the rest of their drinks.

Bree and I savour the last of our wine, until more people go to the disco; until Silvia and Sam are ready to go.

We all go inside the room to cheers, and clapping aimed at the bride and groom.

Silvia quickly gathers together the women, and tosses the bouquet over her shoulder. One of the taller girls gets the catch. I was not even in the running to have a chance.

Silvia grabs her husband, and starts off the dancing. People take a moment to watch, before joining in on the fun.

Very quickly, the older people of the crowd start leaving. The bridesmaids and groomsmen, along with some cousins, or whatever relation they are, have no problem keeping the party going.

I think about grabbing Bree to head out. I'm getting tired, and a bit bored of the party. But, Bree looks like she's enjoying herself, so I opt to get a drink instead.

An arm comes from behind, and links elbows with mine. Silvia leans in. "Let's go get a blended drink, and ditch the party." Sam and Will tag shortly behind her.

I nod. "I've got to let Bree know."

I walk over to Bree, and ask her to join us, she declines, and tells me to have fun. I'm sure she just wants to keep dancing with Ryan, and some others. It's more her idea of fun anyway.

Meeting Silvia back at the door, we leave the party to find the bar over closer towards the pool.

"Bunch of old people. Come for the wedding, and ditch before the night is over." Sam complains.

"Us?" Silvia asks.

He looks at her with a chuckle in his eyes. "No, our guests."

"Well, most of them did just fly in today or last night. Jet lag. Long day. Besides, if they stayed, we wouldn't have been able to ditch." Silvia offers a silver lining.

"Don't worry, you'll get to spend all week with them." Will reminds them.

Silvia grumbles. "Why did we decide to do that again?"

"You wanted the destination wedding. You forgot about the part where that means you'll have to entertain everyone for the whole week." Will tells her.

"So do you." She counters.

Will holds up both hands. "Not my wedding. Not my guests. I'll be off adventuring." He has a bit of a point. Technically his obligations are over.

Silva spits out a sound of disgust. "Can you please cause some drama; it would really help. I give you and Sam permission to cause a scene."

"Yeah, that's a great first impression as your husband." Sam comments.

"Pfft, if they thought things were going to change between you and Will after we got married, then that's their fault." I can't help but giggle a little. Some things never change, and it's great for them all if they can keep their bonds the same after the marriage. Put any thought to bed about the awfulness that is the best friend marrying the sibling.

We order our drinks of four daiquiris, in a bid to make it a bit easier on the bartenders with their crowd.

Silvia leads us over to some tables over near the buffet. She reasons that they might be able to get a little privacy over here. I get the feeling she's trying to avoid run ins with party guests, possibly particular guests.

"Long day." Silvia sinks into her chair. "This wedding stuff is exhausting."

"And just think, you get to do it all over again." Will mentions with bitter cheer.

Silvia groans.

"A destination wedding and a home wedding?" I question. He mom had mentioned something about that in her fit.

"It was a compromise, because so many people couldn't afford to come. Besides, there's too much paperwork to actually get married in another country, so we have to do something to actually get married. Might as well have a wedding to go with it." Sam explains.

"Could have just gone to city hall with a couple witnesses." Will offers a much simpler option.

"Mom wanted a big party." Silvia says.

"There it is." Will calls her out. The real reason why she's having two weddings is clearly from motherly input rather than actual want.

"I know. You don't have to remind me."

I try to steer the conversation into a happier note. "So what do you have planned for the other wedding?"

"Silver, purple, and white. My dress is more classic ball gown/princessy. Lots of jewels to make it sparkle. The bodice is lacey, and heart shaped. I'd show you, but I don't have my phone on me."

"That's okay. It sounds beautiful."

Silvia straightens up her head at an approaching intrusion. I freeze in dread as to who could be approaching from over my shoulder's direction; limited to literally anyone at the hotel. "Hi dad."

"I come in peace with tequila." He sets down a white bottle with blue painted leaf designs, and four matching shot glasses. Old Will places a squeezing hand on Will's shoulder, then kisses Silvia's head. "Good night. Skylar, it was lovely to meet you."

"Nice to meet you as well. Have a great night." I say politely.

The intentions reveal themselves once he's out of earshot. "Who wants bribe tequila? I'm sure it was expensive, and only the best. A sipping tequila because all the best and most expensive alcohols are made for sipping." Silvia bites out bitterly.

I bite my tongue, wishing to say that their dad might just be being nice. But, they know him better than I do. If they say it's bribe tequila, then he might have a history of buying their forgiveness, and possibly even their love.

It's overcompensation that's all too common in many parenting relationships.

Bree's dad did that with her, and chocolate and shopping.

Every time he came home from work, he would bring her some chocolate, and give her a hundred dollar bill to go shopping with. That meant every four days to a week, maybe two; depending on where he was scheduled to drop off shipments.

If he thought she was upset with him, they would go make a day out of something special together: expensive dinner, movie with all the food fixings, water park, or anything she would want.

All it does is work to create resentment, and expectation within the children. Bree has used it to her advantage many times in her life. Well aware of exactly what he was doing.

They don't have the best relationship because of it. More like a daughter for hire tone.

"So, how much longer do you have here?" Sam asks.

I have to think about it for a moment, counting the events of each day, in order to count my days here. "We leave the day after tomorrow, I think."

"No chance in talking you into staying longer?" Silvia pouts. She hands me the shot glass. Then quickly clinks together with her own. We clink all the glasses, and take a swig. I keep in mind what she said about sipping, but after seeing the other three shoot their whole drink down, I follow by example. It's not especially burn-y, but a grimace at the contrast between with sweet daiquiri, and this.

I answer once I get my bearings. "If I did, my parents would be on all sorts of calls convinced I was kidnapped or was convinced to join a cult or gang or something." I also wouldn't be able to justify the extra expense.

"They sound protective." Will says.

"Very." I quick point at him to let him know he nailed it. "And I'm an only child, so no one to commiserate with me on the crazy."

"Growing up with a brother isn't all it's cracked up to be." Silvia says.

"I could say the same thing about having a sister." Will nudges back.

"But, you two seem to get along at least." I say.

"As adults, yes." Silvia smiles at Will. "It's was more love, hate, and torture as children."

The night moves along as we talk about random things, and drink our drinks. Talking, and talking about everything, and nothing at the same time. Some conversations circling and reappearing in drunken eagerness and insistence.

Silvia gets closer to her husband, and snuggles as well as she can in her own separate seat. Eventually ending up stroking his cheek. "I love you."

"I love you too." Sam returns with a quick kiss.

She looks over to her brother. "I love you Willy." I smile big, and swallow a laugh. I wonder if Willy was a nickname growing up.

Will barely contains himself. "You're drunk. Go home."

Silvia frowns. "Don't you love me too?"

"Yes, but when you start talking like that, you've had too much, and you need to go home."

"That's too far away." Silvia pouts. I can just imagine her asking someone to carry her.

"It's just a small walk." Will tries to reason.

"It'd be next week before I'd get there." She whines.

"The villa, Sil. Not our house. We should get back. Before you start announcing to Sky how much you love her." Sam sets her straight, and agrees with Will.

Lovey Silvia is a too drunk Silvia, and needs to call it a night.

"But I do. I'd love for you to stick around. You're cute, and I like talking with you." I mentally awe at her drunken confessions. "Promise me we'll keep in touch. I'll add you when I get my phone. You have Facebook, and things, right?"

"Yes. Skylar Bryson. I'll make sure I accept your request once I get home. It would be nice to keep in contact. Then, I could see some pictures from your other wedding too."

"Would you like to come?" In exaggerated facial expression, so looks as hopeful as a puppy hearing the word walk.

I almost regret having to say no. But, imagine the upheaval there would be if I showed up to her other wedding. Her mom would have a complete fit. Her dad might start planning Will and my wedding. "There's no way I could swing that with my parent's and the café, but I would love to if I could."

"That's too bad." She pouts. "I'm going to miss you. You'll have to come to visit us sometime."

"That could be fun." I say; though I know it would never happen. Travelling across continent to visit people I barely know would be ridiculous. A week vacation is something altogether different then such a personal interaction.

Silvia comes over, and hugs me where I sit. Putting most of her weight on me as she falls off balance. "Please don't be a stranger."

"I won't. Good night. I'll see you tomorrow." I send her off me with a bit of help from Sam.

"Yeah, that's right. You still have another day with us." Silvia bounces quickly back to being cheerful. "Okay. See you tomorrow."

"Night."

"Night."

"Sorry." Will apologizes once they're gone.

142

"That's fine. She's a lovey drunk, right? I have an aunt who's a super lovey drunk. It's one of the best types of drunks." Much better than most of the other types I've met and experienced. Who doesn't like being told that they are loved and appreciated a thousand times? It's amusing at the very least.

"My butt's falling asleep." His announcement brings about my own bodily realization of the same thing. How long have we been sitting here? "Want to walk around for a bit?"

"Sure."

Will gathers the alcohol bottle, and the shot glasses. We walk out towards the beach.

The night sky is dotted with bright stars. A view which seems duller back home. It's different to be on a beach at night, gazing out to a deep blackness. Hearing, more than seeing, the waves crashing.

"You'd love Santa Monica; I think. Beach, ocean, Santa Monica Pier. Muscle beach, if you're into working out. There's an aquarium. Close to Hollywood, Los Angeles, Long Beach, Disneyland… Tell me when I've sold you on it." Will hits all the known highlights.

"It sounds wonderful. Quite the adventure." The filter I'd normally use to keep resentment, and loss away, is out of order with the alcohol. It would be absolutely amazing to go to Santa Monica, go to the wedding, and all the things Will just mentioned. "But, it was hard to try to convince mom and dad that I should go on this trip with Bree. I think they only let me go because of the situation."

I continue to fill the empty dark. Confessions to myself, with an extra set of ears I don't mind listening. "Tight reins at home. I mean it's not bad all the time, but I'm getting to the point where I think it's starting to become embarrassing that I still live at home. I'm passed university, so that's not an excuse. Everyone I know is out on their own. Or has at least gone out, and then been forced back for one reason or another.

And, being at home with them, I still feel like I'm a teenager. Where I sort of have freedom, but only as much as they let me. I still have to check in and get permission to do things. It doesn't help that I live with them and work with them."

"Sounds like, maybe, you should think about moving out." He suggests.

It's crossed my mind a few times.

"Yeah. I know." I yawn.

"I should get you back. Before I'm the one accused of kidnapping you." I laugh. Quickly silenced when he takes my hand. I adjust my fingers to place them between his. He smiles at my gesture, and brings my hand up for a soft kiss. Cool air helps the kiss linger in the light wetness left behind.

We trudge back to my hotel room. Bypassing all the ongoing excitement happening in the hub of the resort.

Will walks me straight to my door. Disappointment fills me. I wish the walk had been longer. I wish Bree wasn't in the room, so we could continue to talk until we fall asleep. So that his warmth didn't have to leave my hand.

He kisses my cheek and says, "sweet dreams."

"Sweet dreams. See you tomorrow."

I enter the hotel room to find Bree hasn't returned yet.

Drained, and too tired to search, I hope she won't get into too much trouble with the wedding party.

Chapter 16

"Are you sure?" I ask for, what feels like, the tenth time this morning. Mostly, I ask out a faint boredom.

"I told you. We haven't done enough relaxing this whole trip." She takes a sip of her drink, and leans back fully again.

The morning sun reaches her on her side of the cabana, but doesn't reach me; a strategic placement with our sun preferences.

"What are you talking about? I'm pretty sure you've spent three quarters of the whole time sleeping." I joke.

"It's not my fault I got sick."

"Did you want to go shopping?" I attempt.

"Is it actually worth it? The way you described it…" Bree pulls back to our conversation about it earlier. She knows I don't like shopping without purpose in the first place.

"Yeah, I mean. It was okay."

"But you wouldn't do it again, if it was just you." She knows me. She's known me too long not to know me well enough.

There's no point in lying about it, though I know I'm possibly giving up my last hope at doing something eventful today. "Not unless I had a specific reason. An hour there, an hour back. I already have a tequila and a souvenir."

"And I've got a beautiful souvenir jewelry box, and I can get alcohol at the airport. We don't need to go." Bree summarizes.

"You sure?"

"Yes. I'd rather spend the four hours lounging poolside, getting a tan, and stuffing myself with food and drinks." Bree concludes our conversation.

She might be okay lying out in the sun for hours, and hours, but I would at least need a book. Some form of entertainment. But, I hadn't thought to bring anything on the trip.

We've already run out of things to talk about.

The lack of doing anything else, already has me sinking drink after drink. In a passing thought, I think to pace myself going forward, unless I want to deal with a nasty hangover, and a plane trip.

Chapter 17

The bartender hands us more drinks as we finish up our sushi rolls.

Dinner snuck up on us, and by the time we figured out it should be supper time, we were already scarfing down our afternoon snack in larger than proper dinner sized portions at the stand alone drink hut; right outside the buffet building.

"So, what do you want to do tonight?" I ask Bree.

"Hmm, more of the same until the curtain is pulled on us. Then find some drinks, and some company? We haven't seen Will or Silvia all day." I'd like to see them all one last time before we have to leave. "Or Ryan."

"Ryan had to leave this morning. Yesterday was the last full day for most of the wedding party." That explains why I haven't seen any of those recognizable faces.

"Is that why you took so long to get back last night?" I joke.

"Maybe." Bree sing songs coyly.

I nearly choke on my bite. "Did something happen last night?"

She smiles unabashedly. My eyes widen in shock. Bree was never one to have random hookups, or hook ups at all.

It makes me wonder if what I'm imagining she's alluding to, really is what happened.

"Well, it is a spite vacation." She shrugs.

"How is this, the first I'm hearing about this?"

"I was processing." Bree says with a quick shrug.

"Are you okay?" I start to wonder if something bad happened. Processing is rarely a good thing.

"Oh, yes!" She outbursts, and relieves my worry in an instant. "Nothing like that. Last night was great. 100% would do it again. I think, at least for now, I'm coming to terms with what happened with what's his name."

"Well, that's good." And surprising. I guess processing is better than another meltdown.

"Ryan was way better anyway."

My mind works in quick stages of questioning, and realization, thankfully, before I can voice my question.

Oh. She's talking about the sex. Oh. Okay.

Done with our food, we decide to walk back to the cabana we staked out for most of the day.

Though, when we get there, every lounge chair and cabana is taken. I recognize a few people from the wedding, and some other tourists we've been sharing the resort with.

"Did you want to swim?" Bree asks.

My mind is already turning. Swimming would take another hour or so. It's after supper, and going to be dark soon. Night and sleep follow after. I doubt we'll be able to get to sleep sooner than normal, so that means a very short night for us. I would like to get clean. "Showers? 4 am pick up, right? Maybe we should shower, and pack up. I don't think we'll want to do it at 3 am."

"Are you turning back into the responsible one?" I can almost hear her inner voice groaning in disappointment.

"If we do it now, we can sleep in later." I reason.

"I guess so." She hums.

148

Bree and I go back to our room to shower, and pack up. She goes for her shower first.

I tidy up the room, and pack up my things. I never fully unpacked, unlike Bree. So it doesn't take long to pack up. I leave out a set of clothes for tonight, pajamas, and a set of comfortable clothes for the plane.

I'll need to grab my phone, and charger, and bathroom supplies in the morning, but that will be it.

My tequila bottle is tucked in the middle of everything with clothes wrapped around it. I hope it doesn't break on the way home.

My pyramid should be a bit hardier, but it also gets wrapped in a shirt for good measure.

The pictures should safe inside a large pocket in the cover of the suitcase.

Bree finally exits the bathroom to a burst of steam, so it becomes my turn to get clean while she tidies up her things.

She manages to get most of it thrown into her bag, and clean up our room significantly at the same time.

It's dark by the time we emerge from our room.

It's a different atmosphere in the night than in the day. No one is in the pool. No one is lounging on the deck. It's too dark to be out on the beach.

People are back in their rooms, at the disco, out on the town, or at the main hub. There aren't many other options.

I stamp my disappointment when I don't see Will or Silvia at the bar or where the mariachi band is. They are probably with family in their villa. It's a bit different with family around versus just friends.

Bree orders me something at the bar. It comes to me as a blue slushy, and is sort of tropical tasting. It tastes fine, so I don't mind it.

Bree parks us at a table nearby, right outside the mariachi room, and steps away from the bar.

"I hate that we have to go back tomorrow." I break our silence.

"Yeah, I'll miss it. We'll have to come back some day."

"Yeah." I hope so.

There is something magical in being somewhere out of your ordinary. The air is warmer, the mood is lighter, and the view is like a dreamscape.

Bree and I talk about our adventure. Reminiscing on the past few days, as they seem so far off now despite still being here.

There's a slight regret that this will soon be over. A large feeling of not being able to do enough while here. I would have loved to have done more, but that likely would have required many more days.

I'm lucky to have gotten to be able to do what I did. Bree, not as lucky, as she was put out of commission for a day and a half.

She would have loved the pirate ship; guilt still nags at me for that.

I would have loved to check off many more of the excursions on the pamphlet. There was a pyramid and cenote adventure that would have been amazing. Or, even the water park theme park. Might've been nice to visit a few places not offered in prepackaged excursions. Nice to go out, and visit local non tourist places.

Might've been nice to stick around the hotel, and gone swimming a few more times. Would have been nicer if we had been able to swim in the ocean without fear of being debilitated for the rest of the trip.

A larger crowd walks by. Will and Silvia in amongst them, and in full conversation with some other people.

I guess they must've been out for the day. They walk by us, busy entertaining their people.

Bree stares off in a thoughtful state, not seeming to have noticed them or anything. Neither smiling nor frowning.

I debate asking her what's wrong. But, I'm not sure of the timing, or whether something really is wrong.

She had said she thought she worked things out earlier, but maybe she's rethinking about it. I don't imagine sex and a week in Mexico is enough to get over such a monumental life change.

Her entirely manicured, and thought out life, has been completely rerouted on a different course.

It would be best to get it out and talk about it.

Then again, if she's just pondering our vacation or taking in the moment, I could ruin it with my question.

I settle for waiting for a visible sign of pain, or for her to mention something.

Peaking inside the large room, I watch the mariachi band preform for the people. Walking around, and taking requests, giving a sort of personal experience to each customer.

I kind of want to grab a plate of nachos to snack on, but not enough to actually move from my spot.

However, I don't seem to have the same issue when my drink needs a refill.

I could get used to this sort of vacation laziness. A more laid back style of living.

But, I'd need to win a lottery I don't play in order to make that happen.

"Oh, thank God, you're still here!" Silvia exclaims. "Mom and dad took forever to go back to their rooms." Silvia hugs me.

Our table for two becomes overcrowded with three additions

after they each find a drink. We pull over chairs from another table to fit everyone.

"When do you leave?" Sam asks.

"4 am pick up." Bree says.

"Ewe."

"Yeah, but at least we don't have much of a layover this time. Just a quick stop, we don't even have to get off the plane. Not like when we were getting here. There was a three hour layover in Toronto." I lay out the flight plan. It shouldn't be too bad. Won't take as much time to get home as it did to get here.

"Ewe." Sam repeats.

"How long is your flight?" Will asks.

I try to count it out. "Eight hours, I think. Not including layovers."

"Ouch." Silvia hisses. "Ours is five hours, and that's rough."

"So you have a long day tomorrow, then?" Will says. "Should we let you get to bed early tonight?"

"No. We can sleep on the plane if we need to." I don't correct Bree. She'll sleep on the plane just fine. I likely won't be able to. I think the next time I come, I'll book a red eye, so I can exhaust my way into sleeping the whole way. "Our timing sucked because our first day here, was us basically getting here, just so we could go to sleep."

"And the screw up." I remind her.

"What screw up?" Will asks.

That's right. I haven't mentioned it to any of them. "They had given our room to someone else, so we walked in, and someone was in the shower. They had to work things out while we ate some nachos. I think we had gotten here at ten thirty or so, and got to bed finally around midnight."

"That's awful. We got here, got settled, and grabbed lunch." His first day sounds so much more relaxed than ours had been.

People drift by as we talk through the night. Even as the bartenders call last call, we sit, and talk. Grabbing one last drink to hold us over.

At some point, it becomes useless to think about getting any sleep before our pick up. Not one of us wishes to end this needlessly.

Our last chance to talk, and hang out before Bree and I leave. Possibly the last time we'll ever talk again.

Vacation promises to keep in touch don't work without the intention, and tenacity of all the people involved.

We have them escort us back to our room to grab our things. Silvia easily forces us to exchange acceptance on our social medias, so that we are sure we have the right contacts in place.

Walking to the bus, we check in, and load up our bags.

Saying good bye to friends we only made a week ago. Exchanging hugs that no longer seem one sided or awkward. Wishing to leave a piece of us lingering with these people, and take a piece of them with us.

Will tightly holds me against him for longer than the others had. He lets go, only to pull back.

At the touch of lips, I flush in embarrassment. I place it on hold to wrap my arms around his neck and indulge.

Igniting a fire in my heart.

We part to hoots and woots. And, an annoyed looking bus driver.

"We should get going. I'm sure they have other people to pick up along the way." I dismiss us with my embarrassment.

Our final chorus of good byes cheers us on to the bus. We sit down on the right side of the bus, so we can wave.

Quickly the bus roars, and pulls around the bend, sending us, and them out of sights.

Hot tears surprise me.

Bree notices as I try to hide behind my hair. "Are you okay?"

"I don't know what's happening. I just- I think I'll miss him. And it hurts." Confusion sweeps my mind as I speak the issues as soon as I figure it out. I'll miss him. This has never happened before. I don't just cry at leaving people. The undertones of what's happening scare me. "Just ignore me. I'll be fine. It's the alcohol, and lack of sleep doing weird things to me."

Bree lets it go, thankfully.

Chapter 18

Bree guides me through the off white expanse; searching for something specific yet intangible.

She'll know it when she sees it.

I'll believe that when I see it.

We find it in the form of an old style looking diner called Johnny Rockets. I've never heard of them before but Bree promises me the best burger and milk shake I've ever had.

I have my doubts. Every company boasts having the best of whatever they sell, but no one really has the best.

The 'best' is extremely subjective. It changes between people, taste buds, atmosphere, moment, hunger levels, and many more variables.

I tell Bree to order me whatever she's having. I don't feel like making a decision about burgers this early in the morning. I would have rather found a breakfast specific place.

With the larger crowd, I find us a couple seats just as a couple leaves, while Bree braves the lineup. Ignoring the looks from people who eye me up for our seats, I hold them until Bree finally makes it back with a tray of food.

She ordered us bacon cheese burgers, fries, and orange milk shakes.

The food is average, but the milk shake is dreamy. The orange creamsicle flavouring is quite pleasant, and not something I would normally order myself.

It can be a wonderful experience when you let someone else choose for you. Bringing you out of the ordering rut of choosing comfortable go-to items.

I would have chosen chocolate, because that's what I normally go for, but this orange shake is definitely something I would order again given the chance.

Our chatter is kept to minimums, and has been all morning. The silence proving to be a little mourning side effect of going home.

I'm exhausted from doing nothing much all week, and want to sleep in my own bed tonight. Not that I'm excited to go home, but would rather like to stay longer. Explore more. Continue this mood, and personality reprieve.

The lighter pressure of the vacation has gravitated as time creeps closer to our departure.

I cross check my ticket with the closest clock for the tenth time since I received it. We have an hour still before departure. I'd like to be at our gate in a half hour.

We trash our garbage as soon as we're finished, and move onto other things.

The duty free shop provides Bree with the bottle of tequila she wanted to bring home. The experience is nothing like mine with the Tequila Museum. She straight up looks at the options, and buys based off her budget, and the look of the bottle.

My experience has spoilt me. There really is no other way to shop for alcohol when you are looking for something new. Liquor stores might make a killing if they decided to do tasting nights.

I purchase two books to read off their Manager's Choice table; two vacation themed romance novels. Maybe, I can prolong the vacation feeling a little longer. Or, escape my reality into them once I get back home. Two books should last me about six to seven hours of the trip, with an hour for whatever else.

Bree has magazines and the inflight movies planned for her entertainment. A nap is likely in her future as well.

We arrive at the gate to an open door, and people going through. They don't look like the type of people who would be priority boarding, and no one else is sitting close to the gate.

We board with no hassle, and find our seats next to each other about mid plane.

There are a few minutes to spare, to spread out what we want for the trip, and leave the rest in the overhead compartment.

The plane is half filled up as the last stragglers board. With a full plane coming here, it's odd to think this may be it for the flight home. But, the flight attendants appear to be winding things up, and ensuring we're all ready to leave.

Our flight attendants go through their emergency run through in a well-rehearsed spiel before taking their own seats.

The plane shakes as it drives on the smooth runway. Bumping the ground once as it gains enough speed to leave the ground.

Good Bye Mexico.

Chapter 19

Hugs from mom pull the air out of me. She squishes hard in her desperation to get me closer in each hug she gives me.

Dad's hug is a quick one but fierce all the same. They are both eager to know about the trip.

"It was great. We had so much fun. We got there late the first night. I think it was eleven. It was late. They had to switch us rooms because of a computer error. They accidentally gave our room to someone else. But, they got that fixed really quick, and we went right to bed after. We were so tired from the trip.

A lot of our time was spent in the pool or at the beach. The food was great. I ate way too much.

We went on a couple excursions. One was to Xel-ha, and Tulum. We walked around a whole city of ruins for the morning, and then went to a nature preserve where we could snorkel with the fishes.

I saw a huge sea turtle, and got to swim with it for a little ways.

We also went on a pirate ship dinner, and show. It was loads of fun, and great food. I got a steak and lobster."

I leave out the wedding parts, and Will. Bree and I corroborated our stories on the way home, not to include them.

Not that I wish to hide them completely, but my parents aren't the understanding type. They would read more into what happened than what actually did. Bree's dalliance with Ryan would be at the top of that list.

Mom repeats how glad she is that I'm home, but releases me

when I yawn. "Oh sweetie, you must be tired. How about you go settle, and we'll talk to you later?"

"Yeah, I'm exhausted."

"You have work tomorrow, so I hope you aren't too exhausted." Dad's slight warning edges into the end of his comment.

I am definitely not allowed to call in sick tomorrow.

If I did, I would never hear the end of it; I would never be let off to go on an adventure ever again.

"Of course. Just tired from not doing anything all day. Sitting on the plane takes a lot out of you."

We bid good nights, and I lug all my things downstairs.

I stop momentarily in the doorway. My room seems smaller now.

My bed is too tempting to chance falling into it now. I set my mind to unpacking first. All my clothes go in my hamper; filling it completely.

My trinkets find a spot on my shelf. The pictures centered between the coin, and the pyramid. I put the picture of Bree and I in the tube on the top, with all the others underneath. No one but me, will know they exist. I can always look at the other pictures when I wish to remember.

I have half a thought to start doing my laundry now. I'd get it washed, but then it would sit all night. If I forget about it in the morning, then I'll have to rewash it again tomorrow night.

The effort, and thought involved seem too much at this point. A reprieve period is needed before bringing myself back up to normal levels of function, and responsibility.

Instead, I change into pajamas, and bury myself in bed. Taking the moment before sleep to appreciate the comfort only my own bed can bring.

Chapter 20

Monotony.

Tired from my vacation, the day just drags. But, it's also more than that. I miss the excitement of the unknown for each day. I miss the freedom of doing anything and everything in the exact moment; living completely for my wants in that moment.

I understand that it can't be that way all the time, but it doesn't make it easier to come back to Earth.

A slow customer day doesn't help time move faster. No one has come in for more than a two minute serving.

I'm a bit disappointed that no one asks where I've been. Life moved on without me, and no one realized I was gone. It's humbling but insulting when you think yourself indispensable, and a required aspect of the establishment.

Dad comes out of the kitchen with two plates of sandwiches.

He sits down at an empty table near the kitchen. Without customers to deal with, I had begun spot cleaning to pass time. I put the cloth inside the soapy water pale under the till.

"Thank you." In a practiced movement, I slide in to the seat, grasp my sandwich, and take a bite.

"How were things while I was gone?" I ask him. We haven't had much of a chance to talk about them. My arrival was about me, and then I went to bed.

Mom was still sleeping when I got up for opening shift, and dad always arrives an hour earlier to prep the food.

"Could've used your help, but that was to be expected. I think the long hours exhausted your mom a bit."

I try not to take his words personally, but it makes me feel bad that they had to work so much harder while I was gone. "Should I take the closing shift too?"

"I'm sure you mother would appreciate it."

"Okay, I'll give her a call later." It's the least I could do to help out, and thank mom for working that much harder.

"I'm sure you could use the money anyway. You probably depleted your savings with your extravagant vacation. Spent more for a week of fun, than what we pay in two months on essentials. You'll be needing to make up what you spent." Each comment from out of his mouth is more bitter, and passive aggressive.

"It wasn't too bad. Especially since Bree had the flight, and hotel paid for already. The food and drinks were all inclusive with the hotel, so I didn't have to pay for any of that either." The whole vacation would have been around two thousand dollars, I think, had I paid for my portion of everything. What I actually paid was significantly less than that.

I stew on his comment a little miffed. Reasoning it wasn't all that much considering what it could have cost; an admin fee to change the name on the plane ticket, passport, and the photo, express fee for the passport, airport food, souvenirs, and my portion of the excursion price.

"Was it worth it?" He asks.

"I think so." Even if I had paid the full amount, I think it would have been worth it. Worth it enough that I want to do it again.

"If you have to think about it, it wasn't worth it." He leaves with the rest of his sandwich, putting an end to the conversation.

I shout within my head at him that it was worth it, but I would never start that conversation with him. No point to arguing with my dad about money or word choice versus meaning. I lose that argument every time.

Eating my sandwich, I gaze around without looking; occupied within my head.

My vacation was worth it; I deem.

I got to go on the adventure of a life time. I relaxed, and, for one in my life, went with the flow. I was spontaneous, and took risks.

I met a boy that I really like.

I was so much *more*…

Colours pop through my memory. Loud music. Smiling joy. The wedding. Burning lips and electric hugs. Warmth.

Vibrant. I was so much more vibrant.

The café is much duller in comparison. This has been my life. Is going to be my life.

It sinks a pit into my heart. I don't want this to be my life anymore.

It's not enough anymore. I want to explore. I want more. I want to *live*.

Chapter 21

A message chimes on my phone, scaring me from my concentration. I jump in my seat and quickly turn to the direction of the unexpected noise.

I frown at the phone from its position sitting on my bed. It's not a normal message noise and I can't recall ever hearing my phone make that noise before.

Maybe some application is trying to get my attention.

I save the presentation before I leave my desk. There's no telling what might happen in any length of time that I'm gone.

For all I know, my computer will pick this exact time to decide to shut down for an update. Or, the power goes out at the same time my battery has decided to no longer hold a charge.

Anything could happen. It's happened before.

I go over to my bed, and simultaneously sit on the bed while picking up the phone. Clicking the power button, I find a notification from the chat portion on my social app.

Clicking on the square takes me into the message. I accept the chat after I verify that it really is Will messaging me.

Will: Hey

Hey, aren't you still in Mexico? I question him. I thought they were supposed to be there almost a whole week after we left; there should still be a few days.

Will: Stole Silvia's Wi-Fi.

Will: You made it home alright?

Yeah. Some plane turbulence, but nothing horrible. Should I ask him how Mexico is? How his hosting is going? Or rather, how Silvia's hosting is going?

Will: What are you up to? Unpacked yet?

Yes. I unpacked as soon as I settled in.

I'm making a presentation for my parents. Trying to persuade them to open a second café, and make me an equal partner.

In talking about it, I move back over to my desk. This conversation could take a while. He's got all the time in the world.

Will: Sounds like a lot of work

If I want to run a café, and be a partner I better be willing to put in the work. This can help show them how serious I am, and the work I'm willing to put in.

I'm offering up my savings as a down payment investment, which can be put towards a new location. I want partnership so I can have equal say in things. And, so that they can't pull the "we're your boss" card when I want to do things.

I plan to hire a competent manager, and staff, so that I can eventually be able to take yearly vacations, and travel the world a little.

The little dots signal him writing, stopping, writing and stopping. Nervous, I fanaticize bout his possible responses. Maybe I revealed too much crazy and ambition in my message. It really didn't need to be so long.

Will: Sounds reasonable.

The short message confuses me. Did he write something longer and delete it; possibly multiple times? The actions of the dots suggests that. Who needs a couple minutes of stop and start dots to write two words?

Will: Where do you want to go?

Everywhere. I might've caught a bit of a travel bug. Would love to get out there, and see the whole world.

This town is nice, but feels a bit cooped up now.

Our conversation dies with my last message. I wait a couple minutes staring at the messages over and over, but don't receive anything back from him. I contemplate writing another message to him. Maybe I dead ended the conversation and he has nothing he can say back.

He might also just be busy.

Placing the phone on my desk, I feel a bit snacky.

I leave my room, and to my fright, mom is downstairs doing laundry. I hadn't noticed her come down the stairs. Usually the sound of feet padding down them is quickly picked up by my ears.

I go upstairs, and to the fridge. Staring at it for a minute, before switching to the freezer, and then the pantry.

I repeat the cycle when nothing jumps out at me. I don't feel like anything that's readily available.

Mixing up the three in my mind, I eventually decide on making tuna salad and cucumber on crackers. A bit of work, and a little more fancier that a normal snack, but it's the first appeasing thing I've thought of.

Gathering together the ingredients, I cut up the cucumbers, and place the slice on top of some multi grain crackers. Then open up the can of tuna, and drain it before mixing in some mayonnaise, dried chives, and pepper. Dolloping some of the tuna mixture on top of the crackers, and sealing the rest off for later.

Returning everything back to where it belongs, I go back downstairs with my snack, as I crunch on one of them. Spilling cracker crumbs down my shirt as I bite into it before awkwardly shoving the whole thing in my mouth to avoid more of such mess.

Mom walks out of my room looking pale.

I know instantly I should have shut down the presentation before going upstairs. Quickly, I can feel my own blood leaving my face.

"Who's Will?" In her question, she reveals that she snooped on my phone. A whole other issue I was similarly not prepared for.

"Bree and I met him, and his sister at the resort. She got married there. They both added me and Bree to their socials."

She nods. "Umm," her voice cracks. "Let's go out for coffee.

My throat is dry. I struggle to respond. Nothing good comes from mom wanting to speak privately in public. "Sure."

Mom steals one of the crackers from my plate, leaving me with two. I palm them both after shutting down the lights in my room, and placing my phone in my pocket.

Following mom upstairs, I grab my purse. The whole time wondering what she wants to talk about. Is it just Will? Did she see the presentation? Both?

I can feel the pressure of being in trouble weighing heavily on me. Dreading whatever she has to say. Drumming up every possibility of her response.

Chapter 22

Mom finally sits down at the table with two teas in hand. I get one and she gets the other.

She opens the lid up on her tea, and I do the same to mine. Both will be too hot to drink for the first five minutes after it's served. Her straight tea won't be drinkable for ten minutes, unless she wants to risk tongue burnings. Mine will be slightly less only because of the cream and sugar I get added.

Mom instructed me grab a seat far away from staff, and other patrons. Off in a corner where we could expect a reasonable amount of privacy.

The other corner of the coffee shop had a couple acquaintances of dad's, so I had to switch sides quickly to the one without recognizable people.

I stare into the steam of my tea. Mesmerized for a moment. Perhaps, I muse, the steam will give me a response before my mother does.

She finally clears her throat, and speaks softly. "I saw your plans. The answer is no, and don't even think of bringing it up to your dad."

She holds her hand up when I open my mouth to argue. My chest chokes.

"Don't. Stop. Listen." She reprimands me in the same tone she's used throughout my childhood. It alone makes me stop. "Don't say a word to your dad about me telling you this, but…" Mom looks over her shoulder in a bid to ensure no ears are leaning in. "We are inches away from bankruptcy and foreclosure."

I lean back, unprepared for the news. I thought the café was doing great. Maybe a little less busy than we would hope for, but nothing so desperate.

Mom doesn't stop there. I remain speechless as the confessions keep coming. My heart dropping with each new revelation.

Mom looks down at her tea, and speaks to it. Perhaps a bit easier to do than look me in the eye.

"We took a second mortgage out on the house to get us through the recession, but never really recovered; not to the levels they were before.

Your dad made some bad investments, and lost eighty percent of fifty thousand dollars. A sure thing; he promised. Reinvested that, and lost another fifty percent of what was left.

We've been fudging the books for the last ten years, so we pay fewer taxes; can claim more expenses.

We've gone without so many things, just so every cent can go into paying things back. But, it's never enough.

That's why you started paying us rent the moment you turned eighteen. Not obligation, but because we desperately needed the money.

Why you had to pay your own schooling.

Why you've had to pay entirely way too much for things you should have had help with, or shouldn't have had to pay for at all.

Why if your dad wants to go out for coffee, he forces you to buy out of obligation, and saying that you should buy him a cup of coffee because you owe him." She pauses to collect herself, and her thoughts. "I'm not expecting to get out of this with the shop still standing."

"Wow." Is all I can say when she looks up to me. Stopping at least for a moment to see my reaction. My tongue is frozen for all but one question. "Why haven't you said anything?"

"I wanted to. Your dad didn't. You know how he gets his way." I do. "But, after I saw your plans, I didn't want you to invest too much time, and energy into a whole presentation, and then resent us for telling you no without explanation. Or, without any good explanation. Without the whole truth."

I rack my head for solutions until a natural progression comes to me. "Then sell me the business. We'll relaunch, reorganize, and update things. You and dad can be managers, but I get final say in everything. You and dad file for bankruptcy, if that's still necessary, and we'll see how things go." I'm mostly sure that that wouldn't be illegal in any way. It might be good to consult a lawyer about it.

"No." Mom's immediate answer infuriates me to her lack of thought around it.

"Why not?" I bite.

"It's not that simple." She says simply. Gazing back down at her tea, mom reigns in her volume again. "I don't want you to have this life."

Rage fuels me. How many years, and how many conversations about exactly that, did I have with Bree, until I finally accepted it? My entire childhood, it was beaten into me that my future was the family business. "Then why would you make this my life? My whole life has been about me taking over the family business."

Her eyes meet mine. A snarl on her upper lip. "And my whole life has been concessions, and pushing things off until later, but.." Mom holds her tongue, and looks around again. "I've recently come to the realize that later may never come. I have too many regrets; little things to big things.

I let so much life pass me by with the reasoning that it could wait, that there were more important things in life than what I wanted, and I could always do it later. It would get better later."

She slows down, and calms her tirade a bit. "I put aside dreams to chase your father, and his dreams became mine. We got married. We traded my cute corvette for his crappy muscle car. I got pregnant on purpose, despite your father's wishes. That's why you grew up thinking you were an accident, because he couldn't know that I planned you.

He got a vasectomy against my wishes; he knew I wanted more kids, but he didn't want another accident, and said we could reverse it when we wanted more, and a better time came; it never came; according to him.

We've sank every cent into his failing dream. So we couldn't ever do anything; no vacations, amusement parks. Doctor visits not covered by basic healthcare. Or anything not completely necessary.

I had to steal from the grocery money allowance and skip meals so you could go on field trips for school, and didn't have to stay at the school while your classmates went on adventures.

I missed most of your life because of that stupid café.

Your dad has forced you to think that his dream is yours too.

This isn't what I want for you.

I want you to be financially stable. I want you to move out immediately, and find a real job that will pay you consistently, and fairly. Without constant fear that in one month, three months, six months, you might lose your job, and your house."

I choke on my breath as a tear rolls down both sides of mom's face. She quickly wipes them away.

"I want you to have fun.

Explore."

Her pointer finger comes up to wag at me. "And, don't think I haven't forgotten about the boy you never told us about. We'll come back to that." She smiles briefly. The action has me feeling better about that. I don't think I'm in trouble about the boy. I smile back to her.

Mom breathes a deep breath and she turns serious again. "I want you to figure out what you actually want from life, not what we've told you you want.

I don't want my legacy to you to be dooming you to my life.

You may not understand, at this time, but that would be the worst thing I could leave you."

A silent apology hangs on her lips.

"I'll help you sort things out. A job, a new place. I'll talk to your dad, so you don't have to." Always trying to protect me from dad's closemindedness.

Mom places her lid back on her tea, so I do the same. She gets up and leaves, and I follow her in a daze.

The whole way home is deafening. She doesn't offer to speak. I don't want to talk. My whole world has been upended and the aftermath has left me empty and raw.

I beeline straight to my room. Each step bringing me closer to tears. Letting loose only once I've shut and locked my bedroom door.

I place the tea on my dresser, and lay down on my bed. Grabbing up my pillow as my breath increases. I gasp for air as all the information slams into my chest repeatedly.

Moving out. Quitting the café. Losing our house. Losing our café. Getting a job.

Mom hates her life. She regrets her life. She doesn't want me to have her life. Mom is miserable.

It's all too much to handle in such a little amount of time.

Gaining little control, I make to text Bree. I need help. Typing brings on a new onslaught of tears.

Mom and dad are going bankrupt, and are losing the house and the café.

Mom's told me to move out, and find a stable job. She regrets her life and mine, and doesn't want me turning out like her.

She basically made it sound like she was apologizing for my entire life.

Bree: Good. She should be sorry.

I can always count on Bree to be bluntly supportive. She did have to sit through all my rants through the years, so her reaction isn't surprising.

Bree: So what are you going to do?

Mom said she would help me move, and find a job. I think, before we tell dad anything.

Bree: I could talk to mom. You can take over my room if you need out immediately. You know she'd let you.

I couldn't do that. Bree said she wanted to move back in with her parents. She shouldn't have to give that up just because I' having a bit of a crisis moment. I'll figure things out.

Thanks, but I don't think it's that urgent. Mom made it sound like she wasn't supposed to be telling me yet, that dad didn't want me to know until everything was final.

I don't want to make things rougher on my parents than things already are. They'd feel horrible if I moved into your parents' house.

Chapter 23

A vibration in my pocket has me looking over my shoulder; Dad is in the kitchen assembling a couple sandwiches with fries. Customers are busy at their tables, and there's no line up.

I feel safe to take out my phone to check the notification. Clicking the power shows me Will's text message.

Will: Hey, what's up? Silvia says you're moving?

Clicking into the message, I type back. *Yeah. Long story.*

How does Silvia know?

Will: Bree told her.

Ah.

Dammit Bree, I curse her. Talk about blabbing things to people that's none of their business.

Will: What happened?

I slip my phone away when someone comes in through the front door. An older man, white hair, orders a coffee with cream and sugar. He takes it in his to go thermos, pays, and leaves.

I reach for my phone, but dad pops out of the kitchen briefly to pass off food to the pick-up counter.

Attending to the customers takes a few minutes, but soon enough I'm back behind the counter.

Mom says it's time. She doesn't want me to miss out on life trying to chase their dreams.

Will: That's very wise of her. What made her come to that

conclusion?

She said she was having regrets about her life. She said she hadn't seen me so happy as when I was talking about the trip.

A rush interrupts my conversation, and then again for the supper rush. Customers flow through until after dad leaves for the evening kitchen closing.

Will: There has to be more to it then that. Maybe she's been thinking about it for a while. And this sort of tipped it over so she finally said something..

Maybe..

I suppose my trip could have changed something. Maybe it made mom realize that she could have done something like it, if she wasn't in this situation. Jealousy through realization on the same level of living vicariously through someone; wanting to do it yourself.

It being hours since my last message to him, I don't expect an answer right away. I don't expect any sort of answer with the type of message I leave the conversation on. Maybe I'll text him tomorrow with a light conversation starter.

Setting about cleaning the café, I sort around the items on the tables, then sweep about.

My phone buzzes.

Will: So, what's the new place like?

2 bedroom, 2 bathroom apartment. Nothing fancy. Hoping to find a roommate, make things cheaper than a 1 bedroom by myself. I get possession in a week.

Will: What about Bree?

I think she's probably going to move back in with her mom after she sells her condo. Bad karma. Doesn't want to live there anymore. Why pay half my rent, and bills when she could live at her mom's for free.

Skylar Bryson

Besides, I've heard it's never a good thing for friendships when they move in together.

Will: Bullshit.

I smile and shake my head. Of course he'd think that. It's just a generalization anyway. I'm sure there are friends who can live together. Otherwise, no one could ever live with anyone, ever.

The messages keep coming in.

Will: It only doesn't work out when the friends are bad for each other in the first place. You, and Bree would do well living together.

Will: Ask her.

Will: She's starting a new life too.

Will: You can help her, and she can help you.

I'll think about it. I promise him.

I set about nightly duties to close up the shop. Leftover display food, is tucked away for discount in the morning, while today's discount food is packed away to take home with me.

I clean the machines, wipe down the counters, and take the garbages outside to the bins. A spray of something wet follows the swing of the bag.

Some idiot put a cup in the garbage while it still had some coffee inside.

Of course, tipping over the cup when I took it out for the garbage, a trail leads all the way back to the garbage bin inside.

I sigh at people's idiocity. It should be common knowledge not to put a cup of liquid in a bag of garbage. As soon as it tips over, there is going to be a mess.

I mop up the cold coffee, and start cash out later than I had wanted to, all due to one customer.

Chapter 24

Will: Silvia apparently needs at least two girls to go with her to go pee.

Will: She thinks it's hilarious.

I think it's hilarious, and completely normal. I muse, imagining Will confused with the right of passage women have come to accept. Big wedding dress equals interesting bathroom situations.

It's a very big, and beautiful dress. I'm sure it's that or she would have to completely take off the dress in order to pee.

Bree had me block off the bathroom whenever she had to pee. I had to zip, and unzip her. She would get naked in the main part of the bathroom before going into the stall to pee.

Letting myself out of my car, I look at Boston Pizza sign; number fifteen on my list. They have a Help Wanted sign up in their window, so hopefully I'll have some luck here.

Inside is a bit dark compare to outside. But not so much that my eyes don't adjust within seconds. The hostess welcomes me with her rehearsed greeting.

I answer back. "Hi I'm Skylar. I was hoping to speak with your manager or supervisor. I would like to drop off my resume."

"Oh, you can just leave that with me." She says.

I look at her name tag; personalize the ending to make a better impression. "Okay, thank you Nicole." I hand my paper to her. "I hope you have a wonderful evening."

"Thank you. You too." She says.

I leave with lingering hope that Nicole will put in a good word about the lovely polite girl who dropped off her resume. Sometimes, it's the impressions of the receiving person, no matter what position in the company, which can get you an interview. At least that's what my mom said.

Back in my car, I check in with my list, and cross off Boston Pizza. I'm exhausted already. Dropping off my resumes, even with a list, and a strategic plan based on their locations in town, feels like it has been taking longer than I thought.

Pulling out my phone, I check my messages.

Will: Mom's invited a bunch of people we've never met. Silvia doesn't recognize 90% of the people here.

Will: Silvia says Hi, and she wishes you were here.

I text Will back with an answer for Silvia. *Hi! Wish I was there too. Sounds like a better time than packing boxes. Have an extra slice of cake for me.*

Turning the phone off and my car on, I realize it's past five. The last couple hours have dragged away.

Weighing the options on both hands, I quickly decide to go home. It's better to try to hand my resume straight to a manager, than to the underlings; where resumes are known to get lost accidentally and on purpose. Those positions traditionally, especially in large companies, are gone by five.

I drive home feeling the messages coming in. Knowing I'm missing somethings along the way temps me into checking my phone, but I resist until parked in my spot.

Dad would never let me hear the end of it, if I ended up with a distracted driving ticket.

Will: All the bridesmaids are so drunk, they're throwing up in the bathroom already.

Will: Waiting on supper to be served to sober them up a bit.

Will: Silvia is pissed!

Will: I've had to confiscate cutlery from two of the bridesmaids. They nearly knocked over a bottle of wine onto Silvia.

Will: One of the bridesmaids just told a story about Silvia sneaking out to get high and drunk when she was 16. No one could get up there to stop her fast enough. Everyone now knows. Silvia is mortified. Mom looks PISSED. Dad's amused. He thinks it's funny.

Oh no...On my end, the running minutes on the dramatics of the wedding are entertaining and fun, but I can also imagine Silvia feels like she's having the worst wedding ever.

Mom waits for me in the kitchen, supper beeping in the microwave. She looks over her shoulder, and a bit around the corner to the living room.

Grabbing the plate from the microwave, she adds a fork to the plate, and hands it to me.

In her best hushed voice, she tells me, "best to eat in your room. I spoke to your father. He didn't take your moving out well." She looks over her shoulder again. In mom speak, I know this means he had a major freak out.

"Thanks mom." Ever grateful that she would take that on for me, I mental note that I should get something nice for her.

I slip downstairs, and into my room, shutting the door behind me.

Will: Someone stepped on the dress, and ripped a hole at Silvia's butt.

Will: The world is imploding.

Will: Silvia's fine. She's changed into a spare dress, and consoled the bridesmaid who did it.

Will: Mom is freaking out. She was apparently going to preserve, and frame the dress for Silvia's house. Whatever that means.

Will: Silvia says it doesn't matter because the rip is in the back. No one will know.

Will: Mom says SHE will know.

Will: Mom tried kicking bridesmaid out after she refused to buy the same dress new to replace it, but said she'd pay to get it fixed. Silvia stopped that bullshit.

Good. After pressing enter, I instantly realize the message could be construed wrong.

I mean, not about the dress.

That sucks. It was probably expensive.

Good that Silvia stopped your mom from kicking her out. All it needs is a good sew, and the dress will be fine for displaying.

Why would your mom prefer to display a replica dress that Silvia didn't even wear, over a dress that now has memories attached?

I eat my spaghetti while looking over my socials. Nothing important to look upon yet. I expect all of Silvia's wedding pictures will start showing up tomorrow from her guests.

The professional photos could take months to get back. Unless Silvia's mom has something to do with it, and I suspect she will.

I leave my empty plate on my desk. I'll clean it up later; once dad is in bed and there's no chance of running into him.

Looking upon my room, specifically all my things, I sigh at all the work that still needs to be done.

How does one room have so many things in it?

Probably because it's my entire life, packed into one room.

Sighing one last time, I figure now is as good as ever.

Getting to it, I pull out boxes and newspapers from underneath my bed, and set about packing up my things.

Now that dad knows, I don't have to hide it as much. Bigger things can be packed up, and my boxes can be left out, and about.

Will: I may have just fucked up a kid for life. Some random teen came up to us earlier. Never seen him before. He looked old enough for a special wedding drink so we asked him to toast with us. He says can't he's allergic to all alcohol. I'm like, that doesn't make sense. I've never heard of that. Bad reactions to certain alcohols sure, but not everything. Kid thinks about it. Never been tested. Never had any. He just says his moms always told him he's allergic. As far as he knows, it's not something that runs in the family. No one else has this allergy.

Will: So 30 minutes later, mom pulls me outside. Some Mrs. Something from her volunteer group front for drinking and gossiping is pissed at me. Her son is piss ass drunk, and it's MY fault. He left us and went and tried some sips of alcohol. No reactions. Sips turned to ten drinks.

Will: Turns out he's not allergic to alcohol. His mom has lied to him his whole life because his dad is a major alcoholic, and she didn't want that passed down to the son. So she lied, and told him he's deathly allergic. And it's my fault that he questioned that. Mom says I've doomed his life, and doomed him to alcoholism.

Will: Not his mom's fault for lying to him at all though. That couldn't have possibly had anything to do with his reaction.

I have to reread his message over a few times. There's so much to it, so many things I could pick a part.

I eventually settle on a series of well thought out responses.

That's not exactly your fault. Someone was eventually going to give him the idea, and he was going to try it eventually.

His mom shouldn't have lied to protect him. It's better for kids to know the truth so they don't spiral, and can learn how to appropriately handle the situation before it happens.

She should have been talking to him about responsible drinking from the time he was 14 or 15, or sooner, and let him know about hereditary addiction risks. And maybe he would have decided on his own that he wasn't ever going to drink, or he could have placed strict limits. Or something.

Maybe he would have become an alcoholic, but she could have at least tried.

Not your fault.

I hope he won't be too hard on himself.

How was he supposed to know the situation, if no one told him? How was he supposed to know that he shouldn't call someone out when they come up with an allergy that he's never heard of before?

I probably would have done the same thing.

There's no guarantee that the kid is going to resort to alcoholism after this. Especially, if his mom handles this right and has an honest heart to heart.

Will: Silvia's upset. One of the bridesmaids left. She's apparently been fighting with her boyfriend all night for talking publicly at the bar with his ex. Who he cheated on with the bridesmaid.

I'm a bit disappointed that he doesn't continue on about the boy. It doesn't give me any sort of gauge about how he feels about it.

I pick through the last message for a response.

Sounds like trust issues there.

If he can cheat on her with me, then he could cheat on me with her.

Will: I don't think they're going to last anyway. Silvia's

talking about them fighting constantly.

I debate lingering longer on the previous message. Did I say enough to him? I go over his long message, and my responses.

Is it too late to say more? We're already on another drama. But, I feel like there needs to be more said.

Will: Jennifer has officially gotten herself cut off. She's so drunk that the bartender cut her off. He's never, in five years, had to cut someone off.

Impressive or sad? Both?

How'd she manage to get cut off?

Now I couple dramas removed from the boy, I decide to put it to rest. If he's not going to say more, then I won't, even if it leaves a lingering nag in my brain.

Will: Jennifer left in Jennifer fashion. Fell down getting into the taxi while storming out. She's going to find a bar that will let her drink as much as she wants.

I hope someone's getting all this on video. The play by play is impressive. I regret not going now, not that I would have realistically been able to pull it off, but there is so much going on that I'm getting jealous from missing out.

Will: Found out she's been flashing everyone all night. Somehow managed to avoid that sight myself.

Will: I don't know if I should be insulted. Finding out that she flashed everyone but me. Like the entire wedding party except me. She even flashed the girls.

Lack of opportunity? I offer a possible reason. It bothers me more than I'd ever admit that he might've wanted to be flashed by Jennifer.

Will: SHE EVEN FLASHED MY GRANDMA!!!

LOL!

Will: She won't stop talking about the poor girls nipples being pierced. HELP!

Laughter bursts out of me until my gut hurts. Not knowing his grandma, I imagine my own in the same situation. *I can't... That's hilarious.*

My right eye starts leaking tears. *I'm crying I'm laughing so hard.*

My phone buzzes again, but another message doesn't appear under mine. I drill down into my main messages screen, and into Bree's highlighted name.

Bree: How's it going?

Good.

Packing up some boxes. Messaging Will. Major drama going down at the wedding.

My list is getting longer. Why didn't you tell me moving is so expensive?

Bree: Go get a bunch of things at the dollar store. You'd be amazed at what they have for the house. Replace with the expensive crap once you have the bigger stuff bought.

Bree: That's what we started out with.

Bree: My favourite spatulas are all from there.

Cool. I'll take a look there first. Thanks.

I update her on some other news to keep our conversation going. *So mom told dad I'm moving out.*

Bree: Oh SHIT!

Bree: How'd he take it?

Mom said it would be best to try to avoid him for a few days... Not exactly, but it was implied.

Bree: Does that mean you have a few days off?

I shake my head; of course not. I'd get in trouble for missing a shift, even if I was dead. *What do you think? Regular shift as usual.*

Bree: That's going to be awkward. I'll visit tomorrow, and give you moral support.

Thanks.

Chapter 25

"Hi, what can I get for you today?"

"My usual."

The familiar voice has me looking up from the register. Bree looks at me amused. "Oh. Hi."

She raises her eyebrow. "Oh hi, to you too."

"Sorry. Everything is a bit off today." I whisper.

"He's still mad?" I nod. She hands me a five dollar bill for her food and drink. I knock on the FIVE, and CASH buttons. The till shoots open for the money, and I push it shut again once the money is in there.

Walking to the back, I open the kitchen door.

Stirring his pot, dad doesn't bother to look back at me like he usually would. The ignore treatment is worse that the silent treatment.

"Hey, Bree's here. She ordered a Bree Salad. Thanks." I back out. I know he heard me, not that he acknowledges it.

I knock back into a body. "Sorry," Bree whispers. She backs away a bit, and gives me space. "That was icy."

"Yup. He's been like that all day." Thus I've felt like crap all day.

Bree pulls up a stool behind the counter at an open part of the surface. Her usual spot, when she shows up when I'm working.

Dad and mom have never minded. Bree helps out sometimes

while she's visiting. I never could figure out why they never offered to give her a job here, but I guess with bankruptcy on the brain, they couldn't afford to have her.

My phone buzzes. I ignore it. A Bree Salad never takes long. Dad throws together some random vegetables and lunch meat, and goes easy on the lettuce. No dressing. Sometimes he'll throw on some garlic toast too, but only if there's some aging and convenient.

By the time I grab Bree a cup of coffee, Dad comes out of the kitchen with her plate. "Hey Bree. Did you have a fun trip?" Dad hugs her with one arm from behind.

I can't look, so I pretend to make myself busy cleaning a spot on the counter. It hurts that he'd be so friendly with her, while being a jerk to me.

Luckily, a new customer comes in the shop, so I can have a better reason to ignore them.

"Wonderful. I'm so glad Sky came with me. She absolutely made the whole thing better. Thank you for letting me steal her away for a while."

"Yes, well…" He trails off. "I have work, so I need to get back before anything burns." Dad exits to the kitchen.

I look over to Bree. She gives me a gritted yikes frown. I return the look with a defeated smile, then check on some customers, and serve some more while she eats.

In a lull, I check on Bree. "How was the salad?"

"Good."

Remembering the text from earlier, and now with a chance to look, I check my message with coverage from the counter, and Bree's body.

Will: There are 8 books in the series, 2 of them are kind of spin offs but are a small part of the storyline too. I didn't read those 2 because I hated the characters. Was a bit lost with some of the mentions but I got by.

It's hard to get into a story when you already don't like the character. Spin offs seem hit or miss. A hit, if the character is already popular, and likeable. But a miss if they aren't.

My biggest hate on spin offs is when they continue the story with the people's children as the main characters. Just because it's their kids, doesn't mean I'm invested in them, and their story. It's never as good.

"Will again?" I jump when my shield speaks unexpectedly. "Do you ever stop texting each other?"

"Yes! And shush. Dad doesn't need something else to be mad at me about."

Chapter 26

No one's called back yet. Getting anxious.

Will: It's only been a couple days.

Will: Relax. I've had places call me 6 months after I sent in a resume.

Will: Maybe send out some resumes to other places. Look for jobs out of your field. Take whatever you can get, until you get a call from one of your more desired positions, and companies.

I mull over his advice. I've never done this before. Job searching is a stressful practice. There's too much waiting and unknown involved.

I'm on a limited timeline, but I don't know the limit. For all I know, I might not even be a contender for any of the companies I applied to, and I'm waiting for a call that will never come; one determined immediately after I had left the building. I could be waiting for nothing.

They could have all thrown my resume in the garbage immediately after my departure, for all I know. Or, a manager might be ready to call me any minute now.

My situation isn't dire yet, but I do know that I can't sit around for six months waiting on a possible call.

"Sorry, that took so long. The printer got jammed." She hands me back my ID.

"Ah. That's okay. It happens." I answer politely.

Mrs. Spratt places the paper on top of my other paperwork and picks up a set of keys off the desk. "Shall we check out your new place?"

"Yes please." We leave the building's multi-purpose office room to enter into an elevator close by.

Mrs. Spratt fills the empty elevator with chit chat. "I bet your mom is happy you're sticking close to home."

"Yeah. It was time to move out, and get my own place. But something still in town for the café." My rehearsed speak sounds natural to me.

It wouldn't do good to have one of mom's friends know anything is amiss with the café. I wouldn't do good to let my new landlord know that I will likely be losing my job in the very near future.

Besides, Mrs. Spratt would have the information spread across town faster than I could apologize to mom and dad.

Maybe the information would be good to get out, in a save our town's beloved family owned café sort of way. I've heard it work for some companies. People love a family owned shop. It might pick up business if people know we're in risk of closing down.

"They'll miss you. We did with our kids. Homes feel less homey once the kids leave, but you're so proud that you were able to raise them to a point that they are comfortable without you."

"Yeah." Her words hit a contagious somber mood. I will miss seeing having them always there; a comforting consistency. "At least we'll still see each other every day" – until the café shuts down. I leave the last bit unspoken.

"That'll be nice for you, and your parents. I haven't seen my youngest in a year. Busy with school, and work. We talk on the phone, when she's got a minute here and there, but it's not the same. Seems like she calls less and less as time goes by."

Her continued melancholy has turned the conversation awkward. I make a sort of affirmation noise that nearly gets drowned out by the elevator's ding.

There's nothing I can really say about her daughter not calling. That sucks for her, but her daughter is probably busy and moving on with her life.

It sounds horrible to put it that way, but many kids leave home and don't look back.

She brings me around the hall to the second last room on the right. "So this is it." She lets me go inside first.

I find a light switch immediately to my left, so I flick it, and bring the lights on.

"Oh shit-shoot. Sorry." She corrects herself a little late. "I left the inspection papers behind. I'm supposed to go through the place with you, and mark down scratches and things, so that we know what's here before, and after you are. I'll have to go back to the office, and grab those. Have little look around."

Mrs. Spratt leaves me to my snooping. I pull out my phone, and snap a picture from the entry. The kitchen island, fridge, pantry, and living room are visible in the picture. I send the picture to Will with the caption *Getting my keys today!*

I take off my shoes, and put them to the side.

The kitchen has a light wood finish to all the cabinets. I can't imagine what I'll be filling them with. It seems like too much space for the very few dishes, and cutlery I'll have for move in. But, I suppose they always end up filled eventually. Mom's always complaining she doesn't have enough space in her kitchen.

The whole apartment is filled with tones of brown. I suppose it must be a popular style since it goes with many people's things. The carpet is darker than the kitchen's hardwood, but not as dark as the tile in the bathroom. All the walls are painted in a very light brown.

There is a clear difference in the two bedrooms, which surprises me. One is strictly a bedroom and closet, on the right of the living room. The other, on the left of the living room, is clearly a master styled bedroom. The room is about the same size, but it connects to bathroom through a walk through closet.

I claim the master bedroom. No sense in giving it to a renter, but I don't know if I can completely justify a 50/50 split of rent, when I clearly have a better room. I could always give them the other bathroom, and call it even, but that might be inconvenient for me, and my guests. Then, they'd have to walk through my bedroom to get to the bathroom they'd be allowed to use.

I'll figure it out later.

"Sorry." Mrs. Spratt surprises me in the bathroom. "Bill is usually the one to handle these things. But, since Maggie asked for a spot for you, I figured I'd handle this personally. But, it's been a while since I've handled this part of the business, so I guess I've forgotten a few things."

"That's alright." Mrs. Spratt's explanation doesn't leave too much confidence in me. I hope she doesn't forget anything important or crucial. I'd hate to have not signed something, and have them able to kick me out or charge me for things I shouldn't have to pay for.

She walks me through the rooms one by one. Pointing out marks she notices, and asking me to name anything I notice. Her eagle eyes spot everything I take no notice to.

There isn't anything bigger than a few scuff marks on the walls, though I'm not worried about them. Mrs. Spratt mentions a few times that she doesn't want me to get dinged with them when I leave.

I imagine if they were that important, they would have been fixed in the switch over. Isn't that why they have damage deposits? So they can fix all these things before someone new moves in?

Unless, they charge the one set of renters for the damages, and then leave them until the whole room needs a painting or something.

At the end, we circle back to the kitchen island, and I sign away on the marked up sheet for all the scuff marks.

With everything else signed already, Mrs. Spratt hands me over the keys. "That's all then." She lets out a wide eyed noise. "Oh. Don't lose your keys. You'll have to pay for a locksmith to change out your lock, and get a new set of keys. Easily $250."

Not an expense I wish to incur. Seems like a lot of money just for a lost key. I mentally add get more keys cut to my list of things to do. Maybe I'll leave the original in a safe spot and use the cut keys for everyday use.

"I will guard them with my life." I say with all seriousness, holding the key to my heart to swear it.

"Alright, I will get out of here. I'm sure you'll want to soak it up for a bit. If there's anything else you need, please let Bill know. If he's not getting back to you quick enough, well, I'm sure your mom will let me know." She laughs as she leaves and shuts the door behind her.

Standing in my new place alone, I can't think of anything else I really want to do other than just start moving things in.

Bree is helping me move my room over tomorrow, but I have all my shopping to do. I can bring everything straight here, and have those set up before tomorrow.

The thought makes me giddy.

Turning off all the lights, I leave, and lock the apartment. Saying a mental goodbye to my new empty place.

There is another exit on this side of the building in the form of stairs. I decide to take them down, and directly out of the building.

The guest parking, where I parked is closer to the main doors, but this door is closer to half of the assigned parking spaces; closer to where my spot is assigned.

A wave of disappointment comes over me, there is no way to open this door from the outside. I guess that's a good thing for security sake, but not so good for taking the shorter way back to my room.

I pull out my list once I get inside the car. Basing my stops off the list, and where I preferred to get each of the items.

NEED LIST

<u>Dollar store</u>

Kitchen stuff – cooking stuff, knives, dish soap, dishes, and utensils, ice cube tray

Bathroom stuff – Soap x2, trash cans x2, plunger, tooth brush holder

Picture Frames – 10x12, 4x6

Broom

<u>Thrift store</u>

Vacuum

Pots and pans

Blender

<u>Walmart</u>

Kitchen stuff – Paper towel, garbage can

Bathroom stuff – Towels, toilet paper, shower curtain, and rings

Curtains

Groceries

Chapter 27

"You can't put your desk in the living room." Bree protests by putting the desk down where she stands.

"Why not?" I look over, just a few feet away to the spot I had wanted to place it; in the middle of the one wall lining the guest room. The spot seems just fine to me.

"Okay, you can, but not there. That's where your TV will go."

"I don't have a TV or a TV stand." No sense in saving a spot for items I may or may not get anytime soon.

"Go on the Buy and Sell, and I'm sure you can find both for really cheap. In two days you could have it here, and all set up." Bree has a point, but I can't justify the expense right now; no matter how cheap I may get it. A TV is one expense which leads to another, which leads to another.

"I don't have cable." I reason with her. "I barely watch anything on TV as it is."

"Movies."

"I don't have a DVD player, and no movie collection; at all." Another expense which could quickly get unreasonably expensive.

Picking up my side of the desk, I pull onto it a little. It moves with some pull on the far side. I would prefer her help, but the desk should be fine to move this way a few feet.

Bree rolls her eyes, but picks up her end to assist me.

"Buy and Sell one, or Netflix it." Bree has an answer for

everything, but all I can see is more dollar signs jumping out the window.

"Internet couldn't come for two weeks." I inform her.

"Two weeks!" She bursts, and in doing so drops the desk. "That's insane."

I shrug. "They're busy." That's what I get for such short notice. "The lady said they had a cancellation slot open, and that's the only reason I got in so early. They typically have a thirty days' notice policy."

I pull the desk into its final resting place without Bree's help.

"What the hell are you going to do for the next two weeks then?" Bree asks as she goes back to the island to handle her drink. She grips both cups there, and hands me mine.

"I upped my data package for the month. I should be good for normal things, if I hotspot to my computer. But, I won't be able to stream anything until my internet is installed."

She takes a long sip. Taking pause, Bree raises her eyebrow expectantly while looking pointedly between my drink, and my face. I sigh but relent to take a sip.

"Well, what about when you get a roommate, they could snoop on your computer."

"I don't know. Are you going to snoop on my computer?" I push not too subtly; she hasn't given me a straight answer yet.

I would appreciate a response so that I know either way. It's a big question, but I'm impatient to know while in limbo. If she's going to move in, great, if not then I need to get on trying to find a roommate. She's been leaving me dancing in limbo, as she's been dancing around my question.

"I do that anyways." She waves a quick brush off wave. "But, I officially can't be your roommate. And, I have to keep the condo."

"Why?" I ask succinctly. Why does she have to keep the condo? She was just talking about the realtor coming for pictures, listing information, and recommendations for quicker and better selling staging.

"The realtor came today, and apparently the market is crap right now. My condo's dropped thirty grand in value in the last two years. So if I sell for what she thinks I could get for it, then I'd end up owing ten thousand to the bank, because we've only paid off twenty in the last two years. Not only that, but I'd have to pay her commission too, and lawyers' fees, and screwed up the ass fees, and-. So, it's not worth it." Her resentment speaks for itself; loud, and clear. Furiously, she downs the rest of her drink.

It doesn't seem right that her condo would drop that much in such a little time. Purchasing homes is supposed to be a safe bet.

"Wow. That sucks." I know how much she wanted to get of the condo, and the memories attached. "Well, maybe, then you should think about redecorating. Make it your own, so that it feels new, and refreshed. I hear even a coat of paint can do wonders."

"Yeah, that's what I was thinking." Bree shakes her cup in the air between us. "I'm out. Want another?"

"No, I'm good."

"What's that? You need a top up?" Her wicked grin spreads. "Of course darling." Adopting a British accent completes her one sided conversation, before she spins around to ignore me.

I roll my eyes. She's going to do what she wants anyway, so there's no point to arguing with her. Only so much can fit into my cup anyway, and I don't technically have to drink it.

Diving back into the spare room, I find my box labelled Desk. Pulling it out from under two other boxes, and bringing it to my desk. I open it up, and start unpacking everything that had been on and in my desk at home.

197

Bree's gasp sounds a millisecond before a wet clang. I look over to her. She stands, holding a now bottomless blender, staring wide eyed at the blue slush dripping off my counter.

"You made the mess, you clean it up." I don't want to know what the red drink is going to do to my cabinets and floor, but I also don't want to deal with the unexpected slushy mess; especially since I didn't particularly want it in the first place.

My words jumpstart her. "This is why you don't buy blenders from the thrift store!" She yells angrily.

"It was a lot cheaper than buying a brand new one." I argue.

"Is it cheaper when you get two uses out of it before it explodes?"

Bree has a point. I tone down my subdued yelling. "On a per use basis, no, I suppose not."

She places the blender glass part into the sink. "I'm buying you a proper blender tomorrow. House warming present." Picking up the chopping portion, she throws it in with the other piece a bit more roughly.

"You can't buy me a blender, you already bought me, like, three hundred dollars in booze for my house warming present." Which she only got away with because she argued that she's probably going to drink three-quarters of that herself. I refuse to let her spend any more money on me.

"Fine!" My internalized party from my win is thrown a bit soon when she quickly retorts. "Then I'm buying me a new blender tomorrow, but I'm keeping it here, because how am I supposed to make you your girly frewffy drinks if you don't have a proper blender."

Bree swipes a paper towel across the counter, sweeping what mess she can right into the sink.

"I can drink other things. I can also go out, and buy a proper blender for myself." No amount of reasoning is going to help us right now.

"Obviously." She gestures towards the sink.

I hold up my hands in white flag defence. "I'll go to Walmart this time." I promise.

"Nope you had your chance."

"I was trying to save money on the initial move in."

"How's that working for us now?" She gesture largely to the sink and mess.

"You brought coolers too. We'll be fine with those for the rest of the night. And tomorrow, I'll go buy a proper brand new blender."

"Nope, I don't trust you with such an important task." Bree swabs up the floor slushy mess with a paper towel.

"At least it worked a couple times before it broke." I take out the glass top, and examine it where the bottom fell off. Nothing appears to be broken off or cracked. The bottom plastic part isn't cracked either. There's nothing to explain why the bottom fell off.

On closer inspection, I see what appears to be a small twist on spiral. Taking top to bottom, I twist. The blender stops a half twist in. Grasping onto both sides, I give a tug. When it doesn't budge, I pull harder.

Taking the chance, I fill up the glass with water, and inspect for leaks; nothing drips out.

"I don't think the bottom was twisted on all the way." I tell her.

"It's not supposed to come off."

I shrug. That's exactly what I had thought too. "Maybe this one comes off for cleaning purposes? Want to give it another try?"

"Sure, but if it explodes again, you get to clean it up."

It's a reasonable clause, but I'm going to make sure there isn't

199

such a large mess if it does. "Sure, but when we pick it up to pour it, we're holding the bottom on until we get over the sink."

Bree hesitantly and skeptically fills the blender up with all the ingredients, and blends the mix together. We both watch the machine intently for any signs of leakage.

"So far, so good." I announce one she turns it off.

"That's what I thought last time." Bree moves to the side so that I can take over.

I pick up the blender by its handle, and the bottom at the same time. Once over the sink, I let go of the lower hand. When the bottom holds, I pour Bree a glass. "Maybe that's all it was."

"I'm buying you a new blender tomorrow. I don't trust that thing anymore."

"Yeah, yeah." I brush her off.

I set the blender down in the sink. She is right. The trust is gone for now. My blender is going to have to prove itself for a while, before I will trust the bottom not to fall off. Maybe I'll Google to find out if it's a common issue with it, or if the bottom is meant to come; I'll know one way or another then. The model number should be on here somewhere.

We finish cleaning our mess. Taking our glasses back to the living room, we continue unpacking, and moving things around.

Will: How's move in going? Have everything unpacked yet?"

Some essentials. Bree's helping, but I think it's taking longer with her here. Lol.

"Will again?" Bree accuses.

"Maybe." I joke coyly. My smile gives away the answer.

"You should invite him over."

I scrunch up my face. "He lives in California."

"Not for like this instant," She says like she was obvious in her statement. "But you're so obviously in love with the guy." I make to protest, but she continues. "And, he won't stop texting you, and I know, it's not because y'all had amazing sex, and he's keeping you open for a booty call. So, I'm thinking he might like you too. He's rich. If he wants to come out, he'd make it happen."

There are all sorts of ridiculousness in what she's saying, but I decide to partially entertain her. "How would I even go about asking him that?"

"Hey Hottie, how about you come keep me company in my big empty apartment?" Her breathy flirty voice makes it worse for me.

"No." I baulk at the notion of being so bold. There's no way I could invite him out like that, with such an obvious sexual connotation and expectation.

"I love how you're not even trying to dispute me. You love him." Bree teases.

"I don't-" All it takes is one disbelieving cock of Bree's head, and I switch from my complete denial. "I don't know if I love him, but I do really like him."

"Awe." Bree pouts out her lips to my tiny confession. Her eyes go round with a sickly sweetness. Her hand comes up to pinch at my cheek, but I successfully swipe away her attempts. "Then invite him to come out, and see what he says. You can be all casual about it, if you want to be boring."

"I don't know." There's one reason to do so, and a million reasons not to. "I mean, we had fun in Mexico, and it's been nice texting him, but it would never work. Long distance relationships never work. He wouldn't move here, I wouldn't move to California. He's got infamous commitment issues-"

Bree cuts off my trail of excuses. "You could be the girl to change him."

"People don't change that much."

"Better to have loved, and lost, than to have never loved at all." Bree reasons with a cliché.

"Christian." I name in a low blow.

"Fuck you. And he doesn't count, because he was an asshole the whole time." Her scowl doesn't last long. "What's the worst that could happen if you tried to pursue something with Will? He says no. Or, maybe he comes out, and you guys have fun. Maybe it turns into a romantic relationship, and he settles down; you have babies, and run a successful café together, and live until you die days apart from each other when you're a hundred. Or maybe you figure out you like you better as friends."

"Or he comes out, and I find out he's a creep or a weirdo, or a murderer." I switch from one extreme to a more plausible possibility. "We have sex and I never hear from him again except when he's bragging on the internet to his buddies about banging that girl he met on vacation, in her home town, because she couldn't get him out of her head."

"You're just scared because control freak you, doesn't have control over the outcome in this. So, you're pushing him away. Creating reasons why it wouldn't work. When it, very well, possibly could in one way or another."

I can't deny her that. She knows me too well. But, I can't get it out of my head that statistically the odds are completely against me. I'd rather always wonder what could have happened, than to get my heart broken.

"You could be happy. Isn't that worth the chance?" I quickly shut down a single shout of yes, until everything in me screams no. "I mean I could also just text him myself, and tell him how much you love him, and you've made a shrine to him."

My stomach sinks on her threat. "I did not make a shrine to him."

"What do you call what's on your dresser?"

"Pictures and things from our trip to Mexico. You're in more of those pictures than he is."

Bree shrugs and takes a quick sip. "Still, I can't be responsible for what I text him drunk."

While I don't want to text him myself, I know for certain that I don't want Bree dabbling in things. I'd never be able to face him again if Bree did text him. "Don't please. I'll text him myself."

Despite telling her such, I still have no intentions of doing so.

"And ask him to come for a visit?" She pushes.

"And ask him to come for a visit." I repeat.

"Good girl." She commends. Her eyes don't leave me the whole while she finishes the rest of her drink.

She obviously eyes between me and my phone.

"Well?" She drags out expectantly.

"You mean now?"

"Yes! Or else you won't do it." I roll my eyes to her like that hadn't been my plan all along. "Come on. I want to see it."

Maybe it wouldn't be so bad. He's going to say no anyway.

An idea flickers in my mind. Recalling his invite attempt in Mexico, I open our messages, and write out a text to him.

You know, there's lots to do around here too.

West Ed Mall, and Waterpark, Galaxyland, Museums. All within an hour's drive.

Calgary, Banff, Drumheller and the Tyrell Dinosaur Museum are all under five hours drive away.

I show her the written out message by holding the phone out towards her. Bree dashes her finger into my phone. The force and surprise knock the phone out of my hand. With a speed I hadn't known I could muster, I pick the phone up off the floor.

First I check the screen for cracks, there are none. A bit of

203

relief floods me, only to recede a moment later.

"You pressed send!" I shout.

"Someone had to." She shrugs and makes her way to my fridge.

I bite my tongue; close to shouting back to her. My blood heats up in anger. She shouldn't have done that.

The phone vibrates in my hand. I force myself to look at the screen. Staying tears of anxiety as my heart thunders.

Will: I'd have to find a place to stay, if I came for a visit.

Well, it wasn't a no.

It wasn't a no.

I glance up to Bree. My legs move before I can process and think. Locking myself in my bathroom, I stare at his message again. Rereading it a few times.

I know I have to respond. I don't want to seem too eager. All this is moving too fast for me. I feel faint from speeding blood.

He answered so fast, and he has to be waiting on a response. Rereading his message again, I directly respond to that.

I think I could buy a couch that you could crash on.

I wouldn't be able to entertain you the whole time though. I've got work. I could probably work it out to have a couple days off in a row while you'd be here.

I don't want to give him any false ideas. If he were to come out, I can't just take off time to show him around everywhere.

Maybe I can dissuade him from coming out at all.

A notch of disappointment changes my mind. I've gotten this far, I should go through with it and see where things end up. He didn't say no.

Will: I can entertain myself for a few hours every day. I'm self sufficient.

Will: No need to buy a couch. I could sleep on your floor.

Well I've at least got a few blankets and pillows for you.

Will: Deal.

I nearly drop my phone. Is that a yes?

My face betrays me. On its own accord, my smile widens as large as it can.

He said yes. I hold my phone to my chest. He said yes.

A couple tears shed from the corners of my eyes. My brain tries to keep up to the confusing effects of pure joy and fear.

Will: I could come sometime after dad's birthday.

I don't know when his dad's birthday is. I assume it's sometime closeish, but also maybe weeks to months away.

That could be fun, but are you prepared for snow?

Will: Is it snowing?

Not yet. But snow tends to start in October, and lasts until May.

His typing dots appear and disappear a few times, until finally a message comes through.

Will: Would it freak you out if I said I've already booked a ticket?

No. My finger hovers above the enter button without pressing down on the screen.

I freeze.

In a moment of shear terror, a piece of me knows that if I press that button, there is no going back. But, a large part of me is urging my finger closer.

Will: Kidding. Relax.

Sky's The Limit
In Devon

Chapter 1

Will: Good morning. Have fun at work today.

Will attached a picture of the beach and sunrise to his message. I have nothing of the sort to return in kind, so I take a smiling selfie at my door and send it along.

Good morning. Just heading out the door now. Have a great day. Say Hi to Silvia.

I lock the door and head down the hall. Two steps in, I remember my ordeal of the night before. Turning about, I begrudgingly head the other way.

I write a mental letter. To the idiot who parked in my spot last night, if you aren't gone by the time I get back from work, I will call someone to tow you. Sincerely, the person you ticked off by forcing her to park over in the visitors' zone; where you should have been.

Maybe I should have left a note. I'm still relatively new here. Someone might not realize the spot is taken now.

Benefit of the doubt and all that.

Benefit of the doubt flies out the window when my face is met with harsh chilly air. It bites at my skin. Frost covers everything in a sparkly sheen. If it wasn't so cold, it would be pretty.

"Skylar!" Mrs. Spratt springs over from her car. "How are you doing dear?"

"Great, just on my way to the café. How-"

She interrupts my polite return. "Oh, I thought you'd be taking some time off to spend with your mom. Make some memories while you can. The café will be there after."

"What," I pause briefly, "are you talking about?" Wracking my brain, I try to figure out what I'm missing.

"The cancer progressed." My mind shuts off all else. Tunneling unto the one key word. What cancer? Her expression morphs to shocked horror. "Oh dear, was I not supposed to say anything?"

I choke on my words to cover for myself. "I wasn't aware we were telling other people." I wasn't aware she had cancer at all.

"Oh good." Mrs. Spratt clutches at her chest and let's out a quick breath. She seems almost relieved by the information, a stark contrast to the whirling inside me. The cold air constricts around me. "I was afraid, for a moment, that I said something I wasn't supposed to. It's a shame that she won't be here much longer. Well, I don't have to tell you that. You're the one who won't have a mom for much longer." My heart skips a beat, and my lungs collapse in on themselves. Nausea floats up to settle in my throat. "I'm sorry. This is still new to me and I'm being insensitive. Please, don't worry about next month's rent. I understand that you'll need to take the time off to grieve. It's the least I could do. You're mom's been my best friend for years. It'll be hard living without her."

I can't hear anymore.

It seems dumb, the moment I have the thought, but the only thing I can think of is how I'm going to be late for my shift; I have to get to the café. "I'm sorry. But, I have to go.

The information overloads my mind. It can't be true. She would have told me.

Almost like teleporting, suddenly I'm parked outside the café. I know, somewhere inside me knows, that I drove here, but I can't remember driving or anything that happened along the way. My brain too busy analyzing the conversation with Mrs. Spratt; did I even end our conversation or did I just walk away?

Looking over my memories for clues of cancer, I can think of anything which isn't explainable in other ways. It's hard to think of any clues in the first place.

The warm air inside does nothing to warm me.

Did I turn off my car? Cold metal in my hands signal the likelihood of that. Did I lock the door?

I glance around. Mom isn't out here, again. No one is in the dining room at the moment.

"Dad?" I call out. "Dad!?" I call louder.

He comes out from the back rushed; startled by my abruption. I never call out to him. I usually meet up with him in the back.

"Where's mom?" I ask him.

His expression doesn't crack. "We weren't busy, so she went home." The words sound plausible, but I don't believe them anymore. The excuse has been used too often lately.

I get straight to the point. "Does mom have cancer?"

He frowns and hardens his stance. "No." Dad moves to turn away from me. He wants to escape to the back room, but this is too important to bury my head in the sand.

There's something wrong between his answer and his actions. "Then, why does Mrs. Spratt seem to think mom has cancer and only has days to live."

He doesn't have to say another word. The way his face falls, I get my confirmation. My heart sinks into my stomach.

Face contorting, the first call of anguish slips out as a whimper.

Dad turns and forces his way through the kitchen door. Something crashes and shatters to the floor. His faint cursing reaches my ears.

Home. I have to go home. I have to see mom.

211

Part of me still needs to hear it from her. I need to see it with my own eyes, until there's no doubt that it's true.

Such devastating information is truly unbelievable. This can't be happening to me. She's not supposed to get cancer. She's never supposed to leave me.

Just the same as my arrival here; I'm at home memoryless of the drive over. The information is too much for my brain. It doesn't want to compute useless information like my travel.

But, I'm greeted with an empty house; a dirty empty house. Mom would never leave it like this. My mind puts the information together. That must mean she hasn't been here for a few days; possibly longer.

Where would she be if not the hospital?

"Hi, I'm here to see Julia Bryson." The girl behind the desk doesn't miss a beat in instructing me where to go. She's supposed to check her computers. She's supposed to tell me she's not here. Anything, but this.

I follow the line she tells me too. I look over the room numbers. I don't remember her giving me a room number. She must have, but I wasn't listening; not completely.

An older woman says something to me from behind the desk. The words fail to register.

"Julia Bryson?" I desperately beg her to say she's not here.

She smiles sadly sweet, and points me towards a room two doors down.

With her lying in bed hooked up to a couple machines, at a passing glance, I'd almost not recognize the woman in front of me.

"Mommy?" My eyes burn in tears. I still hope against reality she'll tell me she's not her.

She holds out her arms for a hug. I wrap my arms around

myself. She looks thin and gray. Fragile. Like if I hugged her, she'd break. Her arms shake, skin loose around shrunken muscles, then fall back to the bed.

"I didn't want you to see me like this." Mom admits. Her voice is gravelly and hoarse.

"Are you dying?" I have to ask. I need to know.

"Yes." I choke on a sob. My face scrunches on it's own accord as tears start to flow. "Skin cancer. We caught it a month ago. Tried to treat it aggressively, but nothing helped. It spread rapidly. They said that I don't have long." Mom looks down to her lap. "Leave. I don't want your last memories of me to be like this."

I choke bitterly. "Too late."

"I'm tired, Skylar." She patronizes me with the same tone and words she'd used on me as a child.

I can't do this. I don't want to be here. I take the out she gave me. She doesn't seem to want me here either.

But, I can't just leave. I need a hug from my mom. This person is still her. Somewhere in there is my mom.

I lean down to hug her gently. She wraps her arms around me tightly. When she releases, so do I. I pull way to see tears falling down her sunken cheeks.

She snatches my hand as I move to leave.

All her last strength used to hold me there. Her hand hurting my own. Hollow eyes pierce into me. "Promise me, you will never end up like this. Promise me, you will not end up like me."

"I promise." I choke on the binding words. Her ferocity frightens me. I have no choice but to promise.

The grip loosens enough I snatch my hand away. My legs carry me out fast as my mind loops in a nightmare.

Chapter 2

My butt aches. Legs, numb, crossed in front of me.

Responsible drinking left the moment I sat down at the foot of my pantry. All the alcohol at my finger tips more readily available to reach my lips.

I swig another few gulp of rum; trying desperately to numb the pain and forget the insanity.

"I'm sorry. Your mom. She's passed away."

I pressed the red button on my phone to end his voice, but it hasn't stopped those same sentences passing through my brain over and over and over.

Did I cause this with my visit today? Soon was not meant to be today.

My body spasms in fear as shrill ringing pierces my thoughts.

NO! My heart screams. I look over to my side, to my phone previously forgotten and abandoned on the floor.

Bree's name rings for a few seconds. Then again. And again. I can neither bring myself to answer, nor to turn off my phone.

I just stare and cry as her name pops up. Again and again. Chasing each ring with a gulp of whatever bottle is in hand.

Then something new happens. Will's name and picture show up in time with a different ringing. A video call from the app. He's never called me before.

My hand reaches towards the phone for a moment before I pull back. I don't want him to see me like this. He has to know, that would be the only reason why he would call me.

Will calls two more times before he gives up.

A clinking metal gives entry into my apartment. I know who it is before she even has to call out; there's only two other keys to out and about. I doubt my landlords would find reason for forced entry with this.

Bree calls out quietly, "Sky?"

She's around the island to the pantry before I can say anything, before I can decide whether to voice anything.

Her body pounces on me to tightly wrap around me like a blanket.

A wave of sorrow gushes from me. The dam breaks wide open.

Mom's dead.

This is happening.

Chapter 3

The hum of people outside our private room quietens over time. It's silent by the time we're retrieved for our entrance.

The church worker stands to the side as the attention falls on me. Why did I have to go first?

I walk forward. My eyes on my seat. I don't dare let them wander onto anyone else. The room is filled, that much is obvious. I would bet half the town's older population is here. Other family add to the numbers. Some of the younger crowd, my age, would have come too. Anyone she impacted through the years at the café.

These are all the people who care enough to attend her funeral.

I take up the pack of tissues left on my seat, before sitting down. No choice but to look up now, a giant image of my mom flashes off the screen to another with her holding a baby me.

Dad arrives right after me. He takes my hand into his after he sits down. Something urges me to pull my hand away, itching through my whole body, but I don't dare to actually try to take my hand back. Not that he would let me even try.

The pastor greets everyone, welcoming them to the service today. He asks them to celebrate her life, rather than mourn her death.

His words are practiced and kind. I drown him out as I watch the casket. Nothing can be seen from here, but I know she's in there. Her body is in the shiny wooden box on stage, right behind where he speaks; open to the whole room.

It's unsettling to be in a room with a dead body; my mom's dead body. But, no one else seems to mind; they came here willingly.

I haven't dared look inside, but dad has. From the moment we came here, hours ago, to when they ushered us into the small family room he cried over her body.

He held her and adjusted her. Begged me to go see her; how pretty the coroners had made her. I refused, despite his attempts.

I know she's wearing her favourite blue dress. I know they recreated her make up look from pictures we had to provide. I know she's wearing her fanciest jewelry. Dad's made sure to describe as much. Trying to reassure me.

But, I don't know if I want to see her like that.

It's hard enough not to picture her frail and gray. I don't want to look in the case and see her perfectly still.

Dad's hand tightens in pulses. Pulling me out of my head. I look over to see tears trailing down his cheeks.

The sight is enough to bring tears to my eyes. I had thought I had nothing left to leak, but I was wrong.

A first in my life. Such an unusual and striking sight to see my dad cry. Even in terrible physical pain, I have never seen him shed one tear. My dad was always inhuman in that way; something I was always told I should strive for.

The pain in my hand becomes my focus. In his pain, he's causing me pain. I don't move. It feels good in a way, to have a physical manifestation for what I'm feeling inside. Somewhere else to hold focus for a few minutes break.

I convince myself that squishing my hand to the point of possible bruising is helping him in some way. He likely doesn't realize how hard he's gripping me.

The lights brighten. An overly happy song plays in the room; dad's choice leaves an unsavory taste in my mouth. He reasoned

217

that she would want people to leave on a happy note, but it seems distasteful to me to play a upbeat party song.

It was all meant to be part of the celebration of life party. Not a funeral. Dad refused to call it that.

I don't want to be happy. My mom is dead. We are going to put her dead body in the ground today, and I will never see her again. I want to be miserable; it's practically my right to be as miserable as I want. Yet, no one wants to let me be miserable.

People get up to leave or mingle; give their condolences to each other. They'll wait to speak with us too.

Dad pulls me up out of my seat with him. His hand tightly wrapped around mine. When he moves, he pulls me with him. I realize what he's doing as we approach the stairs for the stage. I tug my hand to get away.

His grip tightens in a quick squeeze. A reprimand to tell me not to make a scene in front of all these people. Dad's grip is too tight, and I have no choice but to follow.

I tell myself that it won't be too bad. I have to do this for dad. He drags me with a willing appearance to the top of the stage and over to the shiny wooden box.

My heart thunders. It's too late to close my eyes and pretend I looked.

"She looks like she's sleeping." Dad tells me.

She looks wrong.

Her face, neck, chest and hands are completely painted over. The people would have had to change her colour to more of a natural tone, but to me it appears off and unnatural.

Her make up is darker and heavier that she would have liked. I know enough about embalming to know that she's been stuffed and sewn shut.

The chilling part is how still her body is. There is no mistaking her for sleeping. She's an unmoving body.

Slight movements give away life. Twitches and chest raises are completely absent. She might as well be a statue; that would somehow be better.

Dad repeats his statement as a direct question. "She looks like she's sleeping; doesn't she?"

I want to shake him- slap him. She doesn't look anything close to sleeping. She looks dead. She is dead.

You're fucking delusional if you think she looks like she's sleeping.

"Yeah." I respond softly, knowing that's what he needs to hear.

Will: Are you okay?

Will: I heard about your mom. I'm sorry you're going through this.

Will: How are you doing?

Will: I'm so sorry. I couldn't possibly imagine what you're going through.

Will: Please let me know if you need anything.

Will: Bree says the funeral is today. I'm thinking of you.

Will: How are you doing?

Will: Are you okay?

Will: Please take care of yourself.

Will: How are you?

Will: Bree says she's concerned about you. Please answer one of us to let us know you're okay.

Will: It might not seem like it, but you'll make it through this. You have people here for you.

Will: If you need to talk, I'm here for you.

Will: I wish I knew the right thing to say, but I don't suppose there is a right thing to say. I'm sorry you're going through this.

Will: Hope your day goes well.

Will: Thinking of you.

Chapter 4

Bree

I'm doing the right thing.

I have to tell myself again, like a mantra, as I let myself into her condo.

The smell hits me first, like a garbage can with week old food inside. Turning on her lights, I figure it's coming from the take out containers on the counter and island. I'm too scared to open them up and find out if there is molding food inside.

At least I know she's eating. Eating crap food, but eating all the same.

Her pantry is hinged open. I walk around there, and find empty alcohol bottles. Everything I bought her, empty or missing.

She must've had one wild party. I joke to myself solemnly. I know she drank all of it to herself. There was enough there that miss lightweight should've had last her a whole year.

Her phone silence prompted my visit, but I hadn't expected an alcohol binge. Maybe I should have. I found her wasted the night Mrs. Bryson died.

My heart skips a beat at a disturbing thought my brain doesn't wish to entertain; what if she OD'd on alcohol?

The condo is small, and thus has very few places to search. I can rule out more than half of her place in a glance, which leaves her bedroom and the big bathroom.

Breathing deeply, I steel myself for whatever I could encounter in there, before I open the door.

The room is darkened, but not completely. Her blinds let in some light. Enough to see a lump in the bed with food boxes and alcohol bottles surrounding it.

I approach slowly.

Her room gives way to more mess as I go in deeper. Used up tissues dot the floor.

My eyes sting from unshed tears. My heart breaking from the pain in the room.

I get close enough to see her. Her hair is slicked in a bun. Frayed hair crowns her, with what has fallen out of the elastic.

From the bitter body odor smell, I doubt she's showered in a few days.

Her chest rises and falls with breath. It's the only sign I get that she's alive, but I'll take it.

"Sky?" I call quietly and gently. Not wanting to startle her. But, her name gains no response, so I try again a little louder. "Sky?"

I touch her shoulder lightly, but she makes no movements. Shaking her shoulder makes her move, but only as she changes positions to her back.

"Sky, wake up." I push on her shoulder again.

Her eyes pop open in fright. I pull back. She digs further in to the mattress as she tries to get away from me, the intruder. As she realizes I'm not a robber, she scowls but relaxes. "Go away."

"Sky-"

Her voice crackles. "I don't want to see you right now. Go away." She rolls over to her other side, with her back facing me.

"You haven't been answering me, so I came to see if you were still alive." I explain. Is she mad I'm here? Embarrassed of her condition?

"Leave!" She shouts. Her hands come up to cover her ears. She curls in on herself. Shaking and shuddering as fresh tears come to her.

I stand frozen. I want to comfort her, but I don't know how. She's told me to leave. She doesn't want me to be here.

"Just leave, please." Sky begs.

I don't know how to help her. My heart pounds and my mind is blank. Tears of my own stream down my cheeks.

I can't take seeing her like this. She's asked me to leave, so I do. Out to her living room, and out through her door.

I make it to my car before I let my tears slip free. I need help to help her.

Pulling out my phone, I call up Will.

"How is she?" No hello. No, how are you? He knows why I'm calling. Both of us have been concerned for her for days. Neither of us getting responses.

My voice cracks. Face contorting in anguish. "Awful." The only word I can get out to describe what I just saw.

"How bad?"

My voice cracks again. A lump holds in my throat. "I've never seen her like this. She screamed at me to leave. There's empty alcohol bottles everywhere; garbage everywhere. I don't think she's showered in days. Her place smells like rotting food and she's got all the curtains drawn. I had to get out of there."

"How is she? Put her on speaker." Silvia's voice comes on the line faintly.

"She's bad, and no I'm not putting you on speaker." Will tells her.

"Tell Sky we're thinking about her." Silvia shouts.

"You don't have to scream in my ear!" Will shouts back to her. Both have me pulling the phone away from my ear.

"Are you going to go out there?" Silvia asks quieter.

"I think so." Will responds.

"You will do no such thing. And, get off the phone. This is family dinner and it won't be ruined with some phone call." His mother is there. It sounds like I disrupted supper.

A slew of people talking over one another gets gradually quieter. I hear an door shutting. "Do you think it would help if I came out?"

"Yes." I choke. "She was pretty upset when you rejected her invitation to come out. I think she loves you." Sky will kill me if she ever finds out I shared this with him, but I'd take that over how she is now.

I need help. She needs help. And, if she won't accept help from me, then maybe she'll take it from him.

"I'll come." There's a pause. "I just have to go home and grab my passport and a few things. I'll book the earliest flight I can. Do you think you could pick me up from the airport?"

"Of course." I answer. Hopefully that means he'll get a flight in tomorrow. "Just let me know when you're supposed to land."

Chapter 5
Will

"She's still sleeping?" I ask.

"Yeah, looks like it." Bree backs out of the bedroom and closes the door. "Should we wake her?"

"No." I look around the kitchen. "Clean first. We set her life in order, then we deal with her."

"I don't have time to clean all this up. I have to get to work. I already used up all my sick days." Her reasoning sounds like a lame excuse to leave, and get out of cleaning, and helping her best friend. No wonder Sky's gotten so bad. Bree's too selfish or clueless to do what needs to be done.

I simmer my anger. Maybe she'd get fired if she takes the day off, I reason. Maybe she can't afford to lose her job. Maybe she's been taking off time between Sky's mom's death and now.

The other party to my inner conversation fires back stating that it's a risk she should be willing to take for a best friend in this kind of dire need. I give myself a mental shake. "Leave me to it. I'll clean it up, you get to work."

I'll get her well again, if I have to do it myself.

Bree hands me the key she used to get inside, and leaves without another word. Her head down.

I look around at the mess again, before getting to work. It takes a little fumbling around, but I find the garbage bags under the sink with the small garbage can. The bags are nothing like what I would need to efficiently pack everything up, but it appears to be

225

all she has.

The pizza boxes won't even fit inside, so I stack those up on the island. One tall stack of pizza boxes and eight little bags fill up fast. Once they are removed to a bin outside, it makes the kitchen look ten times cleaner.

I make work cleaning the counters, emptying the sink of dishes into the dishwasher, then sweep the floors.

She's going to need food when she wakes up. I check in her fridge. The milk is expired by a couple days, some veggies are starting to grow fur, and I generally start not to trust anything she's stashed in here. Each item gets an expiry check before getting tossed out.

I text Bree. *Can you grab her some fruit, veggies and milk? Her fridge was molding. I'll pay you back."*

Bree: I'll pay. I'll grab it after work, and come over.

Bree: Is she awake yet?

No. Just about to get in there to clean it.

Bree: Good luck.

I enter into her room. She's still sleeping, or completely ignoring me, but I'd bank on the first option. Her room is stuffy, and suffocating. I leave the door open as I clean up her garbage.

It feels wrong to go inside without her permission. Worse, knowing that I'm in her place without her permission, cleaning up her depression mess. It feels like I'm crossing all sorts of boundaries she's set up to keep people out.

She's mentioned her depression and anxiety issues a couple times, but only in passing. This seems like a full onset episode. It's no wonder, likely triggered by her mom passing away.

I don't know her well enough to know if all this work is going to make her worse or better. Bree's no help. She's never seen Sky like this before. Sky may have never gone this deep before; I don't know.

When Tom has a full episode, he needs someone to buffer him from the world; a good apartment cleaning, a good hygiene fix, before some coddling, followed by a swift kick in the pants to get him going again.

I can only hope the same strategy works with Sky.

Working quietly, I get all the garbage gone, and a load of laundry in the washer.

I do a final check around, before deciding that it's finally time to wake her up.

Steadying myself, I take a deep breath, preparing for her reaction. However she reacts, I doubt it's going to be good.

Chapter 6

My shoulder is forced from it's spot; an irritation in my dream world.

I just about bite back at Bree, when another voice entirely calls out. "Skylar, it's time to get up." My eyes spring open. I better be dreaming still.

Standing at the side of my bed, with a hand reached over touching me, is Will. I have to be dreaming still.

"Will?" My voice rasps. It's dry. My throat feels like needles have coated the interior. "What are you doing here?"

"Making you take a shower."

I pinch myself to ascertain dream from reality. With pain comes my answer. This isn't some steamy dream with shower antics. He's here to make disgusting me take a shower. "You flew across the country to make me take a shower?"

"Yes. I'm really here. You're awake. You didn't need to pinch yourself. Bree said you needed a babysitter, so here I am." I throw myself deeper into my bed with an eye roll. "Look, I was worried about you. Bree's been giving me updates, and you haven't been answering. I'm sorry if I overstepped my bounds."

I hide my face from him, as an uncontrollable pain rushes from my heart. A small whimper lets loose into my hands just as my tears come out fresh again. I didn't know I could cry anymore. "I just want to sleep." The words come out so quietly I don't think he could hear.

"You've been doing that. So it's time to do something else.

You need to take care of yourself if you're going to get through this." He says softly.

I hold in my noises, but my shoulders shake with quiet crying; betraying me.

"Do you think your mom would want you to sleep your life away?"

His quiet question makes my heart stop. "My mom's dead. She doesn't want anything." The bitter dead tone comes easily with anger. How dare he bring her up and use her against me.

"I don't want you to sleep your life away." My heart flutters confusingly, but I easily push it away in my rage. He's just saying that. "Bree doesn't want you to sleep your life away. Your dad doesn't want you to sleep your life away." He finally gets to his point. "If you can't do this for yourself, pick someone to lean on and do it for them."

The covers lift off of me. With my hands up at my face, he's able to pull it off halfway, before my hand can shoot down to grasp it. "Go for a shower. It'll make you feel human again."

As much as I don't want to, I don't think I can just shout him away. I don't think he'll leave me alone; not after travelling so far.

I don't want him to see me like this, so I bolt to the bathroom and lock him out.

A glance in the mirror starts tears a new. I can't bear to look at myself. Slick hair wild and knotted. Red strained eyes. Puffy under eyes.

An upturn in my stomach throws up everything into the toilet. My head feels fuzzy still, but no headache. I wonder if I'm still drunk, or really lucky without a hangover headache. The answer relies on a timeline I don't have any knowledge of.

I turn the shower nob to the right area, and get ready while I wait for the water to warm.

It takes four rounds of shampoo and scrubbing to make my hair feel like it should. The build up of oils and grime come off in layers of bubbles.

Disbelief ebbs away as I go; Will is outside waiting for me. He and Bree have both been in my condo, and have seen an embarrassingly large amount of slobbery.

I don't know where to go from here.

Do I clean and apologize for the mess? Do I go out and tell him to leave? He has no business being here. Why is he here? He made it pretty clear he wouldn't come out to see me.

The only thing I do know, is that I don't want to face him yet. I do all I can to stretch out the shower; conditioner, two rounds of body soap, shaving everything, and sitting under the stream as it beats at my back.

Exhausted from all my emotions, I will them away. Numb somber is what I'd prefer. Everything hurts less when I'm numb.

When thoughts of my mom invade my mind, I stop. Turning off the shower, and peeking out behind the curtain.

There is no towel on the hook I reach out to. I forgot a towel. I look to the counter. I forgot clean clothes.

Of course I did. My nose stings with the threat of more tears. I'm an idiot. I can't do anything right.

I ring out my hair of most of the water clinging to it. Swiping my hands over my body, to get some of the excess water off, before leaving the shower stall.

Towels are right outside the door and so are my clothes. Holding up my bath mat as a shield, I unlock the door and peek out. My room is lighter, the curtains are now open.

Quietly, I call out for Will. When he doesn't respond I feel confident enough to open the door more. Tip toeing a bit further out, I grab two towels and dive back into the bathroom.

Step one complete. I wrap my hair in the smaller towel, and wrap my body in the larger one. Both cover me far more than the bath matt shield. A bit more comfortable now, I repeat earlier swift actions to retrieve my clothes. Will is still nowhere in sight or sound.

I grab a set of clothes respectable enough for public viewing, and curse Will that I won't be as comfortable with these as I would be in pjs.

Finishing getting ready, I put on all my clothes, brush out the rat's nest from my hair, and brush my teeth.

After what feels like ages, I'm finally completely done and physically ready to emerge.

Mentally, I am fully prepared to just crawl back into bed and go back to ignoring the world.

Eventually, I know I'll have to leave. It's not like I could wait him out until he gives up and goes home. I doubt he'll leave without seeing me again, and his house isn't ten minutes from here, so he's not going to just stay an hour and leave.

I can't exactly hold up in here for days.

Leaving the small room, I check for him in my room. He's not there. As I get closer to my opened bedroom door, I can hear him opening and closing my laundry machines.

It's then that I take I look around my, now spotless room. All the garbage is gone, bottles have disappeared, bed sheets have been changed, clothes gone, laundry baskets gone, curtains are drawn, and the window is open.

He's cleaning my house. My mortification reaches new levels. I know I haven't cleaned in a week or more; how many days has it been? I hadn't even tried to keep some semblance of cleanliness; just leaving everything wherever I had been at the time.

I silently close my door, then my window and curtains.

231

Crawling into bed I, by long lost habit alone, grab my phone and click the screen on. Hundreds of notifications for unread messages, missed calls and voicemails scream for my attention. Ignoring those, not even my social medias are safe; more notifications await me with condolences.

My lungs constrict with each rapid beat on my heart. I do only what I can think of at the moment, throwing my phone as far from me as possible.

I dive deep into my blankets and hug the second pillow to me. A new onslaught of tears starts, and this time I cannot seem to damper the noise. Wailing whimpers call Will to my attention.

The door creaks open. Hyperaware of him, I wonder what he will do.

I track him as he goes to the phone on the ground and picks it up. He moves to put it back on my nightstand, but I can't handle it anywhere near me at the moment. The reminder is too strong.

"Can you, please, just take it away?? I don't want to look at it right now." I plead.

He nods and escorts the phone away, closing the door behind him.

Chapter 7

An earthquake zoned to only my bed jostles me out of my mind. Some wild animal leaps on top of me, deeply inhales my hair, and declares, "Will works miracles. You smell so much better now."

Maybe if I ignore her, pretend to be asleep, she'll leave. It seems to work for opossums. It's a small hope.

My embarrassment of the way I spoke to her earlier quickly clouds in anger. She's the reason why Will is here, or at least how he would have gotten inside.

"And, he's cleaned your condo. I think you need to keep him." She teases.

"I didn't ask him to do that. You shouldn't have brought him." I practically growl.

My harsh comment earns me a hard slap to my back. "Okay, little lady. Your mom died. We get that. I couldn't possibly understand what you are going through. But we are you're friends and we hate seeing you like this. We are going to help you. The least you can do is not be a bitch about it. I've already tolerated this for long enough and babied you, but I think it's time for tough love." She rips the blankets off me. "Get the fuck out of this bed right now."

The world turns in a harsh push to my side. I open my eyes as the world falls from me, or rather I fall out of bed.

"What the hell?!" I shout. My butt and head hurt from where they had connected with the floor and my nightstand.

"You are leaving this bedroom. You will thank Will for the crap he's put up with because you were disgusting." Bree highly emphasizes the word disgusting. Shame heats my gut. I know that much to be true, I am disgusting. "Then, we are going out for supper."

I stand up and try to go back onto my bed. Bree appears ready to push me back out, so I step back onto the floor.

"I don't want to see anyone." Going out means running into the whole town, and everyone knew my parents.

"That's why we're going to Edmonton. So you don't run into anyone who could possibly say anything about anything." Bree's thought of everything. Her smirk dares me to refute her again.

"Can't we just stay here and order something?" I plead. I really don't want to go out, but I'm starting to figure out that I'm not going to get much of a choice.

"No. You need to get out of your house for a little while. And, Will just loaded all your takeout containers out of here. I don't think he wants to bring more in. So scoot. Let's go." Bree leaps off my bed to give me a shove in the right direction.

"I have to pee!" I refute.

Her hands leave my back. "Go pee, then we're off."

I grumble all the way to the bathroom and back. When I enter the main living area, I can see the effort Will made in getting my place clean. It's as spotless as it was when I had first moved in.

Will stands ready to go at my door. He smiles small when he looks to me. I avoid his eyes. Feeling guilty and sick about everything he's been privy to. "I'm sorry," for everything. I tell him. I don't know where to start for the myriad of things I need to apologize for.

"Nothing to worry about. Glad to see you up and about, even if it's unwilling." He holds the door open for Bree and I.

"So, what's for supper?" Bree asks.

When Will looks to me, I answer, "up to you guys. I don't feel like choosing."

"Great. I know just the place then." She spins on her heels to start out the door.

"Where?" I ask.

"A surprise."

Chapter 8

The line up gets longer and longer, making me glad we got here when we did. IKEA may have amazing fries and meatballs, but they can also get insanely busy.

Bree finishes the last bite of her chocolate cake, so we can get going. I take my tray of dishes to the tray stacks, and wait for Will and Bree to deposit theirs as well.

I have to admit it was a good thing getting out. The air feels lighter here. I almost don't want to go back. I'd give anything to be able to step on a plane going anywhere right about now.

Even with all that we just ate, Bree ensures we stop for IKEA ice cream before we leave. It's never too cold to get ice cream; not even if there were a blizzard out. Will disagrees.

We pile into Bree's car, but as we leave the lot, she goes the wrong way. I'm happy for a detour; whatever it happens to be.

She's parks us not too far down the road at a building with large bowling pins on the roof. There are many things to do in the large building of many companies, so I try not to get my hopes up for bowling.

Bree turns a bit in her seat to talk in a way that faces more in between Will and I. "I thought we'd play a couple games before we go back. If they're not too busy, at least. The last time I came here, they had a four hour wait for lanes, but that was a Friday night, so it might be different. If not, there's Monster Mini Golf next door."

"Bowling sounds great. I haven't gone since I was a kid." Will enthuses.

"Great, so you're going to suck as bad as we do!" I add. Bowling isn't too common for us. Growing up, we usually only went bowling if someone threw their birthday party at the bowling alley.

We venture inside the dark building. They have black lights on to light up all the whites and colours brightly. The music is up loud and pumping.

Bree talks with the guy at the counter. There aren't many others here. Just two lanes are taken up out of their long spread.

Will pays for the lanes, and Bree shoves shoes into my arms. She got me a size seven. I remember something about bowling shoes needing to be a size smaller than your normal shoes size, and I hope they're right.

Bree leads us to an empty lane right beside a family of four. Our names pop up on the screen; Bree, Sky, Will. I don't know if they chose alphabetical, or if Bree chose the order because it could go either way.

My shoes fit fine, but they feel different than runners. The flat bottoms, also very slippery, make walking feel a bit different.

It takes a bit, but the pins make it onto the floor. Bree shoots all her shots straight into the gutter. I'm glad for the low level bar set. It makes my gutter ball and singular pin down seem great.

As Will steps up to take his turn, I secretly hope he will suck as bad as we do. True to his word, and not secretly hiding a past in league bowling; where his idea of a bad game is getting more spares than strikes.

He picks an orange ball I know is heavier than the ones I had picked. Spreading his legs, he swings the ball between them to granny bowl the heavy ball down the lane. It veers to the right a bit, but manages down three pins.

Between giggles Bree reprimands him, "no granny bowling."

"You're just jealous you didn't think of it first." Will grabs another ball but holds it in his arms.

"Do you need the bumpers up too? I can tell them our man child needs the bumpers up." Bree stands up, bluffing her way a step towards the desk.

"If you need to tell yourself that in order to make you feel better about your gutters, then by all means." He motions his hand towards the desk, calling her out on her bluff while also teasing her. I'm glad for the banter. Its amusing to watch them back and forth.

"Asshole."

"Bree!" I motion towards the family beside us. The parents are looking at us and smiling, but the kids are in their own world bowling and keeping watch.

"Ah shi-, sorry! I forgot- little ears." Bree flubs her apology.

Will comes to sit down, telling Bree to take her turn. She takes the chance to leave before she can swear more.

"Sorry." I tell the father.

He waves and smiles. "Nothing they haven't heard before."

"He's got no filter and swears like he forgets he's at home, not the oil patch. I'm surprised neither of the kids' first words were swears." His wife takes place beside him momentarily, before she walks up to take her turn. The husband turns around to watch after the children.

Bree manages to shoot a pin down on the left side, then creating a mirror image of the other side. At least she didn't hit the gutters on every shot.

My turn.

Bree holds her hand up for a high five on her way by, so I indulge her.

I might as well have a cheer squad behind me. Will and Bree loudly lift me up. My confidence outweighing my embarrassment, until I gutter the first ball. Shrugging to them, I grab another ball. Briefly, I muse the thought of granny bowling, but I stash it away for later. I'm not that desperate yet.

Finishing the round with three pins down, I walk back to high fives and cheers. They are definitely overplaying their joy for me.

It saddens me as my butt hits the slight cushion. The reason for their being so extra, edges at the corners of my happy box; ripping apart the sides as though they were made of paper.

I don't want to cry in front of everyone. I excuse myself to the bathroom to whoever might hear the quick utterance.

I close myself into a stall and hug myself. Trying to calm my increasing breathing.

"Sky?" Will calls.

"This is the woman's bathroom." My voice manages to stay strong, but I don't think that'll continue long.

"Just open the door." I don't get time to contemplate the request before he says, "I could always crawl underneath."

Not seeing much of a choose, I unlock the latch, open the door and walk out. He wraps me up in his arms, not saying anything.

An onslaught of sadness burns at the bridge of on nose. Collecting tears quickly escape before I can start actively crying.

"You can't have sex in here!" A booming voice stops everything. I jump away from Will.

It takes half a moment to realize the male voice couldn't be Bree making a joke, and half another second to be thoroughly mortified of the accusation thrown at me.

"We're not." Guilt riddles my voice without intending such. The intended crying fit effectively stopped by the startle he'd given me.

A worker comes around the corner with a smug grin. "Sure,

239

sure." The look drops as he spots me. "Are you okay?"

Consciousness turns to self conscious, as I know my face must be red splotchy from the tears. A few of those still on my cheeks to be rubbed away.

"Can we have a moment?" Wills asks.

He steps closer, cautiously. "Are you okay, mam?"

I want to tell him yes, but nothing comes out; I'm not okay, but not for the reason he thinks. "She's upset. I'm handling it."

He broadens himself, like one who goes up against a predator, to look more threatening. "I can escort you out of here, if you need me too."

"Are you accusing me-"

I stop Will quickly with a hand on his chest. The words rush out. "I'm sorry. My mom died recently. I rushed off crying, so Will came to check on me. I'm sorry. I'll just clean myself up and we'll leave the bathroom."

Eyes wide and mouth gaped, he attempts multiple words, but never makes a sound. "Sorry." He finally utters and leaves.

I walk back into the stall and clean away a little runny snot that had worked up a minute before. At least my shame has curbed the sadness. I don't even know why I feel like this, it's not like we were in anyway caught going to have sex. The accusation, however is enough to have me feeling guilty.

I walk by Will, I have nothing I can bring myself to say to him at the moment.

Bree greets me with a brief hug, but stays attached with one rubbing arm to my back when she pulls away. "You okay?"

"Enough." I shrug.

Will walks by us to take his turn. No longer granny bowling, he takes an upright shot. The ball rolls with an angered lurch, right into the center. All the pins fall down to earn him a strike.

Our reactions vastly different. Bree maniacally cheers, while my congratulations are more reserved. Will himself seems caught between disbelief and an itching to take another turn.

"Great, now I have to go after that." Bree exclaims before walking up to take her turn.

Three rounds go by with reserved silence, save for the odd accolade.

"Excuse me." I turn to see the boy from earlier with an older gentleman. "I'm the manager, I apologize for the earlier misunderstanding. As you might understand your situation isn't the normal outcome when two people of the opposite gender enter that same bathroom." He trails off a bit awkwardly. "I lost my mom a couple years ago. It gets better. It just takes time. Food helps. We brought you a plate of nachos and three cokes on the house to apologize for the situation and in solidarity for you losing your mom."

He and the other employee place everything on the table and back away.

I say, "thank you," in a lack of anything else to voice. They speed away.

"They just didn't want to get sued." Bree gleefully grabs up a cheesy chip.

"For what?" What could I sue them for? Ultimately, they had a reasonable assumption.

"I don't know, but at least we got free snacks."

Chapter 9

I open the door and say, "bye," to Bree. Making to get out of the back of her car.

Will surprises me when he gets out of Bree's car as well.

"Text me later." Bree tells me. I agree then shut the door. She pulls the car away, leaving the two of us behind on either side of the empty space.

I hadn't realized Will wouldn't be leaving with Bree. But, it comes back to me that at some point, weeks ago, I had offered to house him if he came to visit.

He follows me inside the building. Silence follows us up to my door.

It's my fault that he's here, well, maybe Bree's fault ultimately. But, if I hadn't fell so deep inside myself, then he wouldn't be here.

I run through possible ideas, but nothing feels right. I can't just make him sleep on the floor. That doesn't feel right.

When Bree stays over, she sleeps in my bed, but we couldn't do that; could we? Would it be inappropriate? What if he takes it as an invitation for more?

I open up my door, and let us inside. It's late, and I'm exhausted already. Will locks the door behind us with a finite click.

Will grabs up a small suit case he's hidden in my laundry room. He sets it up on the island and opens it up; pulling out a small rolled up sleeping bag. It couldn't possibly be any good, it's so thin. It might as well be a blanket zipped together.

"You could sleep in my bed; if you want. It would be comfier than the floor. The sheets are fresh and clean." Part awkward offer, part logic, and part inside jest; a three part convincing argument.

"Sure."

We stand looking at each other for a moment. I feel awkward. "I don't have much to do around here, if you wanted to stay up longer. I'm a bit tired though."

"That's fine. We can just go to bed." He digs into his suits case and pulls out a black pair of sweats.

He walks by me to the small bathroom and close himself up inside. I go into my own after picking out some pjs.

I put on my pajamas, while leaving my bra on. It'll be uncomfortable, but less likely for any nips slips as my tank top adjusts through the night.

I leave and slip into bed, turning on my lamp, before he comes out of the bathroom.

Placing my phone on the charger, I look back over to find a bare chested surfer man crawling into bed on the other side.

Settling down, he faces me on his side. I get comfortable on my back. Remembering the lamp, I touch it to turn it off, and go back into my placement stiffly.

"You we're right. It's cold here."

I look over to him. "We haven't even gotten snow yet. This is nothing. This is less than nothing. Wait two months and it'll be minus twenty and three feet of snow."

"At least you'll have a snowy Christmas." He says. It's weird to think that he wouldn't have snow at Christmas. Hell would freeze over before we had a snowless Christmas.

"Do you get any snow through the winter?" I ask. He's in

California, I doubt they get any snow that far south.

"It's extremely rare where we're at. Northern California and the mountain usually get snow. I couldn't even imagine three feet of snow back home. The whole city would stop. We wouldn't be able to handle it."

I realize what he's done. We could have just said our goodnights, and laid in bed until we fell asleep, but he started an innocent conversation. That light conversation starter, tested my tiredness levels, and showed a lacking.

I find myself wanting to keep the talk going for whatever he's willing. "Here, three feet of snow only allows for you to be a little bit late, and only if they haven't plowed the roads yet. Otherwise, you best be on time. Which means leaving up to double time to get anywhere on time."

"The world doesn't stop when you get three months of snow." He agrees, but he's missing some information.

I correct him. "Up to six months of snow."

Will's upper lip furls in distaste. "Why do you live here?"

"Have to live somewhere. And at least we don't have to deal with so many poisonous bugs." My neck starts to ach with the angle. I think to stop looking at him while we talk, but decide to roll over to my side for a while.

"At least we don't have to worry about walking outside and freezing to death half the year. Do you even get a summer?"

"Yeah, one weekend in July. Blink and you'll miss it." I joke with a common saying around here. It goes nicely with another saying we have about living in Alberta. Don't like the weather, wait five minutes and it'll change. "Usually June, July and August are warm or hot. But people start wearing shorts as soon as the snow starts melting in April or May."

"You still have snow when you wear shorts." Acclimatization makes a big difference in what people wear. There's jokes, I've heard, about Canadians who go south. That you can always spot a Canadian, because they'll be wearing shorts while the locals are wearing pants.

"Yeah, like melting stage. Like it's above zero and the snow is starting to melt." Though I have seen people out in shorts before that too.

"You're insane." Will exaggerates.

"After six months of snow and minus thirty, zero is a jacuzzi."

"Your jacuzzi's must be different up here. Our jacuzzi's don't give us frost bite."

I smile at a passing memory of an anecdote Harold told Bree and I. "Actually, I know someone who did get frost bite in a Jacuzzi. They went in one during a party in the middle of winter. Usually, it's the fun trick of hey look how I can style my hair as it freezes from how cold outside it is. But, he ended up staying outside too long; drunk of course. And ended up with frost bite on his ears"

"That sounds awesome and awful at the same time." Will impresses.

"It is."

"So do you go in jacuzzi's and frost style your hair?" Will dazzles the end of his question with a smile.

I laugh a little breath out my nose. "No. I'm usually tucked away inside." I'll never explicitly admit to him that I prefer to spend the least amount of time freezing outside as possible. There's Canadian honour at risk when you admit you hate the cold and snow. "Bree's tried to get me out snowboarding, but that failed so horribly that I've declared myself off winter sports."

"What happened?"

"Flipped down the hill. Got a slight concussion. Mom was so mad. She watched me fall all the way down, and thought I

245

must've died or broken every bone in my body." I choke down a lump in my throat. I didn't mean to mention her. Especially, mentioning her and death in the same sentence. It feels too soon for that sort of association. I change the subject to something adjacent and hope he leaves it alone. "Bree broke her collarbone the next week when she ran into a tree. And, she's the expert. She actually had a sponsorship for a few years. They paid for her gear and passes in exchange for exposure and she had to attend certain events."

"That's cool. Does she still snowboard?"

"Not too much the last few years. Either work got in the way, or she'd want to go with someone but no one else wanted to go. Weather and snow conditions can be an issue. It's an expensive hobby."

"So if you don't go outside, what do you do all winter?" Will asks a good question. It doesn't take much thought on my part.

"Work." I say with all seriousness. If I'm not at work, I'm at home existing, or I'm hanging out with Bree. It takes a moment to think about what I do otherwise. "I read books. Bake things."

"What kind of things?"

"Cookies, desserts. All the sweet treats." We'd bake whatever we were craving, or whatever mom decided in advance.

"Did you do a lot of baking growing up?" He presses.

"Yeah. With my mom. She loved to putz around in the kitchen. We usually had some sort of dessert in the house at all times. I love-d to help her, especially when I was a kid." Most of my fondest memories with my mom, and dad, take place in a kitchen; either baking or watching them bake.

"Sounds like her love for baking rubbed off on you."

"Yeah I guess so." I roll to settle on my back and close my eyes, but keep talking to let him know the conversation isn't over. "Both mom and dad did their thing in the kitchen, but I definitely took more to the baking desserts side of things."

"What else can you tell me about her?" There's a pausing hesitation in his voice. He doesn't want to push. I can appreciate that.

"She was literally always there. When I was at home, she was at home. When I wasn't at school or Bree's during the day, then I was at the café helping her. I had a play and nap area in the café when I was really young. If I got sick at school, she would leave the café to dad and immediately come to get me.

She was my buffer between me and dad. He has his ways and can be stuck in his ways. So, I would talk to her about something and she would relay the news to him. So she could take the brunt of it and soften the reaction for later.

I can't remember her having any real hobbies, other than baking. She didn't have the time or energy for it."

"Was she sick for a while?" He asks.

"No. Skin cancer. From diagnosis to death was about a month." At least as far as I know. "She used to tell stories about how she used to put baby oil on and go bake in the sun to get as brown as possible in the summer. That was the popular thing to do then. I guess it finally caught up to her."

"She didn't tell you?" Will sounds surprised.

I thought he would have gotten this information from Bree. Unless he's trying to be considerate, and not go off of second hand information. Or, maybe he's just trying to keep the conversation going. Keep me talking about it.

"Not until the day of." I swallow a forming lump. "I found out from a friend of hers. I went to the café but she wasn't there. When I asked dad, if she had cancer, he couldn't answer me. I knew it was true.

I tracked her down at the hospital. She made me promise her to not end up like her." I swallow a lump. The memory of her pops

247

up in the darkness. I open my eyes to stare at the ceiling. It helps the imagery to pass.

"She looked haunted. It was terrifying. She scared me. The look in her eyes. The grip on my wrist. It felt like she was already dead. Her ghost running through me and shaking me in my soul." As I say it, I can still feel it. Like her hand is still on my wrist.

A few tears grace the corners of my eyes. With nowhere to go, they pool until I wipe them. "I can't shake that. My last memory of her in that damn hospital; like that. I should have just stayed away or left when she first told me to."

"But of course you needed to see your mom. She's your mom. There wasn't going to be anything that could keep you away." The bed dips right before a warm body wraps an arm around me. He cradles me closer with the one arm, to come against his bare chest.

After a moment in hug, he continues. "When we lose someone, we can't help but think of our last memories of them. Like a final good bye. We want closure. But, I think you need to think about your entire lifetime of memories. Remember those and put them before her last day."

"It's hard." My admittance brings more tears with it. My head is pressed against his chest, and the amount of tears I'm shedding is reaching an amount that it starts to track down the side of my face; right onto his skin. I want to apologize, but I don't get the chance before he answers.

"And it might be for a while. But soon enough, with some practice and repetition, you'll be able to do it easier."

"She was always there. I don't know what I'm supposed to do without her." I sob. Holding on tight to my control, I hold in more to hear what he has to say.

Will's arm gets tighter around me. "Live. I think that's what the promise was about. She didn't want you to look back and regret your life. She wanted you to experience everything you want to experience and live."

"I don't even know what I want, other than her alive again." Breathing steadily gets harder and harder. I hold onto the next one, before taking in a deep breath. Successfully resetting my breathing to gain control.

"You don't have to have an answer right now. You'll get it figured out. If you're happy and loving life, I don't think there can be a wrong answer."

"I'm just so exhausted." All the time.

"Then sleep; for now. You've had a couple exhausting weeks. Tomorrow is a new day."

"Yeah." I agree. There's nothing else to say.

"Sweet dreams." Will leans in a bit to kiss my temple. He pulls back a little, but not too much. His head lowers to rest against my pillow, as he settles in to sleep against me. I find the warmth comforting.

"Sweet dreams."

Chapter 10

Dad: Are you coming in today?

The message repeats over and over; once a day, every day, since mom passed away.

I look over to Will as he stirs, then settles.

Oddly enough, if we hadn't talked about mom last night, I don't think I would have had the courage to start going through my messages.

I haven't answered anything, but I have been able to go through them; make them disappear from my messages.

I do feel able to answer dad.

I'm not ready yet.

You shouldn't be going in either. It's not going to help. Mom told me about the bankruptcy.

The phone screen turns dark with a call notice. I stare, not wanting to answer. I feel obligated to. He knows that I'm here. If I ignore the call, he will know it. There will not be any denying it.

I slip out of bed and click the answer icon. Answering vocalizing once I'm out of the bedroom. "Hi."

"Hi."

A long pause follows. I don't think he had planned out what he was going to say. I let him gather his thoughts in silence.

"It's good to hear your voice. How are you doing?" He finally says.

"A bit better. You sound exhausted." His voice comes through gravelly, and I don't think it's just the phone making it that way.

"I am." Dad takes a loud breath. "Your mom told you about the café."

"Yeah, she said it's only a matter of time before it shuts down. That's why she kicked me out and told me to start looking for another job."

Dad gets quiet. "I didn't know that."

"You didn't want to." He's never been easy to talk to about heavy things; I wonder if he knows that.

"I've lost your mother. I can't lose the café too." For him to admit that, is huge and out of character for him, but I'm glad he was able to admit a bit of vulnerability.

While I had been mourning my loss of my mom, I had completely forgot to think that he would be mourning his wife. Grieving the one person he decided to be with for the rest of his life. Someone he's loved for longer than I've been alive.

I hope he found a better way to deal with it than I did. Though I feel as though that would be too much to hope for. It's more likely he poured himself into his work and hasn't dealt with anything.

"You can't keep going like you have. It's obviously not working. You're probably too late anyway. Even if you make changes, it might be too late." I feel like I'm digging a stab wound deeper. My heart goes out to him despite my harsh words; meant with love. A dose of reality mom couldn't get him to take.

"I know." He dejects.

"Sell me the café." The words spill out from long lost ambition. "Let me revamp it. You declare bankruptcy and then you won't lose the café. I'll keep you on, but you have to let me

251

make any changes I need to, and maybe we can turn it around so both of us can keep the café."

"I'll think about it." That usually means no.

Annoyance pings. "Dad, it's either that, or within months you lose the café completely. You don't really have many options here."

"Okay. I'll talk with a lawyer and set things up." The call ends with a pronounced silence. He's never gotten the hang of ending a call properly.

I'm more surprised that he agreed to sell me the café; shocked that he'd agree. I wasn't expecting an affirmative. I was expecting the stubborn man to decline until he was blue in the face and the bank was taking away the keys.

"You want to buy the café?" Will's question jumpstarts my heart. My body moving with the sudden shock. I had been facing away from the bedroom door, so he was easy to miss.

Will stands leaning against the door frame. A sight to behold. Wild bedhead sticks hit hair in odd directions, pulling my eyes up from his bare broad chest. I could get used to walking up to a sight like this.

I stop my trail of thoughts there, reasoning that he's not mine and lives so far away.

"Maybe. I don't know. It was spur of the moment and I wasn't thinking he'd say yes." I take a moment to reflect. It's something that I had wanted at one point. I think I'd like to own my own business. There are so many memories, wonderful memories, in that building. "I don't know if it important because of me or mom, or what. But, I want to."

"Okay." Will smiles, nods, and accepts my answer. "So, what now?"

"I don't know. Dad said he'd get ahold of a lawyer." He takes the information in with more nodding.

"Are we going in to the café today?"

I guess he missed the first part of our conversation. "No. I told him I wouldn't."

A great pause breaks between us. "So, breakfast? How about bacon and eggs?" Will suggests.

Will walks towards the kitchen before getting my answer. I guess he's hungry first thing in the mornings. I usually like to wait a minute.

"Sure." I set forth to the kitchen, but to my surprise Will seems at home finding what he needs. It hits slowly the reason he knows where things are. The whole reason he is here.

I feel like we should talk about it at some point. It's the elephant in the room we've hidden under a blanket.

I thanked him for cleaning, and we managed to talk about mom. But, I feel like I should explain my behaviour. Explain how I stopped caring enough to live clean, to care enough to take a shower. How I numbed the pain with alcohol until the alcohol itself caused issues.

He hasn't asked, or pushed. I don't know how to bring it up. Or, if he'd even want to hear about it.

"I've got this," Will says as he lifts up and down the eggs and bacon he finds in the fridge. "Can you start the toast?"

"Sure." I open my freezer and search, but the bread isn't there. Thinking he may have put it in there fridge, I open that door too, but still come up empty. "Where's the bread?"

"Right here." He tugs on a bag of bread next to the toaster. "Why are you looking in the fridge for the bread?"

"I keep my bread in the freezer so it doesn't mold." Sidestepping him on the way to the bread and toaster, I preform my simple job. Pulling the bread from the bag and place four slices in the toaster.

253

"You just have to eat it before it gets moldy."

I hold up the loaf of bread, and make way for the fridge, so I can throw it in the freezer section. "Clearly, you either eat a lot of bread, or have never lived by yourself, because there is no way I can eat that much bread in just a few days." With my job done, I settle against the island to watch him work.

"Doesn't it get soggy from being in the fridge?" Will cracks some eggs into a buttered pan.

He's already got the bacon going in a different pan. If I had been paying attention before, I would have suggested making the bacon first, then using the fat for the eggs. It adds another level of flavour to the eggs. But, it's too late now. Maybe tomorrow.

"No never. You pop it frozen into the toaster and it toasts just fine. At least in the freezer, it lasts the month or so it takes me to go through the whole loaf."

He looks to me as he juggles egg shells on the way to the garbage can. "It takes you a month to go through a loaf of bread?"

"Yeah, sometimes." I follow through the logic to circle back. "That's why it needs to go in the freezer."

He nods his head side to side in a sort of agreement as he goes about flipping the bacon.

Will finishes cooking, and plates the food. I sit down at my table, and he sets the plate in front of me.

"Thank you." I dip a piece of bread into the egg yolk. Covering a section in yellow before taking a bite.

"I saw your Mexico shrine." Will digs into his food as though he hadn't brought up something potentially mortifying.

"It's not a shrine." I never should have told him about Bree's joke.

"I've got one too." He adds. He hadn't mentioned that before.

Suddenly I feel better about my display. "I've got a couple glass display cabinets with stuff from my travels."

"Yeah?" Tell me more.

I pile one of the eggs on top of my slice of toast. After dipping the yolks, the whites become an open faced sandwich. Something my dad taught me, that always bugged mom. Will doesn't seem to notice the odd habit, or he just doesn't say anything.

"Yeah. One's filled with stuff I've collected around the U.S. The other one is Mexico, with a shelf with other places. One day, I'll get enough to fill more cabinets. Maybe each continent will get their own."

"You're planning on travelling a bunch then?"

"Oh yeah, all over. I bought a huge map and pinned it to a cork board. I've been tacking everywhere I go."

"That's cool." My quick responses let him carry the conversation while I mostly eat. I feel lacking in the topic with only one travel location to date.

"It was that or I was going to get a tattoo of a map on me, and colour in the countries as I went to them. But, mom called up every tattoo parlour and paid them to ban me. By the time I checked the third place out, I figured it was too much work. It's probably a good thing now. The plan was a bit much. It was going sideways on my whole back. I had the idea when I was drunk, and it stuck around the next day."

"I mean, in theory it sounds cool, but yeah, probably a bit much." I couldn't imagine having a huge map on my body. I've never much wanted tattoos, but love how they look sometimes. It's always better when there's a story with it. But, a huge map covering an entire back seems like overkill. "Definitely like the cork board map idea better. I guess you've got a new pin to put in when you get back home."

"Yeah. I guess I do." Will's grin lights up his eyes. "Did you know that US has their map with USA in the center and they cut Asia in half?"

"What?" I try to comprehend what he's saying. How does one just cut a country in half for a map?

"Yeah, I grew up with a map that looked like this." He busies himself on his phone. "It was in all my textbooks. "They've probably changed it by now."

Will shows up his screen. The map does indeed cut countries apart so the USA can be in the center. "That's so weird. I thought all maps were standard to cut through the Pacific Ocean."

"No, not all. Didn't you hear? USA is the center of the universe? Really, if you follow any other map of the world, you're clearly wrong and hate the US." Will beams with exaggerated pride.

My eyes widen at his display. "Wow, going to go that route then?"

"Of course. USA! USA! USA!" He chants loudly. I'm afraid of my neighbours hearing this, though I doubt they'll complain about one outburst.

"You're being a stereotype." I tell him, in hopes he'll quieten on his own.

"Stereotypes have to come from somewhere. I'm sure you'd be amazed at all the stereotypes you could spot in just one day back home."

"I'm sure you'd know exactly where to go to find all those stereotypes too. Friends of yours?" I tease.

"Of course." I can't tell whether he's telling the truth, or going along with the joke still. Maybe, it's both. "You really aught to meet them. I've told them all about you." Will voice tightens up.

That stops my heart for a moment. "Have you?" Why would he tell others about me? What would he even say? I don't have to wait long.

"Yeah. Well, Silvia and Sam did most of the talking at first, but I had questions to answer afterwards. They're probably going to be like dogs with a bone when I get back." He says the last bit quieter and more to himself, I think.

I press for more information without asking him directly, exactly what it is that they've been told about me. "Inquisitive about me, are they?"

"Not every day I jump on a plane to go see a girl." Will gazes directly into my eyes. Heating up something in my heart.

My battered soul becomes overwhelmed with the feeling immediately. I distract myself by teasing him. "That's not normal behaviour; shocking." But I'm glad that it's unusual.

"Not every day, that I text a girl through the whole day either, or at least it used to not be normal."

"I'm flattered." I look down to my empty plate, urging my cheeks to remain their usual colour despite a warmth tickling at my heart and burning at my eyes.

Will takes my plate away. Stacking it on top of his to take to the sink. "Well, what do you say? Shower, change, and get on with our day?"

"Sure." I reply.

Chapter 11

Flour dusts my hands, and I dig into the dough. Turning and molding the dough to work all the ingredients together.

Will pours a splash of olive oil into the big red bowl and swirls it around a bit.

The ingredients mix together to form a sticky ball, too sticky for what we need. I add just a little bit more flour and work it in. When it's just a little tacky to the touch, rather than globs sticking to my hands, I place it into the bowl and cover it with plastic wrap.

"So now, we wait fifteen minutes for it to rise." Walking over to the sink, I turn the tap on to warm. A bit of soap and water breaks down the dough under my nails and pieced around my hands. It takes a thorough scraping under each nail to get them clean.

Turning around, Will waves his phone. "Do you mind if I grab the recipe from you?"

"Sure, go ahead."

Will takes a picture of the recipe in my book. It's handwritten; recipes I've stolen and rewritten out of mom's mass of cookbooks.

All her recipes have been edited from experience. She was always scratching out measurements to make her own. Other times, she'd add or remove whole ingredients from the list.

Mom's edits to the instructions were always the funniest. She'd take a long list of instructions and reduce it to "mix all" and baking temperature and time. Black lines reduced instructions and created a classified document appearance.

Spotting the mess of flour and dough bits on the counter, I grab a paper towel to clean it up. First, dry to get most of the mess swept off, then wet to clear away the remaining particles.

Will has found a new spot on a chair, playing with his phone. There is a bit of relief in that little brick; I won't have to figure out a way to entertain him for so long as he is on there.

Continuing the trend, I keep cleaning. Unloading the clean dishes out of the dishwasher, and loading up our breakfast dishes into it from out of the sink. Then, wiping down the other counters and the stove top.

I keep a glancing eye on the digital stove clock until the fifteen minutes pass.

The dough has grown two times its previous size; if not more. Unsealing the bowl, I take the dough out. It starts deflating immediately. I knead it a little and place it back in the bowl for a second round.

Will seems deeply committed in whatever is happening on his phone. A frown gracing his lips as he types something in. He must be texting someone about something.

I don't want to disturb an important conversation. Keeping my mouth shut, I make work out of nothing to look busy until five minutes are left. I set the stove to heat up to 375°.

Collecting the rest of the ingredients brings Will back to the kitchen from phone world. He pulls over the glass dish to set it beside my workspace.

I grease the pan with olive oil before placing the dough ball inside. The herbs inside are delightfully earthy.

"I think I've actually had foca-ca-chia before. It sounds like this amazing cheesy garlic bread I get from Costco sometimes." He peers over my shoulder at the bread I'm hand rolling into the glass pan.

"I'm sorry. You called it a what?"

"Foca-ca-chia? Isn't that what you called it?" He looks down at my recipe book, and to the word itself: focaccia. "Foca-kia. Foca-shia. Help."

I look back to what I'm supposed to be doing. Kneading the dough to fit into the pan, without taking it all the bubbles requires careful work and the least manhandling possible. "Fuh-cachia. Well, at least that's how my dad's always said it. If it's wrong, blame him."

"See, you don't even know what it is."

I pour olive oil on top and brush it around. "It's delicious bread. That's all we need to know."

A tickle itches my nose. At first I think I might have to sneeze, but I realize it's an outside skin itch. Wriggling my nose doesn't help. My hands are uselessly oiled up, and I don't want to contaminate the dough with a visitor around.

"What's happening with your face?"

"My nose is itchy."

He reaches a finger and scratches on the center of my nose. "There?"

"Yes, actually. Thank you." While his fingers are no longer there, his touch lingers.

I sprinkle the top with crushed garlic, shredded marble cheese, and shredded parmesan. Washing my hands before I place the pan into the oven and I set the timer. The click of the oven sets off a question.

Now what?

The question echoes in my mind.

Flitting my eyes to Will, to the clock, and around the kitchen.

I've already done the tidying. The one dirty bowl is practically nothing to deal with.

Quickly, I'm left to wonder what to do to fill the rest of our time. I had suggested baking to fill the time up, but now that there's a break in that I don't know what to do.

I wish I had more group entertainment things here. One person is fine to stream shows on a laptop, or spend hours surfing whatever on social media. But, with two, things get a bit harder. Hours of phone time could be rude. Streaming off a laptop could get uncomfortable fast.

Unfortunately, that might be the best I've got, without resorting to the liquor cabinet. I'd rather think I should be done day drinking for a while.

My phone buzzes against my thigh. It's dad sending a message.

Dad: Meet me at the café after 6.

"Guess we're meeting my dad at six." I tell him.

"Yeah?" Will asks.

"He doesn't say why." I type back telling him *Kk*.

"Would he have been able to get ahold of a lawyer that fast?"

"Maybe. He knows everyone in town." He's probably made friends with some lawyer or another over coffee. He's always taken the time to visit the other old guys over coffee when he's had time at the café.

There's still time before the focaccia is done, but the baking herbs are permeating the kitchen. The best part of baking bread is the smell.

"Want to watch a movie?" I ask Will.

Chapter 12

"Who are you?" Dad gruffly interrogates the man beside me.

Will doesn't miss a beat. I have no chance to introduce him myself. "Will Bogtrotter. A friend of your daughter's." Will sticks out his hand to shake it with my father's hand.

Dad eyes Will suspiciously, but moves on rather quickly.

"I suppose you'll need a witness. Better to get it done now. Sign these." He demands. Dad holds out a manila envelope thick with papers.

"What is it?" I ask him. I lift open the seal.

"I'm gifting you the café." My head jerks up in surprise. "These are the legal documents to signing it over. You get the café, and I keep the debt."

"Gifting." I reiterate. "You're just giving it to me? Can you do that?"

He nods. "My lawyer ensured me I can."

"Why?" Why just give it to me? Why keep the debt?

"As an inheritance given prior to my death. You would have been getting it anyway, so there's no use arguing that I should sell it to you."

"Thank you." I say, remembering manners suddenly, though the two words do seem like they are enough. Dad wanders back into the kitchen without another word.

Opening the envelope, I take out the papers to stare at the papers in hand. All the words and legal jargon swirl through my head. I can understand the concept, but I can't help but think of legal implications; maybe also tax implications.

Can he really do this without blow back to me? Is he going to apply for bankruptcy after? Can he do that without it looking like some sort of fraud?

My worrying thoughts take over until none of this make sense.

"What are you thinking?" Will asks. I realize I've just been standing awkwardly staring at the papers for some time now.

"It's overwhelming." I look to him, then around the room. With new eyes on the building. It's a different feeling, going from being my parents café to my own. An urge fills me to make it my own place. Prideful want to make this place the best it can be. "What do you think of the café?"

"It's," he pauses trying to find a word, "nice."

I know he doesn't really mean nice. "But…"

"Dark."

I look at the room as a whole. "Yeah, I noticed that too." Recently.

"You'll need a small facelift. Your customers will want to see something, if they're to think anything is changed. You'll have to change their mindset about this place. More employees. An updated modern fancy coffee set of options. Something for those who don't drink coffee. Give people a reason to come in and stay for a bit. People like to see shops that have people in them." Will shifts into business mode quickly. "You'll want to do an official relaunch. Get the word out there about it. Have signs for it. Specials. Maybe a tasting night, to give out samples for your best tasting food and drinks."

"Lots of work and lots of money." I summarize.

Will stops gazing at the room to come back to me. "You were expecting that."

"Yeah. Of course." I feel like I need to reassure him. I can only imagine the trouble I'd be in if I didn't think I'd have to spend money to change things around here. "It's just different now that it's a reality."

"If you need help, you could always look for potential investors." Will's comment simplifies the notion too much. I can't just find investors behind the couch or on a store shelf.

"Who would want to invest in another café?" I'm incredulous. The market has probably been saturated enough with cafés. We're going to need something to set us apart for just another café.

"I would." Will squares up with me. "I'll put up half for a half partnership."

What? No. I have to dissuade him. "I couldn't do that to you. It's a bad investment."

"All business ventures can be swung in such a way that it can be a bad investment. It's rare to find a truly great investment. And have nothing go wrong. There's potential here."

He sounds certain, but I'm not so sure I want to risk his money too. "I'd need to think about it."

Why would he even consider investing in an already once failed café? I have family ties in my reasoning. He has nothing.

"You need to make it official first. Read, then sign the papers. I'm sure your dad's lawyer will be needing it back."

"What are you going to do?" I ask.

Will shrugs. "I'll find things."

I mix the next hour between reading the papers and watching Will scurry around the café cleaning and helping the occasional customer. It's prime supper time, but there is no rush.

He seems like a natural, but then I remember his long list of job titles; barista was somewhere in there. I'm sure he didn't mention everything either. He could have other waiting experience.

If I do take his partnership offer, at least I know he's comfortable in the environment and not just a pretty face newbie with money to burn.

I take the signed papers into the back where dad is stirring something in a pot. "Hey. I've signed the papers. Do you think you could get me a copy of all the records? Suppliers, expenses, accounting, and anything else."

"Most of that should be in the office." I nod and turn, but then think about what mom told me about fixing the books.

"Is it the undoctored version?"

He speaks without looking to me. Just continues to stir. "There is no undoctored version. Your mom would take the cash out sheets and transfer the information into a book. We'd claim a few days and weeks of closed days each year, when the shop was really open. The books will tell you, we were closed and didn't make anything. The food made was expensed as wasted food. We shredded the receipts and cash out sheets for those days."

"I guess, I'll work with what we have then." The accounting books will be useless for all except the template. I can try to budget off them, but I don't know if it'll be a true vision.

Will comes into the back room. "Hey, Bree says she wants a Bree salad?"

"Of course she does." I leave to the till with Will. Dad rustles about starting to make Bree her order.

"Hey." I greet her.

"I'd like to complain." Bree musters up a stern voice, but her smile reveals her true jest. "Newbie here, has no idea how to work the till."

"Can't blame newbie for not knowing the procedure for when our most spoiled rotten customer comes in." Turning to Will, I

265

make sure he's paying attention, then I ring in the order. "A Bree salad and a drink is five dollars. So, just press the FIVE and CASH." Bree hands over the money, so I can finish the transaction.

Will asks. "And, what's a Bree salad?"

"Leftovers from the kitchen toss together into a salad." I say.

"Don't put it like that." Bree admonishes. "I don't like salads with a lot of lettuce. So, there's a bunch of cut up veggies and whatever for meat in there. Sometimes other things. No dressing. Her dad makes it differently every time."

"Because it's made from whatever he happens to have on hand at the moment. Hence leftovers salad." We come full circle.

"Oh, shut up and just feed me." Bree huffs in mock anger.

"Dad's making it now." Dad exits the kitchen just as I mention him. He places the salad into Bree's regular spot after wordlessly checking with Bree.

"Mr. Bryson, how about you go home? We've got the café and you look exhausted." Bree tells him.

I look him over. His eyes appear puffy and glazed over, and hair a bit wild from finger combing. Bree has a good idea. "Yeah, dad. I've got this. There hasn't been too many customers. We can close down the kitchen for the night for anything more complicated than a sandwich."

"Alright. You have yourselves a good night." Dad walks into the back for only long enough to grab his coat. Bree's mouth drops down as he walks by and out the door.

"He must've been exhausted. Normally he'd fight tooth and nail to stay." Bree's right. He wouldn't normally leave until he's good and ready.

"Did he take the soup off the stove?" Will asks. I remember that he was stirring a pot a minute ago. Will doesn't wait for an answer and goes to the kitchen to see for himself.

I realize I never got the mind to tell her yet about the café. "Could be the change up."

"What change up?"

"I own the café now." I tell her.

"WHAT?" Her exclamation fills the café. I look around for someone to apologize to, but we have no customers.

"Dad gave me the café. He's keeping the debt." I tack on the last part before she asks and had a chance to be concerned.

She thinks for a moment. "Can he do that?"

I shrug, still unsure myself. "Supposedly."

"Wow. Alright Sky. Boss guy now. Can I have a job?"

I can't tell if she's joking or not. "I can't pay much. You have bills to pay."

"Part time, silly."

"I don't know." I stretch out in sing song. Of course I'll hire her. She's worked here tonnes of times. "Do you have experience? What about your references?"

"Sky." She hits my name hard in warning.

"How's your cooking?" Bree glares at me. She's a horrible cook. I'd never let her anywhere near the café kitchen. "Yes. You can have a job."

"Yay." She bounces up in a little dance.

"Are you going to eat your salad?" I remind her.

She jerks, suddenly pulled towards her food. "I almost forgot." Bree stabs a bit of chicken and shovels it into her mouth. "Do I get a food discount now?"

"You always have."

Bree hums as she knows I'm right. She eats her food in a hungered hurry. I've stopped worrying about her choking ages

267

ago.

Will comes back. "I put the soup into the container, and into the fridge. I wasn't sure what else he'd be doing with it."

"No, that sounds right. It was probably a stock for tomorrow." It concerns me that he'd just leave the soup on the stove. Maybe he's more exhausted than I'd thought. He should've said something as he was leaving at the least.

Maybe I should go visit him. Check in on him and see how he's doing.

Bree loudly clears her throat for attention. "Well, what do you think Miss cafe owner? Is there a use in keeping the shop open when you have no customers?"

I channel what my dad would say; has said at one time or another. "There could be an argument made for keeping open for the possible customers who might show up. Can't make any money when closed. But might make money while open. Then, again when you counteract the expenses to stay open versus-"

"Sky." Bree presses.

"We'd still need to cash out, and clean up the shop for the morning. If no one shows up by the time we finish cleaning, then I'll cash out and close up. Sound fair?" I make the deal terms, but I don't really see a point in keeping it open either. It's dead during a time when we should be busy.

"We'll help with the cleaning, then party party." Bree whoops a couple times before taking her empty plate into the kitchen.

I assign Will a list of jobs to be done to close to the dining area, while I close up the bar area. Bree eventually comes back to help Will.

Chapter 13

There is no click to my key turn. I turn the other way and try the handle, but the door doesn't budge. Did I forget to lock my door? I turn the key again and open my door.

The lights are on and Bree flits around the island with my blender. Some bottles are already deposited there. She hasn't had too much time ahead of us, but it was enough.

"I thought Will had your key." I say. I thought maybe we had beat her here, since she wasn't outside my door, but I guess not.

"I made him a copy of my key."

"Don't let my landlord know that." I lightly reprimand with a stern tone. I'm not supposed to have extra keys cut for my door. Especially, not ones to be given out to random boys. The thought of Will having an illicit spare key doesn't disturb me as much as I thought it might.

We take off our outdoor gear and settle up inside. Grabbing an assortment of drinks for the visit. We sit in my living room. Getting comfortable as we talk.

"So, are you going to have to go in early tomorrow?" Bree asks.

"To work?" Bree nods. "I hadn't thought about that." Should I go in early to help dad out? Or, would we keep our same schedule? Would dad assume to keep the usual schedule?

"Are you going to shut the store down for rebranding?" Will asks.

"Yes, but I hadn't thought so soon. I think it might be best to wait until I have an idea for what it should look like first." Numerous tasks and dollar tags add up simultaneously in my head. Maybe Will was right. "But, I think I'd have to discuss that with my investor-partner. If you still want to I mean."

Will's grin grows. "Of course." I feel like I should shake hands with him, or make him sign something, but he doesn't move and it would likely make it awkward to pounce on legalities right now.

Bree takes a breather from drinking. "What?"

I catch her up on the deal Will offered. "Will said he would 50/50 with me if he was an equal partner."

Without missing a neat, Bree smirks and asks, "so, when's the wedding?"

"Not that kind of partnership," I shout back. If I had a pillow, I'd throw it at her for making the suggestion I front of Will.

"Oh, come on. You'd make a cute couple." She gushes.

Words cannot express the rush of confusing and conflicting feelings, though my mouth opens to try. I completely avoid looking towards Will. Part of me wants to know how he's reacting to a relationship suggestion with me, but I don't think I could handle any sign of rejection.

For all I know, any sign of interest doesn't mean much to him.

"Maybe we'll figure out rebranding tomorrow morning. Figure out a timeline to close down, renovate and rebrand, and when the reopening will be." Will places our conversation back on track, and I am thankful for that.

"That sounds great." I brave meeting his gaze.

"Good. It sounds like I'm going to have to leave tomorrow afternoon though. My dad is calling an emergency meeting. I should be able to get back in a few days to help out. But, until then I'll have to work with you virtually."

"Okay. No problem." Little problem. I didn't think he'd end up leaving so soon. Especially after agreeing to invest in the café. I figured he would stick around to help renovate. I'll have to readjust my thinking. He lives far away, I shouldn't have expected him to be anything much more than a silent partner.

"No work talk tonight." Bree declares. "I'm out. Who else needs more?"

Bree helps herself to another round before we start playing cards. Go fish keeps the mood light, and conversations going.

Bree beats Will and I for rounds of drink; though Will isn't far behind. My drinking binge has the alcohol leaving a bitter feeling. Very quickly, my drinks only inhibit a splash of alcohol each. I mix them myself while Bree is distracted. I love her, but she can be a bit pushy with the alcohol.

I snap open another can of coke, then splash a little rum inside.

"Sky was totally bummed you didn't come out when she asked. It took me a whole week to get her out of a funk." Bree audaciously stated.

"No I wasn't." I deny. Shooting Bree death glares, I signal for her to end this topic.

"That's alright," Will chuckles. "Honestly, I was looking at flights, but I thought you might be a bit weirded out by it. I figured it would be better to get to know each other more and revisit it later."

"Awe that's adorable." Bree coos. "Get a room. Please. There's one right there. Sky needs to get laid."

Will beats me in protest. "I have a rule. I don't have sex after drinking alcohol, unless agreed upon before drinking occurred by both involved."

"What?"

"It means that I won't do more than kissing after consuming alcohol."

271

"Yeah, right." Bree scoffs. She doesn't believe him.

"Why?" I ask. People with rules like that, usually have a reason. Something they learnt through experience.

"Because, I was young and stupid once. Had sex a few times with very eager and persistent drunk girls, that I ended up regretting the next day." Will's answer is a bit vague, but it answers the question well enough. "If you set up a strict rule before hand, most women leave you alone. Especially, if you tell them it's for their own benefit."

"I don't know. I think I'd take it as a challenge and try harder." Bree admits.

Will turns to look at me, but holds his palm up in a motion towards Bree. "And, then some girls are like that."

Bree opens her mouth wide, making a dramatic production out of yawning. "I'm tired. I'm going to go home. You can keep the party going. Maybe move somewhere a bit more comfortable." She wags her eyebrows suggestively.

"You've been drinking. You can't drive." Will tells her.

"I'll walk." Bree tells him in a bold faced lie. She's never had a problem drinking and driving. It's reckless and idiotic, but I haven't ever been able to convince her otherwise. She reasons it's such a short distance away and she's careful. The fact that she's never been caught, has emboldened her to continue.

I wonder about calling her out.

"You're not walking alone at this time of night." Will insists.

"It's Devon. Nothing bad happens here."

"You'll freeze."

"She is right. The likelihood of something happening is small. But, he is also right. You can just stay here. There's no point to going home at this point." I reason. Hopefully, I can convince her, otherwise she will just drive herself home. The snowfall makes it more dangerous than usual.

"I'm not sleeping on the floor." Bree crosses her arms.

"I've got a sleeping bag. You can sleep in Skylar's bed." Will suggests.

Bree gives up. "Fine, but just know I'm not taking the blame for being a clock block."

"Alright, I think you need to go to bed. Maybe a bit too much merriment tonight."

Chapter 14

Placing the sign on the door, I take a step back. It seems monumental to put the sign up for everyone to see.

Closed For Renovations

A plan has been set. A small facelift is in order; major cleaning, painting, and décor take the bulk of it. Minimal renovations with minimal money, but things that will hopefully have a greater impact.

I rub my chilled fingers together.

One big moment down, another to go. I hop back into the car with Will.

Silence follows us to the airport. I park my car in the unloading zone. The sign says I have five minutes. Another insists it's an unloading zone only. I'm afraid if I leave my car, someone will come ticket me. Though I do wish I could go inside, if only to stretch out these last few minutes together.

Will grabs his bag from my back seat. I step around the car to meet him on the side walk.

Each step closer, I know I'm getting closer to him leaving. It becomes harder to breath. Once he goes beyond those doors, he's gone.

I shake my head. It's silly. He's only leaving for a few days. Back to his dad's for the emergency thing, then back here. He promised he'd be back to help with whatever renovations are left, and reopening the café.

The feeling won't shake away. It's leaving Mexico all over

again. I just hope I don't cry I front of him.

"Well, this is it." He starts.

"Yeah." I say softly.

"I'll let you know when I land. And, I'll get you the information for my flight back, when I get that figured out." Will sets out his plan.

"Great. Perfect. Hope you have a safe trip."

Will braces me tightly, and kisses the top of my head. I smile big at him when he pulls away.

He turns and the tears fill into my eyes. I scold myself. If I can't stop the crying, then I need to stop watching him walk away.

Will turns around. I smile and hope he misses the tears. But with a downturn, I know he has.

He comes back to me with a magnetic force. Grasping me. "I'll be back."

I'm embarrassed of my feelings and lack of control of them. "I'm sorry. It's weird."

He pulls back enough to place his lips onto mine. A sweet kiss.

"I'll miss you too. I'll be back sooner than you know it." Will loosens his embrace a little to lean back. "In the mean time, we can call or text. You can FaceTime me. Send me picture updates. I'll let you know what a miserable time I'm having with the family, then I'll be back on a plane here."

"You're right." Knowing it, doesn't make me feel better inside, but I put on a show on the outside. "I'm sorry. It's weird. It just happened."

"It's fine. It's not weird." He brushes my lips with his. "Feel what you need to feel and never apologize for your feelings."

"Yeah." I'm torn between wanting this to last and wanting to run away. The latter wins out. "You should probably get going before you miss your flight."

"Are you going to be alright?"

"Yeah."

He gives pause, then points a finger at me. "Text me."

I agree and we part ways.

Chapter 15

Check listing the items on the table, I make sure I didn't forget anything for tomorrow. There's still time to go out and get anything I could possibly need; as long as I make the trip into Edmonton and what I need is open after nine.

Final final details for the grand opening will have to wait for tomorrow morning. Everything else is done that can be done.

Food prep in the kitchen is complete as much as can be done today. Tomorrow morning will bring the bulk of it. Everything behind the counter is set up and ready to go. Helium balloons will have to wait until the morning, and redone through the day as they get acquired by children.

I can only hope the staff are trained enough to be able to serve customers tomorrow. Two days of a few hours of training, doesn't seem like enough time.

I go back behind the counter. My cheat sheets are laminated and beside each station. Running through them, for the thousandth time, I read for simplicity and straightforwardness.

If the shop gets busy, I might not have the time to zip by every time someone needs help with making a drink.

Should I try to keep behind the till? No, I shake myself inwardly. I'll be needed flitting around and making sure everything is running smoothly. I'll need to greet people.

If the shop can even get busy enough.

A knock at the door surprises me out of my thoughts. A small crowd of people stand outside in the darkness.

I walk over to the door, rehearsing a polite, 'we're closed. Please come back tomorrow for out Grand ReOpening.'

The words aren't needed when I get close enough to see the faces on the other side.

I unlock the door to let them inside. "What are you doing here?" I ask with multiple sentiments.

Bree's the least of my concern, when I see the three people she's brought with her.

Will wasn't supposed to arrive until tomorrow. And, Silvia and Sam have come with him.

"Surprise!" Silvia pushes past the others to lunge at me. "We thought we'd surprise you. The café looks amazing. You look great. Sorry about your mom."

I don't really know what to say. I pick out the compliment and focus on that. "Uh, thank you."

Sam chimes in. "And, Katherine didn't trust Will to be back in a couple days for Mr. Bogtrotter's birthday, so we were sent along to make sure he returns."

The two of them pass on by to start their own tour of the dining room. Bree follows them and starts telling them about how it used to work to emphasize how much work has done into the last week.

"See, I need babysitters too." Will jokes softly. He holds up a bottle. "I brought champagne to celebrate."

I don't know how to react to him. I want to kiss him. We left things off with sweet kisses. But, I don't know what they meant.

Was it a comfort tactic? We kissed just fine in Mexico, but that was on vacation. Then, he kisses me, but that could have been just to comfort me.

Now, were business partners and he doesn't appear to be disappearing anytime soon. But, I don't know where that leaves us, and I don't think I want to find out while there are witnesses.

Letting him take lead seems like the safest bet of the moment.

"Thank you." I take the bottle and leave him to go behind the counter. Setting the booze on the counter to pull out enough glasses for all of us. Silvia takes over to put drink to glass and glass to person.

"To Will and Sky. Wishing you a successful launch tomorrow." Silvia's toast is brief, but well enough. We raise our glasses high in mock clinking before drinking.

Bree continues to escort Silvia and Sam in a whirl of excitement to show them around.

Will pulls me in a hug. "Good surprise?"

"Yeah." I try not to be bitter. Of course they all show up after the work it all done, then make a mess. It's just glasses but it's still five more glasses I have to wash now. I pin point the real issue, it's not just the glasses, it's all the work I've had to put in this last week, while they've done nothing.

"Sorry I couldn't make it out sooner." His apology rubs off as well as the purchases, as appreciated as they were.

I take the high road for the moment. I don't want spite to ruin this. "That's okay. You did more than enough to help out. Let me know what I owe you for the machines."

"Those are on me."

"I still need the receipts for taxes and insurance." I insist. I can get tax write offs for it, but only if I have the receipts.

"Right." Will smiles sheepishly. "I'll need your email address, unless you want me to print them off. They we're email receipts."

"Email's fine. I'll text you the address." I send him my email in a quick text, so I don't forget about it later.

"Business talk! Seriously!" Bree smiles mischievously with her

279

outburst.

Will and I part with the new attention.

"Yes, business talk. What still needs to be done?" Will asks me.

"Well, those glasses all need to get cleaned now." I've finished everything else, without the help. If they are offering to help, they might as well wash dishes. "I don't know. I think I've finished everything, but I was going over it all again just incase."

"Sky the worrier. It'll be great. Everything looks great." Bree tries to reassure my nerves.

"I just want to make sure we're ready for anything tomorrow." I admit.

"We will be. Don't worry. You have us coming in ridiculously early, we'll be well prepared by the time we get the first customer." Bree's complaint isn't new. She's been complaining since I gave her her scheduled shift.

I got over it all again. It's practiced speech at this point. "It's not ridiculously early. We open at 6 am. That's the same time as the other coffee shops in town."

"Then, why do I have to be here for five thirty."

"Prep time before go time."

"I have to wake up at four." She complains.

Bree's pining her unrealistic expectations on me. "No one said you have to look ready for prom. You just have to be presentable. I can guarantee you, but the time a month has gone, most of the morning shift will be rolling out of bed fifteen minutes before their shift starts, and will still be here on time and perfectly ready to go."

"It takes time to look like this." She motions towards herself.

"Then lose the sleep, I don't care." I put out harshly.

"Wow. Grouchy. Maybe you need sleep."

"What time are you coming in tomorrow?" Will asks me.

"Five."

"Alright." He pulls out his phone to fiddle on.

"Then I guess you're taking the car keys once we get back to the hotel. I'm not waking up that early." Silvia declares to Will. I guess that she thinks Will will be here at opening. It hadn't occurred to me, but I guess it would make sense he would want to be there since he's here now.

Will shrugs. "Told you we should have gotten two cars."

"Yeah, yeah." Silvia mutters.

Sam looks to her. "It doesn't seem that far from the hotel to here. We can just walk over, or call a taxi or something. Or make Will come back to pick us up."

"I'm not walking out there. Do you know how cold it is?"

"I could pick Will up on my way here, if you wanted to be here for opening." I offer. It does seem like that would solve their issue, and if he plans on being here at opening anyway, then he might as well come here with me.

"Yes!" Silvia jumps on the offer. "We're at the Key West Inn. Make sure to call before hand to make sure he's up. He'll sleep in otherwise."

"I'll make sure to have an alarm set." Will assures me.

"I can call before I leave to make sure you're up." If he really does have a problem getting up in the morning, then he'll have a few minutes to pull himself together.

"Sure. Thanks."

"Well, it's been a long day. I'm ready to get back to the hotel." Silvia comes over to me and wraps her arms around me briefly. "I'm so glad we got to see you tonight."

281

"Yeah, me too."

"We'll see you tomorrow. I can't wait." Silvia leaves a whirlwind behind her. Sam chases after her.

Will apologizes in a half smile. "I guess I'll see you tomorrow morning."

Bree comes over for a quick hug. "Do you want me to come back?"

"No, that's okay."

We say good bye and everyone leaves. I shake off a pit in my stomach wondering why Will got himself a hotel room this time.

Their whirlwind visit created a little chaos in here. I sigh. I guess I have to clean dishes before I leave.

Chapter 16

A steady stream of people flow in and out; they have all day. There's a buzz in the air from many voices talking their own things at the same time.

Each uttering of, "excuse me," is met with small movements to let me pass by. When it's not, it leads to quick conversations and practiced answers.

"Thanks for coming out."

"Hope to see you soon."

"I'm glad you like it."

"He's still here. Very busy tonight, so I don't know if he'll get out of the kitchen."

"I'll let dad know. Thank you."

"That's Will. He's my business partner and an investor."

"I'll take those for you."

Those are the easy conversations.

"I'm sorry about your mom. How are you doing?"

"Your mom would be so proud."

"I wish your mom was here to see this."

Every utterance of "mom" punches me in the gut. All my strength is used up to sound in some semblance of my normal voice. I wish everyone would stop bringing her up today. I've cried three times between my office and the bathroom today already.

Skylar Bryson

It feels like today has been one whole extension of her funeral. A nightmare funeral where I'm forced to host and serve each guest.

The whole town seems like they've wandered in and out at sometime tonight. Which is great for business, but I can't help but feel it's not entirely meant for me.

"My God, watching you flit around here, I thought I saw your mom's ghost for a moment there. You remind me so much of her. What a way to honor her memory." Mrs. Spratt sucks me in for a tight hug.

I choke up. Her words hammer at my heart. The last time we talked started off the worst day of my life. "Thank you. I'm sorry, I need to get something from the back. I hope you enjoy the grand opening."

"Of course. Busy busy tonight. I'll leave you be." She let's me go, not that I was waiting for her permission.

I hang my head down and bee line for the kitchen door. Wisps of hair line my face but aren't enough to hide inevitable tears.

I run into the bathroom door when a quick turn to the doorknob yields nothing. I attempt the turn another time to find the door locked.

Panicking, I leave out the back door. Cold air bites at me. Tears unload while my breathing accelerates.

The door swings open behind me, the creak spinning me around. Apology ready in my throat.

Will wraps arms around me. "Breathe." He reminds me softly. On command, my throat opens up to let air in and out. "Did something happen?"

"Mom." The one word blurts out and takes all other possible words with it. Both explanation and reason, but not heavy on the detail.

His hugs tightens in a empathetic squeeze. "Your mom

sounded like a great woman. I wish I could have met her. She'd be very proud of you."

"Would she?" I back out of his arms but not out of reach. "Isn't this exactly what she made me promise not to do?"

"No. You are doing things differently. You're not giving your life to the café. You are creating a life out of the café. You have plans and dreams. You are making the café what it needs to be. Working hard so you can vacation around the world eventually; do what you love. She just didn't want the café to consume you. She wanted you to live a life you won't end up regretting. I'm sure of it."

I nod. There's nothing else I can do. It's been a long day, and yet it's still not over. "We should get back in there."

"I will get back in there. You need a break. Did you want to come inside so you don't freeze? Go hide in the office?" The way he words it, like I have a choice. But he pulls me with him into the building.

"Okay."

We go into the office and he has me take a seat. Will makes to leave but pops his head back around the door for one short sentence. "Please don't shut down again."

Chapter 17

Dropping my keys on the island, I take off my boots and jacket next.

The warmth of the condo air doesn't touch how numb I feel inside.

I leave Will at the door. His insistence on following me back home likely had something to do with my breaking down earlier, but I couldn't bring myself to argue.

My bed calls to my exhaustion, but I know I can't go there quite yet.

"I'm going to clean up. I'll be back soon." I hide away in my bathroom to wash the day away and get ready for bed. Layers of sweat scrub off in a three minute shower.

Another three minutes, and I'm wandering out into the living room. The other bathroom door is closed, and Will's things are still here. I didn't scare him off yet.

My stomach aches. I'd like to go straight to bed, but Will put a wrench in those plans. Searching the fridge, I settle on cold pizza. Grabbing a slice straight out of the box to munch on without a plate, I take it to bed with me.

A hollow flush sounds as I pull back my covers. I climb inside. Holding my one hand under the pizza, I take a bite and try to catch any crumbs that might fall.

Will exits the bathroom and appears in my door shortly after. He's changed into sweats and a t-shirt. I guess that's why he brought the bag up with him. "Any more of that?"

"In the fridge."

Will comes back after a short escapade. He hands me a paper towel piece. "Thanks."

"You're welcome." He sits down on the edge of the bed close to where I sit.

"Seems like we had a successful launch." I start a light conversation. "I had some people mention they heard about us through the City's Facebook page. Did you do that?"

"I took care of some marketing. Figured since I couldn't be here for the hard work, that I could do some extra marketing. Got an ad in the paper, posted on anything Devon related about the opening, looked up and posted to anything I could find for close towns, and in Edmonton. I snapped some pictures tonight to post up on the cafés social media pages. I made a couple social media pages; Instagram and Twitter."

"You were busy." Maybe, he didn't quite deserve my bitterness about him leaving everything to me. He paid for quite a few items I wouldn't have been able to purchase otherwise, and successful marketing. He put in an effort.

"I felt bad I couldn't be here." Will admits.

"Sounded like you were needed back home. Is your dad alright?" In all the times we messaged, he never did get into details about the emergency. Just that it wasn't as an immediate of an emergency as was suggested, but that it would take longer to sort out. Being that it seemed like a family matter, I didn't want to push. If he didn't want to tell me, then so be it.

"Yeah. Everyone's convinced he was just pulling some dramatics before turning fifty. Midlife crisis or something."

"Maybe he got a case of feeling mortal." Could his father be hiding the same sort of secret as mom did?

"We all feel that way sometimes; I suppose."

287

"Especially when someone dies." I mutter a bit too loud.

"Are you feeling any better?" Will asks just as I take a big bite to finish off my pizza. We both realize what happened, and wait for me to swallow.

"Yeah."

"Are you sure?" He presses on.

"I'm fine." I try.

"No, you're not." Will calls my bluff.

Deciding that lying to him another time isn't going to work, I spill a tidbit of honesty. "Well, I'm not crying and I'm not getting drunk, so I'm well enough."

"You can cry if you need too, but I don't recommend getting drunk seeing as we have an early morning." His jesting nudge loosens my lips more.

"I'm more numb than feeling like I need to cry. I don't know if that's because I'm exhausted or because.. I just can't feel anymore right now."

Will ponders for a moment. Leaning in, he pulls me closer so we meet lips in the middle.

A spark ignites in my chest. The effect of our kiss immediate. Perhaps, I can feel things after all.

Will pulls away too soon. "Feel anything?"

"Yes."

He smiles in triumph that his little experiment worked. "We'll blame it on the exhaustion then."

"I guess I should get some sleep then." I urge. One question remains. "Are you staying here or going back to the hotel?"

"I'll stay, if you want me too?"

"Stay."

Will closes the gap between us, placing on hand around the back of my head, as the other indents the bed beside my hip. Our lips mash when I meet him with more ferocity. Actively participating this time.

He breaks the kiss to pull away slightly. "Will you be my girlfriend?"

If this goes wrong, it could risk the café. A thousand no's and reasons could be brought forth, yet I take a terrifying leap. "Yes."

"Good. Or else, this could've gotten awkward really fast." His goofy grin pulls up the corners of my own mouth. I can't help but smile with him. "We really should go to bed though. Early morning."

Will leaves our embrace to turn off the light. When he returns, he let's himself in on the other side of the bed.

This time, he sets himself closer to the middle of the bed. I take it as a silent suggestion for cuddles. Rolling over, I snuggle against his side.

I'm ecstatic of the possibilities. But, mostly, relieved to finally have a concrete answer to what we are.

Will's warmth lulls me to a comforting sleep.

Chapter 18

Ringing wakes me up. I pick up my phone but the sound isn't coming from mine.

Will runs in from the kitchen and picks up the phone on the other nightstand. "Where the hell are you?" Silvia's voice booms loud enough I can hear her despite the phone call not being on speaker.

"I stayed with Sky last night." He mouths, 'sorry' to me.

"Why did we even bother to get you a hotel room?! Never mind, get your ass back here, pack up your shit, we need to get to the airport in an hour." I look at the clock; it's nearly four. My alarm would be going off in about ten minutes anyway. There's no point in going back to sleep.

"I'm already packed. I'll be there in twenty minutes to checkout. That still leaves plenty of time."

"Whatever."

Will looks at his phone, confirming Silvia's hung up. "Good morning. Sorry about that."

"No, that's alright. It sounds like I should be up anyway." If he's got to leave, then I should see him go. It's the polite thing to do.

"It's about that time. Stay here." Will rushes out the door. I'm left for a moment, listening to a couple instances of clinking dishes, before he comes back with two plates of pancakes.

"Thank you." I say as I take my plate.

"You're welcome. I've got something else for you." Will sets his plate down near my feet. Reaching into his pocket, Will removes a little red box.

Inside, is a pink pearl attached at its top to a delicate silver chain. "It's beautiful. You didn't have to get me anything."

"I wanted to. Part grand opening present. Part hoping you'd agree to date me." He smirks with the second part.

It warms my heart know that he had this planned. That he didn't just ask me on a whim last night. "Thank you. It's beautiful."

"You're welcome."

"These look great." I carve out a piece and take a bite. Tastes like a normal cooked pancake. I dip another piece in the syrup he pooled on the side.

"Just box mix pancakes, but I did add chocolate chips." He cuts into his pancake with his fork. "Looks like I'll have to leave right away here. I miscalculated last night. I meant to have more than five minutes for breakfast and goodbyes."

"That's alright. We'll have more time another time." I try to look on the bright side.

Will's phone rings again. "What?" Silvia speaks quieter this time. All I can make out is mumbles. "Eating breakfast." Pause. "I'm leaving soon. Bye." He hangs up.

"I think Silvia's getting impatient." I tell him.

"She's always impatient." Will sighs. "But, she's also never late. Which means I've probably got one more phone call before she's going to track me down and drag me out of here." He very quickly scarfs down the last bit of pancake left on his plate. I do the same.

We take our dishes to the sink before he gets another call. "Leaving out the door now." He says in a one sided conversation. He hangs up right after. "Well, I guess this is it."

291

Will puts on his jacket and shoes. He collects a bag tucked into the laundry room.

"Have a safe flight. Message me when you get there." I say.

"Of course. Have a good day at the café. Tell Bree I said bye."

"Yeah."

Will comes in close. Looping one arm around my back, he loops the other hand to rest against the side of my head; pulling me in for a sweet kiss. Satisfied with lip on lip, neither of us deepen the kiss.

We parts ways with good byes, and I close the door behind him.

I look at the clock. Dad should be at the café. I might as well get ready and go a bit early.

Chapter 19

The warm sandwich melts in my mouth with the jus on it. I immediately give it the green flag to be on the menu. Maybe make it a special to introduce it.

I see my screen light up with a message.

Will: How's work?

Great! Just on lunch. Trey makes an incredible roast beef and jus sandwich.

Dad's taking the day off tomorrow. He's actually taking a day off. Trey's all trained up and is, according to dad, sufficient at making the food.

Will: That's great. Does he know what he's going to do with himself?

Nope. I type asking him, *When do you think you might come visit again?* But, I erase without sending. I don't want to push him. It's been a few weeks already, and I feel like he should be here, but I tell myself logically I can't expect him here all the time. He lives too far away for that.

Will: How's the new manager working out?

Good. I'm actually leaving at 2 today. Leaving the rest of the day to him.

Will: That's awesome. Maybe you can start having regular shift hours.

Will: Even better. This means you might be able to get Christmas off.

Skylar Bryson

Yeah. I'm thinking that we might close for the day. Give everyone the day off that way. Most businesses are either closed or they adjust their hours.

Will: I was thinking maybe you take Christmas off completely. Give yourself a week off to come to Santa Monica. Spend a week here. It doesn't have to be Christmas exactly either. Sometime in December works.

I explode in giddy excitement. Telling myself I had nothing to be worried about with him. The gesture isn't enough, I have to follow through on my end. I can make it work.

Yeah sure. I think I can make that work.